THE YEAR OF THE KNIFE

Also by G.D. Penman

Call Your Steel | a stand-alone fantasy novel
Apocrypha | collected short fiction

other Sully stories

Heart of Winter | novella
"Equinox" | short story in *Apocrypha*

THE YEAR OF THE KNIFE

G.D. PENMAN

Meerkat Press
Atlanta

ISBN-13 978-0-9966262-8-6 (Paperback)
ISBN-13 978-0-9966262-9-3 (eBook)

Library of Congress Control Number: 2017916751

This is a work of fiction. Names, characters, businesses, places, events and incidents are either the products of the author's imagination or used in a fictitious manner. Any resemblance to actual persons, living or dead, or actual events is purely coincidental.

Printed in the United States of America

Published in the United States of America by
Meerkat Press, LLC, Atlanta, Georgia
www.meerkatpress.com

ACKNOWLEDGMENTS

People struggle to work out whether I am being sincere or sarcastic, so I will endeavor to keep this short and to the point:

Thank you to my little family for enduring the long periods when I lived entirely inside my own head.

Thank you to my parents for making the terrible mistake of bringing me into the world and the even worse mistake of enabling my reading habits. You have doomed us all.

Thank you to Erin and Steven for being my literary guinea pigs, even when my stories were awful. Especially when they were awful.

Thank you to the wonderful team at Meerkat Press for making this book into a reality and apologies to my editor Tricia; I have misplaced the long list of compliments that you requested so you will have to settle for my sincere thanks.

Finally, a special thank you to the cats who strolled across my keyboard when I was getting a cup of tea, deleting whole sections of this book and forcing me to rewrite it from scratch weeks later when I finally noticed what had happened. I really appreciated that.

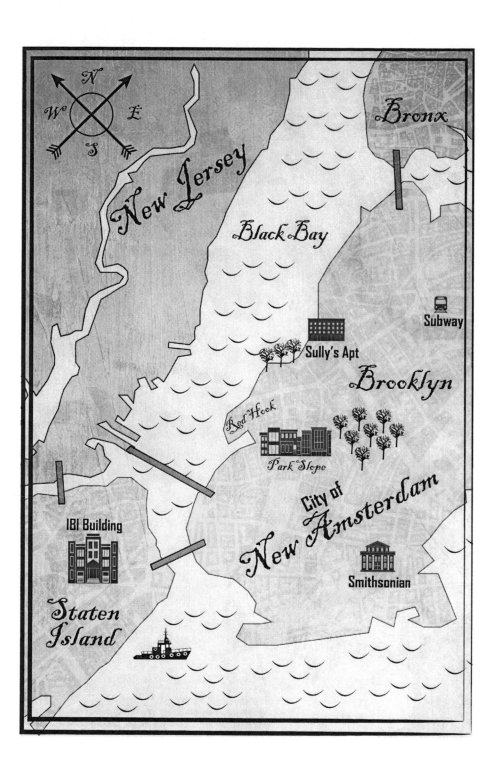

JULY 1, 2015

New Amsterdam was a city the way decapitation was a paper cut. Both could make a person bleed and both would hurt like hell, but only one made bystanders start screaming. It was a quarter past midnight and the streets of Nova Europa's capitol still pulsed with life. Not so long ago, Sully would have been in the midst of that crowd, in one of the clubs that lined Park Slope with the scent of gin on her lips and her arm draped over some silly young wannabe starlet's shoulders. She wasn't in a nightclub tonight, though—she wasn't even in the streets. She was hard at work among the vermin in the subway beneath the city.

The tunnel was pitch black and the trains weren't running there thanks to the New Amsterdam Police Department's order to cut the power, an emergency measure to keep Sully safe. Although *safe* was a relative term given that she was tracking a serial murderer through total darkness. It was a dangerous job, but one that suited Sully perfectly—certainly better than her earlier stint in the navy or the retirement in academia everyone seemed to expect from her. The subway company had made a stink about the impact the outage would have on their business, but they'd been left no choice in the matter. Besides, it was the middle of the night—not rush hour—they would survive the loss of a few hours' worth of fares.

Sully kept her eyes down so that she wouldn't give away her position; they glowed a dull red, the tell-tale sign that she had conjured vision enhancing magic—in this case a modified night vision spell that allowed her to see in the sunless tunnels. She needed the element of surprise; she was in the killer's territory now. The heat signature of a set of footprints led her along the narrow subway walkways. They were getting brighter the farther in that she traveled. The NAPD officers on the scene had warned her that there was a homeless population in the tunnels, so it was possible that she was chasing one of them instead of her killer, but she doubted it. There was a certain cosmic geometry involved in magic, and once you knew how to interpret the angles, it only took simple calculations to work backward from effect to cause. Sully knew that whoever was casting the spells that had been killing citizens of New Amsterdam was doing it from down here.

The footprints were glowing brightly now—she was close. All of the creeping around, the cat and mouse nonsense—it was making Sully tense. If alchemy classes had taught her professors anything it was that there were certain substances that reacted violently under pressure, and one of those substances was Sully. She'd started the night off angry, and it had only gotten worse after dealing with the solid wall of ignorance at the NAPD. The few cops who didn't treat her like an idiot for being a woman treated her like an idiot for being Irish. It was enough to make anyone tetchy.

Giving up any pretense of stealth, Sully shouted into the maintenance tunnel, "That trick with the trains was clever. Simple thaumaturgy, transferring the force from the train up to hit the people above. It takes a twisted kind of mind to come up with something like that. I like it."

In the tunnel ahead, purple spellfire appeared, sputtering from someone's fingertips, presumably the killer's. Sully's face split into a wicked grin and she dropped into a low stance. Her own magic flowed out smoothly. She twisted the flames of it with her fingers and traced jagged glowing sigils that hung where she left them, drifting in slow orbits around her hands. The scent of ozone started to fill the air, the smell of the gathering storm overpowering even the stink of tar on the train tracks. The dust, which hung heavy in the air due to the constant disturbance from the passage of trains in adjoining tunnels, started to take on shapes of its own. Geometric patterns formed in the clouds around the two of them as they prepared their spells.

Sully was ready, but she held back for a moment. She wanted to see what she was up against. A sizzling green bolt burst out of the darkness toward her, some backwater hoodoo garbage that she wouldn't have wasted the time of day on. She slapped it away with a half-formed shield and then returned fire: a sphere of ice that her opponent managed to dodge with a stumble. The spells were the only light in the tunnel, and she had to blink hard when her magic collided with a pillar and exploded in a shower of snowflakes and sparks.

Another green dart was cast at her. She ducked under it with a wild laugh, not even wasting the effort to deflect it, and returned to her feet close enough to see the man in the glow of the sparks trailing from his hands.

He was taller than her—but who wasn't. He wore clean-cut clothes and appeared well-fed. Good, definitely not one of the homeless residents trying to defend their turf. She snapped her fingers and set off a series of small concussions in the air above him. He scrambled back from the din and clapped his hands to his ears in a vain attempt to protect his hearing.

Laughing now, Sully let a long, razor-thin coil of flame trail from her hand, then snapped it up to catch the next bolt he flung. The captured spell swung around her in an arc, charring a long curve into the concrete walls of the tunnel. She flicked it back toward him and watched the man's glassy eyes follow the blaze of light. The green bolt hit him in the chest and his clothes started to disintegrate instantly. He frantically tugged at his coat, trying to get it off before the spell spread to his skin, but it was too late. Bruises blossomed across his newly-bared chest, and blisters rose to the surface in a horrid yellowed mass before popping in a shower of bloody fluids. He screamed and the magic in his hands vanished. Only Sully's fire kept the tunnel lit as she stood and watched him die by inches, the flame of her whip coiling and lashing around her like a snake caught by the tail.

It was only after the man had collapsed onto the ground and was starting to decompose that Sully realized she was still laughing—although cackling might have been a better word. She stopped herself, feeling the build-up of adrenaline start to recede. She sat down on the side of the track and dug her cellphone out of her pocket, hoping for enough signal to call the office.

Lots of women worked for the Imperial Bureau of Investigation these days, but Sully could never quite shake the feeling that, apart from her, most of them sat behind a desk and answered a telephone. She didn't recognize the voice on the other end of the line, so she used her formal drone. "Superior Agent Sullivan reporting."

"What is your status Agent Sullivan?"

"Target is dead. Deceased. Extinct."

The conversation on the other end of the phone was muffled until she clearly recognized the nasal monotone of Deputy Director Colcross. "Agent Sullivan, I need you to be in Winchester Village in Yonkers. Immediately."

Sully found herself straightening up despite herself. "What's the situation, sir?"

There was a sound that might have been the grinding of teeth on the other end of the line. "We may be dealing with a breach but it is unconfirmed. I wouldn't ask you to be there if I didn't think you were required. Please be as swift as possible, there are civilians within the containment area."

Sully had her little leather-bound notebook out of her inside pocket before the call had even disconnected. She scribbled out a formula and tried to be honest with herself about her own weight—it was crucial for the spell. As far as combat magic went, she was acknowledged as an expert by her peers, but traveling spells were not her area of expertise. For Sully, it was a brain grinding exercise in raw maths and she loathed it. Just when she was starting to think it would be quicker hiking back along the tunnel, the last piece of the spell clicked into place. She vanished in a soft thunderclap as the air rushed to fill the space behind her.

* * *

Aboveground, a taxi swerved to avoid the woman appearing out of thin air and nearly plowed into a streetlamp. The driver was out of the car and yelling before Sully had time to think. She tucked her notebook back in her jacket and yanked out her badge instead, shoving it in the cabdriver's face until the torrent of Hindi slowed to a halt and he just stood there panting. She asked, "How fast can you get to Yonkers?"

He looked at her like she'd just appeared out of thin air and demanded a ride; he then carefully said, "Half an hour if Throgg's Neck is clear."

She weighed the information and then nodded. "All right, let's go."

They moved slowly through the Brooklyn streets, only getting up to a decent speed once they had cut across to the road that ran alongside Black Bay. By the time they were over the bridge to the Bronx, Sully had more or less forgotten that the driver was there and was already on her third phone call. The first two had been to different branches of the NAPD, where no one seemed to be able to get their heads around the idea that their serial killer was dead and that Sully had more important things to do than convince them of this fact. The third had been back to her own office at the Imperial Bureau of Investigation to see if somebody who spoke the complicated language of jurisdiction could explain the situation to the NAPD.

The IBI offices were on Staten Island in the midst of the shining towers of law firms, stock brokers and seers. It was the classiest looking place that Sully had ever worked, and she always felt as common as muck walking in wearing her street clothes. She probably should have been doing what everyone else in the building was doing, dumping half of her paycheck into tailors shops so she could blend in, but she was a lot more comfortable in her jeans. She blessed whichever bureaucrat had failed to make the dress code apply to her department.

* * *

The little gated community of Winchester Village was done up in the faux-Republican style that had been popular down south a few years back. The houses looked like big white blocks to Sully—white stucco walls and flat terracotta tiled roofs. Normally, they would have been dark at this time of night; the streetlights weren't meant to reach all the way back past their pretty little gardens, but tonight, they flickered at the edges of Sully's vision under the red and blue strobing lights of police cars.

She paid the taxi driver with a bundle of greasy notes, and he hauled ass away so fast that she wondered if his green card was shaky, or if he knew the meaning behind the big glowing dome over the house at the end of the cul-de-sac. She jogged across to the barricade line where the local residents politely hovered. Sully may not have been tall enough to see over them but she had no qualms about elbowing her way through the crowd.

She flashed her badge at the pale faced boy in uniform on the other side of the barricade and, when he didn't respond fast enough, she hopped right over it and strode toward the group who looked like they were in charge. There were a pair of redcoats in the midst of a sea of blue and black uniforms of the NAPD, and it was the redcoats she focused on. The navy and the army recruited magicians for their power, the IBI recruited them for their intelligence, but the redcoats didn't care if you could barely string a spell together. Redcoats were picked for their blind loyalty to the Empire. Their presence on the scene meant that the governor knew what was happening here—that the government was already involved. Sully groaned.

Covered in cold sweat and sporting a blank face, one of the redcoats had his hands in the air maintaining a barrier spell around the house, apparently with some difficulty. His superior officer was so entrenched in her jurisdictional pissing contest with the NAPD that she hadn't noticed that he was burning out. Sully spun her around by the shoulder and snarled, "Relieve your deputy. He's about to drop."

The silver haired redcoat glowered at Sully but caught sight of her slumping coworker at the same time. She gave Sully a dirty look as she stomped off and Sully took the woman's place in the huddle of officers.

The men fell silent and stared at Sully for a long moment until she rolled her eyes and flashed her credentials. "I'm with the IBI. Give me the situation."

The assembly muttered and spluttered a moment before all eyes settled on an older man with a walrus moustache and an attitude that screamed detective-sergeant.

He huffed. "We have the situation under control."

Sully didn't raise her voice at him; that would be unprofessional. Instead, she calmly said, "If things were under control, I wouldn't be sent out here at"—she glanced at her watch—"half past one in the morning. Now give me a report or I'll find somebody who can."

A sergeant can be many things—he can be rude, he can be stubborn, he can even be reckless—but one thing a sergeant cannot be is stupid. Behind the little eyes in the middle of his slab of a face, there were cogs spinning at high speed, and somewhere in that arcane mechanism, in the region of the brain related to having a career in the morning, a little alarm bell started ringing. He perked up and started reciting, "Our breach alarms went off a little after nine. We narrowed the search down with our magic detectors, I mean, ah, Schrödinger units until we got to this street. Then somebody called in the redcoats and we got things quarantined. They weren't calling in the army until it was confirmed but they said that it looks like, ah"—he glanced around nervously—"one of the gentlemen downstairs may have come a-calling."

Sully almost laughed at the superstitious nonsense. "They only come if you call them by their own name, sergeant. You can say 'demons' until the cows come home, and it won't do any harm."

He flinched when she said the word but went on, "We've managed to piece together a time line from witnesses, scrying, and the family's social media. Mister"—he checked his clipboard—"Mister Underwood left work at about eight, got home just before nine. The family had already had dinner. He ate some leftovers. They all watched TV together for half an hour. That was about the time that our alarms started and the family went silent. We were on the scene about half an hour later."

Sully blew her frustration out between her teeth. "So they have been in there with whatever came through for nearly three hours? What shape is your badge sergeant?"

He scowled at her and said nothing. The other men seemed to be intently studying their own folders or examining the barrier. She spat on the ground.

"How many kids are in there?"

He grunted. "Two girls. Teenagers."

She stepped closer to him, breaking up the circle. "Your badge is in the shape of a shield. It is in the shape of a shield because you're meant to put yourself between innocent people and harm. You had better hope that it killed those girls, sergeant. You had better hope that it was quick. Because if I go in there and have to see what it has done to them, and it has kept them alive for three hours because you were too chicken-shit to send in the redcoats, I will be coming for you. Do you hear me?"

The sergeant tried to posture, tried to answer back, but the weight of Sully's power was behind her emerald stare. He was pinned like a butterfly to a board. Legally she couldn't just kill him for following procedure. They were both agents of the Imperial law in their own ways. But then again, magicians were a law unto themselves. All magicians got a bit strange with time, and rules like "wear clothes" and "don't kill people" seemed to fade in significance when you spent your days trying to puzzle out the equations to create your own miniature star or a cat with a human face. He nodded nervously and backed away.

Sully rolled her shoulders and took off her overcoat, handing it to some poor hapless boy in uniform. She trusted the NAPD as far as she could throw them, so she scooped up one of the Schrödinger units to check the readings herself.

The Schrödinger's Box was a clever piece of equipment. They were originally used to detect when wishes were being made. When the laws of probability were getting skewed, the randomness of the break-down of radioactive material inside their lead-lined core became a lot less random, but with a bit of time the technology was refined, and they could detect practically any magic nowadays. Sully saw that the readings were off the charts, so high that she was surprised white rabbits weren't spontaneously appearing in people's hats.

She found the exhausted redcoat and tapped him on the shoulder. He was still glassy-eyed when he turned to face her, and it was with some sadness she realized that in her report, he was going to be hammered just as hard as the bitch who left him holding the barrier so long it had lobotomized him. Assuming Sully lived long enough to write a report.

She held out a hand. "Give me your sword kid."

He barely responded—whatever channels had been carved into his mind by the spell were cutting through the language centers of his brain—so Sully reached inside his jacket and drew his sword out herself. She strode over to the barrier, casting spells on herself as she walked. The middle-aged redcoat who'd taken over for him couldn't do much more than glance sideways as Sully whispered an incantation, punched through the barrier, then stepped right through, letting it close behind her.

The house was lit up in a pulsing purple tone, and it took Sully a moment to realize that it was the red and blue lights outside being twisted by the barrier. There was no sign of damage to the structure, which gave Sully some hope. Demons were many things, but subtle wasn't one of them. If there had really been one set loose in here, it would have demolished the place and been throwing itself at the barrier long before now.

Even so, something was going on, and Sully, never the quiet and retiring type, was about to find out what. There was an old industrial spell—primarily used in glass work and in the last century for making light bulbs—that Sully had tweaked slightly to create the effect of a grenade explosion. She whispered it then and every window in the house exploded outward. Spellfire was drifting off her fingertips and dancing around her, overflowing and getting caught in the currents of the spells she'd already cast on herself. At that moment, her sight, strength and speed were bordering on inhuman. Demons could swallow even the strongest of spells, so she armed herself with whatever advantages she could.

She kicked the front door off its hinges, and for the first time that night, Sully felt tired. All of the spells operating at the same time drained her reserves faster than usual. Magical exhaustion was serious business—the idiot outside was proof enough of that. Sully needed to make this quick. Whatever monster was in the house couldn't have missed all of the noise she was making. To her heightened senses, even her footsteps seemed deafening.

Nothing looked out of place as she made her way into the home. The hallway walls were pristine and white; the only decorations were a woven wall hanging and a rug from the United Nations. Naughty Mr Underwood, dodging the trade embargo with the Native Americans, he was going to get a slap on the wrist for that, if he still had wrists.

It looked normal. But the smell—she knew that smell far too intimately to relax. There was a metallic tinge to it, like raw meat mingled with the unique sickly-sweet stench of a punctured bowel. The smell was coming from the doorway to the right. Glancing through, Sully took in an equally pristine dining room and a doorway hung with a beaded curtain that appeared to lead to the kitchen. She did not want to go into the kitchen—that was where the corpse stink was strongest.

Sully startled at the sound of a footstep above her—a leather soled shoe squeaking against polished wood. She readied her borrowed sword and crept up the stairs. Straining her ears to catch any sound of movement, any warning of what she was about to encounter, she heard something completely unexpected. First a little sob and, just at the edge of her senses, two heartbeats. Then the unmistakable sound of steel biting into wood.

Sully ran up the remaining stairs, her sword at the ready, the glow of spellfire lighting her way. There was a corridor at the top of the stairs, and some remnant of sanity made her creep along it instead of running. She came to a corner and halted. There was ragged breathing just around it and the regular thumping of metal into wood that gradually ground to a halt.

Sully had heard demons speak before. They rarely had anything smart to say, being more interested in screeching elaborate threats, but when they did speak it sort of sounded like a squid gargling rocks. The voice from around the corner didn't sound like a demon's—it sounded like a chorus of screaming voices all trying to squeeze through one mouth. "WE cAN SMELL YoU litTLE WITcH." There was a staggering footstep. "COMe out anD PLAy."

Whatever this was, Sully had never heard anything like it before. She took a steadying breath then stepped around the corner. It was a man, presumably Mr. Underwood. His clothes hung loosely on his body, everything slightly out of place. His thinning hair had fallen out of its greasy comb-over and was dangling off the side of his lolling head. He moved in a series of twitches; the overall impression was of a broken toy. In his hand was a kitchen knife, a big steely one that was stained with blood. The door behind him was covered in wild slashes, but he had not managed to break through. Sully took another deep breath and his head jerked around to follow the sound. Although his eyes didn't seem to lock onto her, his mouth flapped open and that noise came out again, "TELL yoUR MASters. TELL them thaT WE aRE COMING BacK."

Sully leveled her sword at him and hoarsely whispered, "Drop the weapon."

His head rolled on his shoulders and his face twisted into an almost comical rictus, like he was noticing the bloody knife in his hand for the first time. Sully heard a sound like the wind rustling leaves and slowly realized it was meant to be a laugh. He took one staggering step forward, arms dangling limp at his sides. That was all the provocation that Sully needed. She darted forward and thrust the sword into his chest—close to the heart, if not straight through it. She felt the blade glance off a rib and lodge solidly in one of the bones in his back. When she couldn't tug it free and he wasn't falling, she leapt back, freeing her hands in case she needed them.

The man looked down at the sword sticking out of his chest with all signs of amusement. He took another dragging step toward her and hissed, "It IS tHE YEAR oF the KNIfe."

Then he collapsed. He wasn't bleeding properly yet—it was pooling under him but it wasn't gushing out the way that it should be. Sully shuddered and quickly let all of her spells unwind before they knocked her out.

She heard a loud sob from behind the door, then the screaming cry of someone descending into hysterics. With a barely remembered incantation from her college days, Sully melted the lock then nudged the door open with the toe of her boot. The girls were inside, huddled around each other behind a barricade of towels, cowering under the torn shower curtain. They wailed as she leaned inside, so she had to shout to be heard, "You can come out. He's dead." Sully was talented in a lot of areas, but comforting the children of a man she'd just killed was a bit beyond her, so she beat a hasty retreat back downstairs.

Sully was about to head out the front door when she remembered the smell in the kitchen. She knew she didn't have to go and look. She had done her part—killed the monster, saved the damsels in distress. She could leave now feeling pride in her work. But that treacherous part of her, the part that made her a good investigator instead of just muscle, wouldn't let her go. It called *leaving without looking* cowardice, and if there was a spell to silence that voice in her head, Sully had never found it.

She walked to the kitchen. It was a modern looking room, all stainless steel and brickwork, but now it was accented with the very old-fashioned decoration of blood on every surface. There was arterial spray up over the hood above the oven, crusted on where the electric stovetop had been left running. The mother of the kids upstairs had been a classy looking soccer mum wearing a union jack dress from some weirdly patriotic but trendy designer. She was pinned to the kitchen counter by a couple of the kitchen knives. The husband had obviously gone to work on her. The coroner was going to have a hell of a time counting the number of stab wounds involved. The smell caught in the back of Sully's throat again—she'd taste this woman's death for days.

The shimmering barrier was still in place, the lights from outside the dome writhing purple on its surface like oil on a pond. With one well-placed spell and a bit of spite, Sully tore it down. There were screams and shouts and the sound of a dozen shotguns being cocked. The police were going to go down swinging if a demon came running out. She gave them all a smile. The backlash from the barrier going down had knocked the remaining redcoat unconscious. That was for the best, a hedge witch with a badge could start asking all sorts of awkward questions about now.

Sully saw the Detective-Sergeant making a hasty retreat and caught him by the back of his collar. He shook her hand off and turned to face her and take his lumps like a man. Sully leaned in close, her face twisted into a mask of rage, and whispered, "The girls are still alive"—he paled before she finished—"and unharmed."

He let out a groan. "Jesus fucking Christ lady, my heart ain't that good. Don't do that to me."

She gave him a pat on the shoulder. "You got lucky today. No demons. Something weird. But no demons. Do me a favor, I was meant to be off duty about a day ago, could you get the bodies shipped over to the IBI offices? I want my coroner to have a poke at them. There was something odd going on with the guy."

He was nearly giggling with relief, "Yeah, sure, no problem sweetheart."

She raised an eyebrow at the last word, and he coughed and corrected himself. "Sir?"

Sully went home to do her paperwork.

JULY 1, 2015

Sully woke up to the sound of her cellphone buzzing on the bedside table. She didn't have a hangover; she'd been too tired to drink last night, which was probably a good thing. Regardless, a headache pounded behind her eyes, although she couldn't tell if it was because of magical exhaustion or just the lack of sleep. She fumbled the phone to her ear and managed to hit the answer button by mashing it against the side of her face. She attempted to say "hello" but the sound that came out of her mouth was closer to the one a cat makes when choking up a hairball. She coughed and tried again. "This is Sully?"

The crisp voice of Deputy Director Colcross jerked her awake and into an upright position.

"Good morning Agent Sullivan. Could you visit me in my office at your earliest convenience? I would like to discuss last night's activities, and I believe that Doctor Sharma would like you to shed some light on the ambulance full of bodies that were delivered to him in the early hours."

Sully coughed again but managed to splutter out, "Sure, sir. I'll head over now."

"That would be just perfect. Thank you, Agent Sullivan."

The phone made a beeping noise when it disconnected, and Sully was left sitting bolt upright in her bed. What had she done this time? She let out a long and steady groan as she flopped back down.

Eventually, she stopped groaning and rolled out of bed. Her

apartment was right by the Black Bay, and the ambient magic of the place made anyone who didn't have magic of their own feel uncomfortable; hence, the rent being so cheap. That, and the fact that the apartment only had one room—well, two if you counted the little sectioned off area that hid the shower and toilet—and it rested below street level. There were windows along one wall just beneath the low ceiling that were perfect for watching people's feet go by. In addition to Sully's bed, there was a little breakfast bar which doubled as her desk, a wardrobe stuffed with various iterations of her unofficial uniform, blue jeans and Hawaiian shirts, and a whiteboard with the Dante's Inferno spell written out in longhand.

Sully worked a lot, so the apartment was really just somewhere to sleep, but if she had anything like a hobby, this spell was it. She tinkered with it whenever she needed to keep her mind occupied; whenever she didn't want her attention drawn to the little cupboard under the sink that she knew held a halfway decent bottle of gin. The spell was widely considered to be an abject failure. Any magic involving fire had the risk of getting out of control, and Dante's Inferno was the poster child for that problem. It had been cast a few times over the years, and each time it had proven lethal to the person casting it, draining all of the magician's reserves to fuel the flames.

Dante Alighieri was a vampire hunter over in the Roman Empire before the Great War, and this was his big contribution to the world. A spell that burnt so hot and so powerful that it had practically turned him inside out. Sully was starting to think that she had cracked it. The runes and words on the board were a tangled mix of Enochian, algebra, Old English, trigonometry and Norse runes. They made perfect sense to Sully, but her professors back at the Royal College would have rolled their eyes at her obstinate refusal to use standardized Latin. She stared at the spell for a moment while she waited for the worst of the throbbing in her head to clear. Not that she really needed to look at it when she could recite it, with all of her modifications over the last decade, by rote. When the ache in her head eased into more of a gentle fizzing sensation, she headed for the shower.

A towel hung over the mirror and it was only on dazed mornings like this one, when Sully couldn't be bothered to search her laundry pile for another towel, that she removed it. Mirrors were a risk. Sure, they could be helpful for scrying and for casting glamors, but they could also be used to spy on you just as easily. She had considered throwing out the mirror at one point, but she couldn't because it was a gift from Marie—one of the few gifts she'd ever given Sully. Like most of Marie's gifts, it had really been for Marie's use when she stayed over, but the sentiment was the same. So Sully had found what she considered to be the optimal balance—a covered mirror.

Only this morning it wasn't covered, so Sully, still pink from the shower, took a moment to survey the damage. There were no cuts or bruises that she could see; just the usual freckles and assorted scars, which was a miracle given the night she'd had. Her head was shaved at the back and sides, a throwback to her navy days, and the tumble of red hair on the top was tousled as usual. She blessed her luck that short hair on women was fashionable again and could even pass as professional. Sully still got asked to prove her age at bars sometimes— not bad for a girl pushing forty. The towel could go back on the mirror later.

Sully dressed in the closest thing she had to business casual: a suit jacket tossed on over one of her Hawaiian shirts, but with the slight modification of black jeans, rather than blue. She had the exact calculations for transporting herself from home to the office scribbled in the front of her notebook. Now she would find out if the headache was from throwing too much magic around. The papers on the breakfast bar rustled as she vanished, then the apartment fell back into silence.

It wasn't a straight jump from her apartment to the foyer of the IBI building on Staten Island. That would have had her passing over the edge of the Black Bay and, while it was quite possible to travel over a body of water with a slight modification to the spell and an extra push of power, nobody in their right mind would try it over the Bay. Something had happened there at some point in history that had left the place throbbing with magic. Perhaps some rite performed by the natives or some naturally occurring phenomenon that had gone awry.

She jumped first to a spot about eight stories above the Red Hook district and then cast the spell again before gravity had too much of a chance to catch her. She landed, a little too heavily, in the janitor's closet just off the atrium of the IBI building. The janitor was an old, heavyset Germanic man with thick glasses. He was trying to slyly roll a cigarette while balancing his backside against the little sink. He didn't even act surprised—this was far from the first time Sully had made this sort of entrance. They nodded to one another, and then went on about their day.

Sully sidled out of the closet and into the elevator before the security guards at the front desk had time to notice her and demand that she sign in. It was playful on her part and exasperating on theirs. The elevator didn't actually go all the way up to the Deputy Director's office without a special key, but after unlocking the forces of magic and reshaping the universe with your will, a couple of tumblers in a metal tube weren't too difficult to realign. Sully's professors might have said that she lacked finesse, but never the strength of will required for big magic. With her cunning brain and raw power, they had expected her to stay in academia—essentially as a powerful piece of lab equipment—but she'd had different aspirations.

The Deputy Director's secretary, Chloe, sat in the small room outside his office. Sully gave her a smile and a wink as she strode past. Chloe was a pretty blonde in her twenties. Men could hit on her all day long without her blinking but she blushed scarlet all the way to the roots of her hair every time Sully so much as looked at her. It was adorable. Chloe still hadn't pulled herself together by the time Sully laid her hand on the Deputy Director's door, but she did manage a splutter that Sully took to mean that she had to wait. Sully glanced back at the girl to see her half up out of her seat, mouth hanging open. Sully was tempted to roll her eyes, but held back, knowing that she might well need Chloe's sympathy after the meeting.

She gave the girl a querulous look. "Is he in?"

Chloe shut her mouth and nodded. Today they were playing twenty questions.

"Is he ready to see me?"

Another nod.

"All right then, see you later."

The office was a monument to everything that was wrong with the British Empire. The walls were paneled with walnut, the floor had a thick red carpet. The desk was a colossal antique dominating the far end of the space. But the worst part of the room was perched behind the oversized desk in a red leather chair, smoking a clay pipe. Deputy Director Colcross was an elderly man with prodigious sideburns. His voluminous mass was concealed neatly in a well-tailored three-piece suit. His desk was cluttered with stacks of paper and folders. He didn't have a computer. He didn't trust them.

In front of him was the report Sully had hastily typed and emailed into the office before she'd collapsed in a heap the night before. If he had called her in for her poor typing, it was entirely possible that she would explode. He pointed with his pipe at the chair opposite his desk and then went back to reading the papers in front of him.

Sully sat, feeling like nothing more than a scolded child being sent to the headmaster's office. He kept her waiting, which may have been the speed of her arrival throwing him off his schedule, or it may have been a power play. Colcross and Sully had a complex relationship. He was a man deeply in love with statistics, and on paper Sully solved more cases than any of her coworkers, but on the other hand he was a gentleman of the British Empire and had been taught from birth that the Irish, women in general, and lesbians in particular, were inferior species. He found the reality on his papers and his perceptions of the world a little difficult to synchronize. For her part, Sully thought that he was a stuffed-suit condescending prick who had no business anywhere near a criminal investigation except, possibly, as a victim if he kept on talking to her like she was stupid.

After a moment, she forced herself to relax and looked around for the Director. The reason the Deputy Director had taken on so many of the Director's duties was that the Director had received a curse in the mail several weeks ago and was now a Hyacinth Macaw. The IBI had set up a large aviary for him in what had been his office, and the budget that was usually spent on his fairly elaborate lunches was now spent on a daily fruit delivery. It was the perfect habitat for him in his current state, but he still enjoyed overseeing operations, which was to say that he squawked less frequently and slept more when he got to listen in on Colcross's conversations, providing input in the form of seemingly random words. Sully spotted him up on the curtain rail, wide awake, his beady little black eyes locked onto her.

Sully had a bit of a thing about birds—she wasn't particularly fond of them, but they seemed to be fond of her, showing up in flocks whenever she was upset. Marie was able to judge her mood by the number of seagulls outside the apartment at any given moment.

Eventually Colcross spoke, although he still did not deign to look at her. "I would like for you to know that I am very grateful for your extra work last night. I understand that you were off-duty and took on not one, but two extremely dangerous situations without complaint."

Sully took the compliment stoically. Colcross liked to use the old "criticism sandwich" with praise doled out on either side of a complaint to soften the blow. When more seemed to be required she said, "I enjoy the work sir. I wouldn't be here if I didn't."

He gave her a very thin smile. "Indeed. Well, as to your first case of the evening, calculating the position of the murderer from the locations of his victims, it was very good work Sullivan, very cerebral." He let that hang for a moment, with the implication that he had previously considered her little better than a moron. "Are we likely to see his . . . eh . . . weapon of choice . . . employed again?"

Sully weighed the question before replying, "I don't think it is likely sir, not unless you widely publicize how he was doing it. If we ever have to deal with something bloody massive, I might give it a try myself. Otherwise, we should be safe from exploding investment bankers for a while."

The thin smile remained in place, but Colcross's eyebrows drew down—the death of law-abiding citizens was not a laughing matter. He had never been on the front lines so he had no use for gallows humor. He was here thanks to politics, as were most of the upper echelons of the civil services. If it were war time, he would be a general; if they were in England, he would be a politician.

The Director squawked, "Grapes," seemingly to himself.

Colcross shuffled the papers on his desk and lowered his eyes again. "I can see that there was something of a personality conflict when you arrived on the scene of the second incident, the constabulary did not seem to be overly impressed with you." Sully opened her mouth to argue but he held up a finger to silence her. "I believe that this can be overlooked given the trying circumstances. I only mention it to make you aware that it has been brought to my attention. I do not want you to think that these things are not reported to your superiors. Now, on to more pressing matters."

Sully sat up straight in her seat and started preparing her defenses. Colcross droned on, "I appreciate the manner in which you presented this case. It was very clean: all facts of the matter reported. This makes an excellent official account of events. I would like to move beyond the realm of fact with you for a moment."

Sully tried to keep her face placid but this was unusual. The Director's little black eyes were boring into the side of her head and Colcross's little piggy ones were fixed on her too. She coughed politely and said, "As you wish, sir."

He seemed to deflate a little. "What do you think this was Agent Sullivan? Off the record."

Sully glanced back and forth between the man and the bird. "Off the record? I know demonic possession is a myth, but that guy wasn't acting right. His voice sounded like a lot of people talking at once."

Colcross raised an eyebrow. "As in 'I am legion?'"

Sully shrugged uncomfortably—this was all reminding her too much of school. "Didn't take you for a Catholic, sir."

Colcross tapped out his pipe. "Alas, it is part of the curriculum in diplomatic training. When a significant portion of the world listens to the same imaginary friend, it behooves us to find out what he is saying."

Sully gritted her teeth and pressed on. "It was more than the voice. He moved like a marionette. Not to mention all the alarms going off, as though we had a reality breach. It seems like the simplest explanation."

Colcross gave no sign of agreeing with her. He acknowledged that she had spoken but otherwise there was nothing. Under his silent scrutiny Sully shrugged. "People snap. I'm not saying that he did anything other than that in my official reports, and I don't need reminding not to go spreading rumors around. I am just saying that it bears further investigation."

He sighed again. "You are most likely correct Agent Sullivan. I assume that this is why you had the bodies of both the attacker and victim delivered to Dr Sharma's laboratory: for some further investigation?"

Sully had almost forgotten about that. "Yes, sir. Was that all right, sir?"

Colcross gave her a benevolent smile. She actually caught a glimpse of his teeth for a moment. "I have always found it best to keep the good doctor's time filled to prevent him from . . . eh . . . experimenting too much. Perhaps your unusual man's unusual corpse will keep us all safe from his scientific advances for the time being." The smile thinned again and the veneer of pleasantry faded with it. "You will not be conducting any further investigation at this time. You will return to the usual case rotation tomorrow. You have the remainder of today to rest and recuperate. If you would like to extend that time off, you have my special dispensation. You look like you're in need of a good rest, Sullivan."

From his perch the Director crowed, "Under the rug."

Sully didn't even blink, she was quite proud of herself. "Thank you, sir. I will pay a visit to make my apologies to Dr. Sharma, and then go home."

Colcross returned to his papers as though she had never been in the room. "Good day, Agent Sullivan."

Sully rose up to her full height, barely taller than him sitting down. "Good day, Deputy Director."

* * *

The laboratory was meant to be a mortuary, and Dr. Raavi Sharma was meant to be a medical examiner—one of several employed by the IBI across the colonies. However, Raavi had taken extremely well to having a squad of magicians upstairs dragging home the corpses of whatever weird creature had preyed on the civilian population this time. Some would say that he had taken to it too well, his scientific curiosity overtaking other drives—such as decency and common sense.

This was exacerbated by the fact that his citizenship in the Empire was on thin ice. The subcontinent of India had not officially been a part of the Empire since the Great War, and while there were still healthy trade routes and many strangely interlocking treaties, it was not even a little bit clear if Raavi was allowed to live in a country ruled by Britain, let alone practice medicine there.

Working for the IBI was a convenient way to side-step the issue. As an essential government employee, the immigration office would overlook him indefinitely. Raavi was keenly aware that he could be kicked out of his job and the Americas at a moment's notice, so he took advantage of every possible opportunity to pursue his interests while he still could. He had been in the lab all night. Sully could tell from the bagged and tagged remains from her crime scene as evidence and the fact that his shirt sat neatly folded on a chair by the door.

When Raavi took his shirt off, he got really weird, and that didn't usually happen until he was certain everyone else in the building had either gone home or was going to leave him alone. Seeing a man with four arms usually spooked the interns but it left anyone with an understanding of medicine seriously disturbed. The additional arms had been grafted on when he was still in his early twenties, riding high on the success of his experiments to use doppelgänger organs in transplants to humans. The experiments had been successful, and the doppelgänger species had become a farmed resource overnight; but the world was not ready for four armed men running around, so Raavi was one of a kind.

At the moment, he was working on what looked like the carcass of a spider the size of a terrier. Sully coughed politely and he glanced up at her. His accent sounded oddly English for someone who had never been there. "Sully! Lovely of you to visit. Have you ever seen one of these before?"

Sully found herself smiling despite the smell of Colcross's tobacco still clinging to her. "Can't say that I have."

Raavi had a boyish smile plastered on his face. "Nobody has. It is some sort of magical construct. Somebody cast a spell to create a giant spider. Somebody else cast a spell to kill it, and now I have an entirely artificial life-form, invented by somebody who has no idea how biology works, to poke around in. Today is a good day, Sully. A very good day. Despite the weird dead man that you sent to me."

Sully cocked an eyebrow. "Weird how?"

Raavi grinned even wider. "I knew that was why you were sneaking down here. He was weird in the sense that, apart from your fairly clean stroke through the chest, he also had almost every joint dislocated and a Schrödinger scan showed that he had been at the apex of some pretty potent magic. Either a breach, a wish, or something I have never had the pleasure of seeing before. Oh, I am also unable to give an accurate time of death, despite knowing when you stabbed him from your reports. It is like parts of him died a few hours earlier. Do you happen to know what happened to him?"

In a good imitation of Colcross's monotone Sully recited, "He simply went mad with the terrible pressure of being a wealthy middle-class white man."

Raavi sniggered. "Do you have any better suggestions?"

Sully shrugged. "Your guess is as good as mine. I'm off the case, anyway."

Raavi stared at her intently then nodded politely when nothing else was said. "Really wants this all hushed up quick, eh?"

Sully gave her patented one shoulder shrug again. Raavi sighed. "Well, Agent Sullivan. Off the record, I would guess that somebody else was piloting this man's body and doing a piss poor job of it. But of course, I would keep that off-the-record, wild speculation to myself."

Sully gave a subtle nod of agreement, and he changed subjects without taking a breath. "So, Sully, how's life treating you? You don't come down to see me so often now that my beautiful young assistant has finished her internship. Is it possible that our burgeoning friendship was just a mask slapped haphazardly over your lusty feelings toward that poor creature?"

Sully laughed. "She wasn't so pretty that I'd haul myself down to this godforsaken basement to ogle her. I'm here for the conversation."

Raavi spread his arms. "All part of the service. Come for the corpses, stay for the entertainment."

Sully eased back to a chuckle. "Story of my life."

JULY 5, 2015

Sully woke up in her own bed, partially draped over a sleeping girl who'd said she worked part-time as a bartender and part-time wearing no clothes on the internet. The girl had the smooth tan skin and curviness that Sully associated with visitors from the Republic of America. From the fragmented memories of last night Sully seemed to recall a lot of Spanish being spoken. The girl's wavy purple hair was shaved along one side of her head in a fashion that Sully would probably have emulated if she thought she could pull it off. Last night, Sully had been sure the girl was over eighteen; now, with the haze of smoke and gin faded, she wasn't so sure. The little upturned nose was cute, but it made her look like a teenager.

Sully jerked at the sound of her cellphone buzzing. She cast a quick glance around the spinning room, finding the clock after only two attempts. It was only eight in the morning, and she wasn't due in the office for another hour, at least. The Director had more or less given up on any attempt to track her comings and goings, and like most of the magicians who worked for the IBI, she was on an honor system regarding her hours. Almost nobody had her cellphone number. Even her coworkers had to relay messages through the main switchboard. Sully had learned the hard way not to give out her number after one of her romantic entanglements went publicly sour.

She couldn't reach the phone without waking the girl, and she wasn't sure if she was ready to do that yet. Luckily, she had a few tricks up her sleeve. Technically it was low magic, considered so basic that it wasn't even discussed at the Imperial College, but Sully could do it without speaking or tracing out spellforms. A little line appeared between her eyebrows as she concentrated, constructing the spell in her head and letting a little touch of power into it without the protective layers of ritual. The phone leapt off the table, slipped between her fingers and hit her in the tit. She grumbled quietly and then fumbled it up to her ear. "What?"

She could almost hear Ceejay, her occasional partner at the IBI, smirking through the phone. "You had better get into the office quick, girl. Deputy Dick is foaming at the mouth, even called me 'my good man' this morning."

Sully groaned loud enough that the girl beside her woke up anyway. Stealth had never been her strong suit. "What's his problem now?"

Ceejay's voice was rich and exuberant even at the worst of times, and now, gloating over her misfortune, it was almost intolerably glib. "There's been another one of your funny murders. It's all over the news. It is the 'Year of the Knife.'"

Sully wasted no time getting the girl out of the bed, into the few clothes she had and out of the apartment. She didn't speak a lot of English, which explained in part the ease with which the previous night had progressed. In a fit of bad taste, Sully mentally nicknamed her "Chica." When she finally had her out in the hallway, Sully dithered for a moment, looked at Chica's petulant pout and wished that she could remember a little more of what had happened last night. After a second, she made a decision and pulled her sword out of the umbrella stand behind the door.

It was a saber from back in her naval days; she had never enchanted it, just run a spell over it once in a while that kept it clean and razor sharp. It wasn't a wise choice to carry too much enchanted gear if you intended on using magic yourself. Spells could interact in unexpected ways and Sully had seen one of the other artillery casters from her ship go up in flames in a bar fight once because he was wearing a water repelling jacket.

Chica's eyes widened at the sight of the saber. Sully detected a hint of fear as the girl spluttered out with a thick accent, "Policia?"

Sully stepped out into the hall and slammed the door shut behind her. Sully moved in close and let the girl feel the warm heat of breath on her cheek. Chica didn't flinch but she was trembling—probably afraid she'd get kicked back down south or strong armed into something less like a relationship and more like slavery. Sully gave her a gentle kiss on the neck, just below her ear and then whispered one of the few words of Spanish that she knew, "No. Not police. Brujah. Witch."

Sully pulled back from the girl, who stood stock still, staring at her with big eyes, now clouded with doubt. With a tiny thunderclap, Sully vanished.

* * *

As Sully plummeted through the air toward Red Hook, she realized it had been foolish to pull that stunt with the girl. She hadn't taken the time to prepare the second set of equations for her trip, and now she was probably going to break her legs.

Spellfire trailed from her fingers as she fell, looking like a comet tail as she tumbled. She was almost ready, the words on the tip of her tongue, but she still had to factor in her velocity and the time of day. She held the traveling spell in stasis in one hand, reached toward the ground with the other, then focused and flexed her power. Sully couldn't move an entire planet, she wasn't that powerful although she had heard rumors of a big name magus doing something similar with a meteor before. What she could do was create an equal and opposite reaction from the ground beneath her when she pushed. The pavement cracked and she was flung back up into the air, spinning like a rag doll. She then let loose the traveling spell she'd been holding and landed sprawled on the floor of Colcross's office, with a thump that must have echoed through the building.

By some kindly twist of fate, the Deputy Director was not in the room at that exact moment, allowing Sully to scrape together her dignity and get back to her feet. The macaw was sitting on the back of Colcross's chair, his dull gaze locked onto Sully. He cocked his head from side to side before croaking at her. She gave the Director a polite, awkward nod and then said, half to herself, "Sorry, sir. I made a slight miscalculation."

The bird shuffled from side to side on its perch, scratching the red leather with his claws. He made a weird little choking sound and Sully hoped to god she wasn't about to see her feathered superior keel over dead. She didn't have an inkling of how to give mouth-to-mouth resuscitation to a parrot. Instead the bird squawked, "Forty-three now. Forty-three."

It was her turn to cock her head. Nobody was clear on how much of the old man's mind had survived the transformation. There had been some furor when the curse had first landed on the Director, and every magician in the building was on the case for four days straight. They worked out about half of the spell from the clues left behind: the sigil burnt into his desk and the few remnants of the self-incinerating letter that had contained the spell.

Although they never worked out who was behind the curse, given the political nature of the Director's position, it was no surprise that somebody was gunning for him. The IBI had tried what Colcross described as "good old-fashioned police work" to catch the assailant but, with the letter mostly in ashes, all that they had to go on was the fact that whoever had sent it knew the Director's address and could afford a stamp. It had been a bit of a black mark on the entire branch's record.

Sully asked the Director, slowly, like she would talk to a small child, "Forty-three of what, sir?"

The words seemed to go into the little feather wrapped brain but there was no immediate response. The door opened behind Sully. For someone so bulky, Colcross could move with surprising stealth. He stopped dead when he saw Sully standing in his office, and she could actually see him deflate a little. He drew himself back to his full height and strode over to her. He was like a cat. Every time he stumbled he acted like it was all part of his plan from the beginning. With a forced smile he said, "Good morning to you, Agent Sullivan. I assume that your visit is relating to the . . . eh . . . incident at the Atlas Park Mall?"

Sully answered honestly, "I don't know anything about it, sir. I was just under the impression that you wanted to speak to me."

He tried to force more life into the smile as he strolled around his desk. "Yes, of course. I believe that your insight may be required in the investigation. I have had the file delivered to your desk already."

Sully kept her face as emotionless as she could muster but something must have snuck through because Colcross tutted at her and sighed. "Gloating does not suit you, Miss Sullivan. Please go about your duties."

She nodded politely and started to back away, trying not to let her smile show. She was almost to the door when the macaw chattered its beak and hooted, "Year of the Knife."

Both Colcross and Sully spun to look at the bird. Then Colcross turned an irate stare on Sully. She shrugged. "He picked that up quick."

Colcross frowned again and then shook his head a little, "Sullivan, this may seem like a somewhat odd question but . . . eh . . . what was the Director's name?"

This was more familiar ground. "Don't try to think about it, sir. There is a taboo on the name; it's part of the curse. Nobody can remember who he was, so it takes less power to maintain the spell. It's sort of like a glamor that way: it works better if nobody knows about it. If you try to force the memory, you'll just end up with a headache. It'll be written down in his personnel file or something. But, even if you read it, you'll just forget it again. Better to cut out the middleman."

Colcross had a softness to his expression that Sully couldn't remember seeing there before; he petted the macaw softly on the top of its head and it pressed back against his hand with a shiver of feathers. He nodded to her. "Thank you, Sullivan. Please report to me directly on these killings. Let me know what you need to make them stop."

She felt an odd moment of something like camaraderie from the old bastard, so she gave him a smile and a nod and then left. Chloe, the eternal secretary, looked intensely flustered but still hadn't worked out how to talk to Sully without first passing through ten stages of blushing. Sully did roll her eyes this time. Her reputation might have preceded her but surely it wasn't all that bad.

* * *

Sully found Ceejay loitering in his cubicle, which was right next to hers—obviously waiting for her, or more accurately, waiting for the story. Ceejay looked about forty years old, not that you could ever really tell a magician's age with the way magic extended their lifespans. He kept his head shaved bald and wore flamboyant suits, it seemed like there was a different color every day, perfectly tailored in the loose style favored in Ophir. That African kingdom was where he was originally from, absconding to the colonies in much the same way that Raavi had, although a few decades earlier and with a lot less difficulty. The Empire was always willing to give papers to a decent magician, especially back in the seventies, when Britain was still at war with the Khanate.

Ceejay never spoke about being in Asia, but Sully had heard all of the horror stories over the years. Half New Amsterdam's homeless had been veterans of the wars with Mongolia when she arrived fresh off the boat from Ireland. An insufferable gossip, Ceejay's rolling laugh was the regular percussion that let you know the office was running properly. Sully didn't have a lot of friends—it was a short list. But somehow, Ceejay had squeezed onto it despite annoying her on such a regular basis.

Sully ignored him and sat down at her desk, but he just rotated on the spot, his big shiny head looming over the top of the cubicle wall. He grinned far too broadly. "Well, girl. Tell me the story. Let's hear about your crazy cult killers."

Sully mentally added a cult to her list of theories—it didn't seem likely, but there were weirder things than demon worshipers. The heap of folders on her desk was ridiculous. Every IBI case that had a hint of magic involved wormed its way into their department, and the ones her lazy office-mates didn't want got passed on to Sully. She found the newest file on top of the precarious topography of her desk and settled in to read the NAPD report. Ceejay still hovered over the side of the cubicle until Sully hissed, "Later! Shoo! Shoo!"

* * *

Last night's incident was similar enough to the first killing that Sully knew there must be a connection. There had been no simple knife this time. The killer had gone to town on a shopping center with an army surplus antique Gatling Rifle. He had screamed about it being the "Year of the Knife" in what a few survivors called "freaky voices" before a security guard had cut him down.

Afterward, they discovered that the killer was an, admittedly tall, twelve-year-old. Any observations that could have been gained from having a competent magician on the scene, or even an incompetent one like a redcoat, were lost along with the killer. The other reports were the usual garble of eyewitness statements, interspersed with the reporting officer's theories: drugs, rock and roll, drugs, going crazy, and drugs, respectively. Worse than useless.

When Sully glanced toward the throbbing sound of rock music, she saw that Ceejay was hovering again, eyes just above the edge of the dividing wall like a crocodile on a river. She sniggered. "All right. Come on 'round."

Ceejay practically bounced with excitement. "Is it a new monster? Is it a cult? What have you got?"

She shrugged. "Wish I knew. No idea. Not a clue."

She described her experience at Winchester Village and what she knew about the incident at the mall. Ceejay listened with wide eyes and nodded when appropriate.

"You think it's a demon, squeezing into a person suit? That makes no sense. That's not how demons work. Demons make a deal with you, then, when you die, they get to force their big freaky body into your corpse and come through. They can't come up if you are still alive. It sounds like science fiction; mind control. Magic doesn't let you control people like this."

Sully snorted at that. "Glamors. Illusions. All those love potions we stop from coming into the country. There's a ton of magic that affects the mind. What I don't believe is that some nobody we've never heard of could come up with this kind of spell and cast it twice in two days without burning themselves out. The Schrödingers are showing some major power at work here."

Ceejay gave her a level stare, and his usually jovial tone dipped into a low rumble. "You know who you'll be chasing, then. I would keep the circle small on this one."

Even as he said it, Sully could feel the cold weight settling in her stomach. If a magus was involved—one of the genius magicians powerful enough to churn out the spells that kept the world running—it wouldn't be a straightforward fight. It would be politics and cutting deals and quiet conversations between rich men in expensive suits, and eventually, the blame would be assigned by committee. The cold feeling in her stomach heated up, sharpened. Anger bubbled up into her chest.

Ceejay saw it and his smile came back. "There's my girl. Go kick 'em all up their backsides." He wiggled his eyebrows at her. "Just do it quietly."

Flashing him a smile, Sully headed for the door then called back over her shoulder, "I'm going to look at the crime scenes. If Colcross comes sniffing around, you can tell him where I am and let him know I'm going to need to talk to a magical theorist." She paused at the door. "Ask him if I can have Pratt. He's a pompous ass but he's good at keeping things secret. And Colcross knows I don't like him, so it should be an easy sell."

Her phone buzzed on the way to the elevator: a message from Raavi complaining about all the bodies that were now crowding his lab space. He'd had to set aside the spider project and move the maimed doppelgänger that he used for spare parts into the freezer where it had shifted shape to become a penguin and bitched at him in Dutch. Sully sniggered and replied with a little sad face emoticon.

She traveled to Glendale from inside the elevator, scribbling out the details of the jump in her notepad and double-checking her calculations this time. Skydiving was probably only fun if you were expecting it and wearing the right backpack.

JULY 7, 2015

Neither Colcross nor Sully believed the killings were over. But while Colcross was willing to wait it out and hope that the media didn't pick up on the connections, Sully spent her next few shifts crawling through every crime report in the city, hoping to find something—anything—to shed some light on the what was happening. But she'd come up empty.

So two days later when Colcross called her in for a briefing on reports he'd received from other parts of the colony, she wasted no time getting there.

Colcross received reports from across the whole country, not just the east coast. There had been an incident in Wisconsin: a little diner on one of the highways leading up to the northern province had acquired some gory graffiti across its interior wall: a waitress, a fry-cook and a trucker were dead from single stab wounds to the neck. Another trucker had died on the road, mowed down by a passing car that he'd apparently tried to stab with a hunting knife.

That was yesterday's horror show. Today's show was still in progress down in Carolina. That was why Colcross had called her in, even though it was obvious that the frequency of their meetings over the past few days were causing him pain.

"We have eight civilians and one civil servant deceased so far. One of the province's transport constabularies turned on his partner and has been setting up roadblocks and attacking anyone he stops. He's been heard shouting the key phrases used in the other cases. His current whereabouts are unknown. Our course seems clear at this point. I will deploy you in the field to capture this asset for interrogation."

Sully hadn't sat down. She was standing in a well-practiced "at ease" stance in front of the Deputy Director's desk. She kept her gaze fixed over his shoulder and agreed with anything he said using terse nods, trying to act like she could take it or leave it. It would be just like Colcross to take her off the case out of spite.

The media hadn't connected the killings yet, and she sincerely hoped to get through the week without a press conference. She suppressed a shudder at the idea that she might get dragged into the politics behind these crimes, it was hard enough doing her job without having to justify every step to a committee of Colcross clones. The single Colcross that she had to deal with rolled his eyes and picked up a folder from his desk. "You may join the hunt in Charlotte, Carolina, at your earliest convenience, Agent Sullivan."

Sully swallowed a dozen questions and demands and spat out, "Thank you, sir."

Outside Colcross's office, Chloe was showing all of the stress that her boss wasn't. Her hair was frizzing out of its bun, she looked like she had slept in her clothes, and her make-up, usually so tastefully applied, was missing. It was enough to make Sully smile. The harried girl didn't even notice Sully at first, but when she did, she flushed as usual. Sully gave her a wink before stepping onto the elevator and saw Chloe flop back down into her seat with a barely concealed grin.

* * *

Sully caught Ceejay by the back of his collar as he came hustling out of his cubicle. He was about to swing at her before he realized who she was and what a bad idea that would be.

He grumbled, "Well, superstar, how can I help you today?"

She let go of his collar and dragged him back into his cubicle by a garish yellow sleeve. They weren't face-to-face—there were about two feet of him she'd have to climb to make that happen—but he was close enough to hear her hiss, "I need a long distance portal down to Carolina. I know you have the spells for it, and I don't have the time for any pissing about filing requisitions for a magus or a station. Going to help me out?"

Ceejay's eyes were bulging but he kept a facade of calm. "That's a big jump, little lady. It may be all that I can do for the whole of the day. What'll happen if I'm sent out on a call of my own? I can't admit to knowing illegal transporting spells when our superiors come questioning me."

Sully smirked. "Tell them the evil Irish witch stole your powers. They'll believe that."

Ceejay tried to keep up his serious demeanor for another moment, but Sully could hear the rumble of laughter starting in his belly like distant thunder and then, finally, it echoed out and around the high ceiling of their office.

"Up to the roof then, you mad little beast. Let Ceejay throw you through space and time."

* * *

The bastard called up the portal a short distance from the side of the roof and made Sully jump for it, so when she landed in Charlotte she was running down the middle of a street and she had to swerve to avoid an oncoming bike messenger. When she'd passed through the portal, her insides felt like they were her outsides, and the minute changes in gravity created a weird dizziness, as well. No wonder nobody liked to travel long distance by magic.

The heat in Charlotte was oppressive compared to the crisp air of New Amsterdam, so between that and the aftereffects of the transport, it took her longer than she wanted to admit to weave her way through the traffic and find a taxi to the central constabulary. The fact that cabs weren't yellow outside of New Amsterdam didn't help. At the police station, it took waving her badge in front of eight different faces and more than a little shouting to get face-to-face with the bristly moustache running the manhunt. On her way to what they called the "crisis room," Sully noticed that aside from her, the only women she'd seen in the station were wearing cuffs.

Carolina province was the breadbasket of the Empire: wheat and cornfields as far as the eye could see once you got outside the city limits. It was the perfect place to pull a stunt like this—you could drive off down a farm road and be practically invisible. To make matters worse, every marked car the Carolina police had sent out to help in the hunt was another bit of camouflage for the one they were looking for.

All of the officers seemed to be talking at once, so when several attempts to get a word in failed, Sully silenced the room using another modified version of her concussion spell that had the nearest cops covering their ears and the rest drawing their weapons on her. She spoke softly after that—anything more would have been unnecessary. "If your rogue trooper is anything like the rest of our killers, then he's going to be lit up with magic. We need to locate key areas where he's likely to be active next then deploy units with Schrödingers to quickly narrow them down."

The local cops all looked as sheepish as was possible while still pointing a gun at a person. Sully looked at the map of the province up on the wall. There were a few pins showing where the earlier attacks had taken place, and post-it notes stuck to points on the map that meant nothing to Sully, but that the locals seemed to think were likely places for the killer to setup the next roadblock.

"Looks like you've already picked out our spots. Let's get moving," she said.

Sully heard a cough behind her. Then in the bouncy regional accent one of the officers said, "Miss Sullivan, it's up to the Chief to decide what we do. We don't take our orders from—"

Sully very calmly pulled out her badge and turned toward the young man, who couldn't have been more than twenty, blond hair, probably never been outside of the province. Moron. She read aloud,

"Superior Agent of the Empire." Then she fixed him with a stare. "Is this part of the British Empire?"

He mumbled, so Sully spoke a little louder, "I beg your pardon?"

The chief of police stood up from his place at the head of the table and cut them off. "We will have all three of our magic detectors out in the field as soon as possible, Agent Sullivan. What do you want from us exactly?"

She smiled. "I want you to let me have the first swing at him because I want to keep your buddy alive. How does that sound to you?"

* * *

Sully hit the town in search of a good cup of coffee but eventually settled for a bad cup of coffee at a café with little white painted tables on the sidewalk out front. She had a police radio strapped to her belt, tuned in to the channel set aside for the investigation, one usually used by the province wildlife constables when they were out dealing with poachers. It wasn't likely their target would be on that channel, unless he had been moonlighting as a Venus flytrap thief. Sully sipped the bitter coffee and realized that, in this sort of town, it certainly wasn't beyond the realm of possibility.

One thing was sure: they needed to get ahead of this thing. They were reacting to events as they happened and not even doing that well. The attacks were going to keep happening, and Sully needed to get to the cause instead of just the effect. The radio let out a little noise, like a robot breaking wind, and Sully lifted it to her ear. Through the crackle she heard shouting and shooting. It was showtime.

Sully's own experience with traveling magic was pretty limited. She had the power to make good sized jumps, but she lacked the patience for all the preparation. The killer cop had been spotted a hundred miles away from the city, blocking a main highway in flagrant disregard of any threat of discovery. Sully made the calculations as fast as she could, and then made her first jump to the very limit of her range, straight up.

This wasn't like the journey to work around the Black Bay. She was so high up that the air was thin and she could see the whole of Carolina stretching out before her; rows upon rows of corn wavering in the breeze, like a big yellow vat of butter. This was where Sully's math got hazier, but at least little mistakes weren't going to leave her wedged into a solid wall like it would in the crowded streets of New Amsterdam. Sully gulped in a lungful of thin air and began to fall.

With each jump, she threw herself back up in the air a little farther. She was aching all over from the sudden jerks of gravity snaring and releasing her along the way, and she was burning through her magical reserves at a dizzying rate. She passed through a cloud, tried to wipe the dampness away from her face, and then spotted the motorway below her. For a long, stomach-turning moment she let herself drop, taking in the lay of the land.

There were a lot of bodies on the tarmac—easily distinguishable from the cowering bystanders by the pools of red beneath them. She had the final part of the traveling spell on the tip of her tongue when she spotted the killer hidden behind a burnt out car. He was firing blindly over the hood at the locals. Sully had planned to land on the side of the road opposite the vehicle. But no plan survives contact with the enemy, especially now that Sully's blood was pumping and she had a target in sight. Nobody ever looks up unless they hear something above them—a weird quirk of human psychology that Sully was counting on.

With a wicked grin, Sully cast a freezing spell. A shimmering beam shot straight downward from her fingertips and struck the killer on the top of the head. Sully expected the spell to freeze him in place when it made contact. Instead, he exploded in a shower of blood and a wave of raw magic burst out of him, buffeting Sully with a cushion of displaced air just long enough for her to realize that she was spinning to the ground out of control and had no time to calculate another jump.

JULY 3, 2015

Healing spells existed, but they were in the realm of specialists and were intensely regulated, given that they brushed so close to the forbidden area of necromancy. The universities didn't even teach them anymore. So Sully found herself in a hospital in Carolina. A few deputies had been set to guard her room until she woke up, and now they gave her an even mix of sympathetic and angry stares. She had screwed up, and they knew it. It had cost her a few bruises and a concussion, but it had cost them a coworker—chunks of whom were still being hosed off the highway.

The local chief had debriefed her after she woke up the first time, and she didn't even consider making excuses. It had been her call to take on the deputy alone. It had been her magic that overloaded him. If she had stuck to the plan, it probably still would have happened, but there would have been a bit more transparency. When an Imperial Agent descended on a small town and exploded somebody, it was hard not to suspect some sort of cover-up or conspiracy. Especially when Sully had received very explicit instructions from the Deputy Director of the IBI to not discuss the case with anyone, even the victims' families.

A day in a hospital was more than enough for Sully. After about twelve hours of stewing in her adjustable bed, cursing her own stupidity, and ignoring her throbbing everything, Sully discharged herself and caught the train home. The media bubble was about to burst now.

There were too many small-town cops involved, and it would be all they'd talk about for months, if not years. Civilians would overhear, and with civilians came journalists.

Sully found a seat in one of the train's quiet compartments and buried her head in her hands. If Colcross even let her stay on the case when she got back to New Amsterdam—and after this, there was a good chance he wouldn't—then it was going to be her whole life until it was over. That meant finding out who was really behind it. Not just the killers, who appeared to be victims themselves. This magic was something new, something Sully had never even heard of before, and it was going to be a nightmare to puzzle through.

But at least once it was public, she could tap resources, call in the assistance that she needed and, hopefully, keep interference from the Colonial Government at arm's length for as long as the public were watching.

If the painkillers weren't already flooding her system, just thinking about all of this would have given her a pulsing headache. She slept fitfully on the way back home. In one of her waking moments, against all sense of self preservation, she turned on her cell. The message from Deputy Director Colcross was the politest she had ever heard, and that scared her, asking her to stop by his office at her earliest convenience. She also had a message from Raavi, trying to set her up on another blind date with his sister and casually mentioning that he was finished with the first three rounds of bodies she'd sent him.

The third message was briefer, a throaty southern voice whispering down the line, "I need to see you darlin'. I'm hurting."

The morphine haze lifted in a rush of excitement. Setting up that last meeting was a little further out of her way, but at least it would be something to look forward to, whether she was still on the case or not. Maybe her own aches and bruises would get some soothing while she was at it.

* * *

It was night by the time New Amsterdam's shining skyline was visible, but there was no hope of dodging out of work on an excuse as tawdry as being injured and needing to rest. A crowd milled about outside the IBI building; not the usual suits blustering around, but a proper press of bodies. Cameras and microphones were being thrust in the face of anyone walking in or out.

Sully groaned softly and pushed her way through the crowd. It didn't take long for one of her earlier cases to bite her in the ass—like it or not, she was known to the press. One of the reporters who had followed the Florida dragon smuggling case spotted her and put two and two together. The media were like a school of piranhas. Another reporter spotted the redirected attention of the first, and then they all turned on her in a wave of shrieked questions.

The first time one of them bashed up against her, she gritted her teeth and pressed on, but the next one caught her in her cracked ribs with an elbow, and it was enough to set off her contingency spells. The unfortunate cameraman was lifted off his feet and began a slow orbit around her. The rest of the media scampered away with a slight decrease in volume and Sully strode on toward the entrance, using the slowly drifting man as a shield to keep the rest of them away, until the spell finally dumped him in a heap on the ground. He shouted something about a lawsuit, until Sully glowered with so much contempt that he shut up and scampered off.

She was just about to step through the door of the IBI building, aching and angry, when she did something stupid. Turning to the gathered swarm, she held up her hands for silence. When it came, she said, "The IBI is investigating this matter. I will be taking care of it personally. We will be making official statements shortly."

* * *

Colcross was not amused. "It is my hope that you recognize the uncomfortable position you have put the Bureau in, both in your failure to apprehend the last suspect, and in announcing your involvement in this case so publicly. Especially when you take into consideration that there has been no progress whatsoever under your . . . eh . . . attentive care."

Sully bit back her first three replies before finally grunting, "Hard to make progress when I'm running in circles and nobody's telling me anything."

The director fluttered down and perched on the back of Sully's chair with a loud squawk. Bolstered by the avian moral support Sully pressed on. "If I hadn't landed in the middle of this case, I would never have known anything was going on. The rest of the department needs to be brought up to speed. The constabularies across the colony need to be put on alert. We need to go through all of the murders this year to find out when these attacks started."

Colcross's expression was fixed, his stare glassy. "Do you have any other suggestions on how I should run this department, Agent Sullivan?"

Sully recognized the dripping sarcasm but waded right through it. "Whoever is doing this has more power and magic than any civilian. If we find out that it's not some kind of new demonic incursion, then a magus must be doing it. Either way, this is going way above my pay grade, and I need you to have my back. If you want this put down. Sir."

He gave her a thin smile. "Thank you for your input, Sullivan. I will take your comments into consideration."

Sully smiled back, with just as much warmth. "With all due respect, sir, what the hell does that mean?"

If she didn't know better, she could have sworn Colcross's smile almost became genuine for an instant. The Director hopped down onto her shoulder and croaked, "Put it down. Put it down."

Colcross scowled at the bird, but nodded. "It means that I am already gathering the information that you have requested, and should any solid evidence present itself, then I will pass that information along to you. It also means that this conversation never happened. Are we clear?"

Sully grinned, this was better than the morphine. "As crystal, sir."

Colcross pinched the bridge of his nose and pushed a sheet of paper across the table. "This is a requisition order for the theoretical assistance you requested. Local constabularies have been alerted to the situation. What I need, Sullivan, is for you to find the cause of these events. If we know how this is done, we can stop it from being done again. No more chasing our tails. No more . . . eh . . . explosive errors in our decision making. Do try not to disappoint me, Agent Sullivan."

* * *

The morgue was scattered with body-bags and fast-food wrappers. Bodies were stacked in piles organized by their respective cases, and despite the relatively early time, Raavi's shirt was off and all four hands were full. Although one held a ginger beer, which meant it wasn't quite crunch time yet.

Raavi met her placid smile with a manic one of his own. "This is getting boring Sully. All of these bodies. All killed in such boring ways. I remember when you used to bring me people with their blood turned to molten lead. I remember when you brought me a severed tongue that kept on moving in a jar for three months. You remember?

"The interns thought it was some kind of exotic slug. These are just people who got stabbed or shot. And I won't even get to look at the last body since it is basically jelly. This is a waste of my talents. Go solve this nonsense so I can get back to staying up all night doing the things I like to do."

Sully laughed despite the fresh fire it spread through her rib cage. "Sorry that you're being put out. Have you found anything I can use?"

He shook his head. "All the same as the first one; dislocations all over the place. So much magic one of my Schrödingers actually jammed into full-on panic mode. I am going to say demons. Smells like demons to me."

Sully snorted. "I'm not sure your smells are going to interest the Deputy Director."

Raavi looked up at her again. Blood had dried across his forehead and on his mask in a dark brown smear. "I mean they really smell of something, Sully. Ozone and rotten eggs. Brimstone if you like. I'm doing more testing but this sort of thing is hard to narrow down. Magic isn't an exact science, you know."

Sully rolled her eyes. "Spoken like somebody who never studied it. You really think we have demons involved? This isn't just your weird dissection fetish flaring up again, is it?"

"I derive purely intellectual pleasure from chopping up demon corpses. Don't sully my passion with your filthy sexual allusions."

Sully tried to keep a straight face as she stared him down. Blood trickled down one of his arms from the scalpel in his upper right hand. Eventually he fidgeted, "Alright, so I enjoy my work. That doesn't make me wrong. That doesn't make me perverse. It just makes me happy. Why don't you want me to be happy? I thought we were friends?"

Sully snorted and then gasped, grabbing at her cracked ribs. All humor left Raavi's face, and where anyone else would have shown concern, he went straight to professionalism. "Cracked ribs? Anything else?"

Sully blew out a strangled breath. "Just my everything."

Raavi's perfectly sculpted eyebrows drew together. "Have they given you the good drugs or that cheap nonsense they use on civilians."

Sully winced through another laugh. "Not my first time at the circus Raavi. I know my limits, don't start mothering me."

He scoffed and went back to his work. "Wouldn't dream of it, darling. Toddle off and find our demon, will you? I can't wait to see what it looks like. Some sort of jellyfish is my bet. I love the ones with tentacles. Their neurology is always so fancy."

* * *

The taxi driver who took her home was Irish, and it was no secret his passenger was too. The faint hint of her accent and the bloody red hair made sure of that. So it didn't surprise Sully when about halfway through the trip, he brought up the conversation every immigrant eventually had.

They spoke about the old country, the home of their blood, exchanging stories about what was happening over there. As an immigrant in the British Empire, pretty much anything said about Ireland could be interpreted as sedition. Their countries had a long and bloody history. And every few years there was another failed uprising: some hedge witch would get their hands on a little extra power and lead some glorious revolution, which would promptly be crushed by agents of the Crown. Then came the usual crackdowns, rationing to the point of starvation, and campaigns of dehumanization that the Empire used to keep its colonial subjects in line. All providing a healthy well of hatred for the next would-be revolutionary to tap into.

It was a cycle that nobody wanted to see repeated. As far as the British were concerned, the Irish were ungrateful savages; as far as the Irish were concerned, the British were perfectly nice people when they didn't have their boot on your face. The driver told her about the new bridge that cursed London had started growing across the Irish sea in its never ending expansion, and the rumors that the Veil of Tears was starting to break down.

The bridge didn't concern her, London could go on growing forever for all she cared, but any breakdown of the barrier spell between the demon-haunted, magic-ravaged mainland of Europe and home set alarm bells ringing in her mind. If the Veil fell, every demon that was running riot through the ruins of Europe would have been free to go roaming around the world, slaughtering as it saw fit. It was almost enough to make her call her mother. Almost.

Sully shared a few stories of her own, not quite confidential information, but helpful enough that a few good people who had garnered a little too much attention from the Empire would be fleeing their homes immediately after the taxi driver dropped her off and got to a phone. He wouldn't take her money when they finally arrived—even though she argued back and forth with him for a solid minute—and it wasn't an insignificant fare. He eventually forced her hand back into the passenger compartment with her cash still bundled up in it and then gave it a squeeze. "You remind me of my daughter. I'm not going to take your money. We need to take care of each other out here in the wilds."

She couldn't argue with that.

* * *

It took some digging in her pockets to find her door keys; everything was out of its usual place after the hospital stay. When she finally got them into the door, it swung open of its own accord.

Sully ducked to the side of the door and cast a quick shield over herself but nothing exploded in a flurry of bullets or spells. Her arcane senses rolled out over the room but she could feel nothing alive in her apartment beyond the usual roaches. Nothing alive. Someone inside. That meant vampires.

Vampires had no magic of their own, but if they bit someone, it severed that person's connection to magic too. Even the day after a bite Sully always felt that her powers were weaker. So whoever was in the apartment would probably try to rush her before she could cast, if they had any sense. Sully readied a freezing spell, felt the cool energy crawling along her fingers, then spun around and rushed through the door with her hand raised to cast.

By the bed was a lit candle. The scent of perfume swept over Sully: wildflowers and coconut oil. Cold hands encircled her wrist, and the spell died as her hand was drawn away from her. Cold lips wrapped around one of her fingertips, kissing it all better. A fang brushed over the soft pad of her finger, drawing a gasp out of the depths of her chest. The vampire practically purred as Sully succumbed, kicking the door shut behind them. Marie leaned in close enough that her chill breath tickled Sully's ear and whispered, "Welcome home, darlin'."

JULY 10, 2015

The morning after was as awkward as usual. Their current arrangement benefited them both—Sully provided Marie with enough blood to keep her off the streets, and Marie provided Sully with . . . well, Marie. The benefits didn't overpower their memories though: Marie left Sully at the altar for a nasty little man from the carnival and Sully clung tightly to that betrayal as an excuse for every awful little revenge she'd taken in the years since.

The guilt that came with believing she was responsible for Marie's current state of undeath confused things even further. Love and pain and guilt were so tightly bound together that Sully couldn't puzzle out where one ended and the others began.

They woke up tangled with each other in Sully's bed with Marie purring softly in her ear. In life Marie had been tall, tanned and blonde with a scattering of freckles across her perfect aquiline nose—every inch the aspiring movie star in appearance, even if her acting dreams had been focused on the stages of Broadway. Without light, her hair had faded to almost white, her skin had turned porcelain pale and the freckles had vanished.

Sully missed those freckles. If she hadn't been aching already, Sully would have been now. But it was a different kind of ache, deep in the bones and warm—so warm—even as the body pressed against her was sapping that heat as fast as it was generated. When they untangled themselves, Sully hissed as the movement tugged on the fresh puncture wounds on the inside of her thigh. That whole area was going to be thick with scars if she couldn't get Marie to start turning her head the other way when she was in the throes of passion.

Marie was as curious as she always was about Sully's latest case, especially since she'd picked up one of last night's broadsheets before coming over. It had run with Sully's impromptu doorstep statement in front of the IBI along with a photo and a brief biography. The paper, one of the few that Sully hadn't pissed off over the years, went so far as to call her career in the IBI "triumphant." Marie had always loved the smell of celebrity but she didn't chase after it like she'd done back when she had a pulse. Being part of the most loathed minority in the Empire had put Marie's dreams of stardom beyond reach.

Sully had the first shower, hissing as the hot water touched her scratches, scrapes and the new bite. When she returned Marie was still lounging on the bed, the sunlight filtering through the dirty windows to cast a glowing band over the curve of her back. If the windows were clean then she would have been gently sizzling, which was precisely why they weren't. Sully covered her face with the towel from her hair as if it was to dry herself, rather than to hide her expression when Marie rolled over to look at her. The hooks were in deep. Even after all of the heartache.

"So I hear you make policemen explode now? That's exciting."

Sully grumbled as she sorted through her wardrobe. "It was one policeman. Once. One time. It isn't like it's a hobby. And you know I can't talk to you about this."

Marie pouted and Sully looked away, biting her own lip, before she told Marie everything she wanted to know. The vampire remembered the power that pout held over Sully. She heard the rustle of fabric as the bedsheets fell away.

"Well the least you can do is tell us concerned citizen types whether some crazy person with a knife is gonna start chopping us up."

Sully pulled on a clean white camisole top then turned around. She kept her eyes fixed on Marie's face instead of letting them wander like they wanted to, and the distraction made her more honest than she would have liked to be. "Nothing's going to happen to you, Marie. I wouldn't let anything happen to you."

Marie was briefly stunned, giving Sully enough time to retrieve a pair of underwear and jeans from the drawers. But she rallied quickly. "You're going to take care of me, darlin'? Put me up in a five-star hotel and pamper me? Going to make an honest woman of me yet? Are you?"

Sully's temper flared. "I didn't know you were the marrying type, Marie. You should have said something, and I would have proposed years ago."

There was a steely quiet to the room as Sully finished getting dressed. They didn't look at each other much after that, and they certainly didn't talk. Marie slipped her floral dress back on when Sully wasn't looking. Sully let her out, then locked the door behind them. They went their separate ways, for now.

Sully listened to her cell phone messages as she walked to the subway station. The first message was from Leonard Pratt. In a deep, melodious voice, he said, "My dear Miss Sullivan, it is a delight to hear from you again after all of these years. How goes the great work? You must let me check over the latest calculations when I see you. I would love to be of assistance to you, and by happy coincidence, my book tour will be passing through New Amsterdam in three days' time.

"If your Deputy Director can arrange it with my publisher then we should be able to squeeze in some time together. My understanding is that a number of very well reviewed dining establishments have opened in your neighborhood, and I believe that it is my duty as a citizen of the world to take some time to get acquainted with them. Give me a call. I look forward to your latest puzzle."

It was just like Leonard to use every second of a voicemail message to say absolutely nothing.

The next message was from Deputy Director Colcross, who, to Sully's memory, didn't even like to acknowledge that cell phones existed. The message was less floral than Pratt's, and due to continuous security concerns, it told her even less: there was information on her desk about the latest attacks, and all resources were available to her. Not even a goodbye. The third message was the one she had been waiting for ever since speaking to Raavi last night. It was from the Smithsonian Museum regarding one of the items in their sub-basement. She had an interview there at half past ten. Sully jumped the turnstile and ran for her train.

* * *

If Sully had wanted to speak to an expert on the subject of demons there were few places in the world that had more demonologists than New Amsterdam. The only problem was that every one of them gossiped incessantly, to each other and to their clients. Sully wanted secrecy so she preferred to go straight to the source.

She was met by one of the research associates at the museum. By torchlight, they made the perilous journey down a set of rickety steps into the depths of the inactive exhibits. The researcher was a boy in his early twenties, gangly, with ears that had surely grown to their present size in order to support his glasses, which looked to be about an inch thick.

Upstairs, he had barely spoken to Sully, flushing every time their eyes met, but down in the dark sub-basement, she couldn't get him to shut up. He explained the absence of lights was to prevent the old paintings and tapestries from fading, pointed out every long-abandoned pickled creature, every priceless relic—well informed right up until the moment they stood before the massive solid steel safe that housed the museum's best hidden attraction. Sully patted him on the shoulder in an uncharacteristic bout of sympathy and felt him vibrate on the spot. Even in the dark she noticed the sweat that ran down his forehead, beading on his glasses in the cold air. She smiled. "Don't worry, kid. I won't be long."

He muttered into his chest, "The Director said to give you as long as you need, Mrs. Sullivan."

Sully gritted her teeth. "Agent Sullivan. Sully if you're feeling especially daring. Mrs. Sullivan was my mum."

He handed over his torch and started backing away. "Good luck, Agent Sullivan. Just knock three times when you are done. I will be right here."

Inside the big old safe that was set into the foundations of the Smithsonian were several overlapping circles. The biggest was made of a solid band of silver. Then there was a ring of glass pipe that constantly circulated salt water, powered by an ancient charm that would probably outlast the building. Those were followed by rings of crystal and worked iron. The final ring was made of a brown substance that was unmistakably dried blood. Inside the rings were markings: sigils and runes from an assortment of different cultures and mystical traditions.

The room was kept cool by its position—so deep below the earth's surface that several major fires had gutted the upper levels of the museum, along with huge portions of the city, without ever touching it. The room was as safe a place as could be made for the demon Eugene.

Eugene the Sailor Doll had been found down in Florida, not long after the first settlements were built there, sitting untouched in the burnt out remains of a townhouse. A toddler-sized doll—fairly placid in its little white sailor's uniform, face painted like a jester. Academics and experts had researched Eugene for decades—but eventually the death toll climbed too high, and it was entombed in its current location.

When Sully entered the room and shined the torch in its direction, the doll's head tilted just a little. That was Eugene's way, movements tiny enough to cast doubt in the mind of the observer. Was it a trick of light? A rush of air? The air in the vault was dry and stale, with just a faint hint of rotten eggs. Sully licked her dry lips. "Are you going to give me the silent treatment all day? I thought you'd be bored by now, down here all by yourself with no one to talk to."

With the door closed behind Sully, the only light in the room was from the torch, shining a small circle on Eugene in the center of the room. The only noise was the blooping of the circulating water making its merry passage around and around in the glass pipe. Sully very deliberately took a step forward, despite the electric sensation running up her spine at being so close. She tried again. "Will you talk to me? I have some questions."

The doll's head tilted slightly in the other direction, its voice just as Sully had expected, deafening in the tiny chamber. "THAT IS THE INTENTION? ISOLATE ME TO WEAKEN MY RESOLVE? I AM THE VANGUARD OF THE HELLS. I AM THEIR FOOTHOLD UPON YOUR WORLD. NO SECRET THAT I IMPART WILL SAVE YOU. NOTHING WILL SAVE YOU. SET ME FREE THAT I MAY CONTINUE MY GREAT WORK OR RETURN ME TO DARKNESS UNTIL I AM RESCUED."

Sully laughed at him. She didn't mean to—it certainly wasn't conducive to a successful interview. But it was funny watching this little doll threaten all of human civilization. It had been a tense few days with very little relief, and that was the excuse she made to herself.

The doll bellowed, "HOW DARE YOU MOCK ME? YOU OF THE TAINTED GRACE. YOU, HIDING FROM MY SIGHT BY THE COLD ONE'S TOOTH. RETURN ME TO THE DARKNESS YOU PITIFUL WRETCH. WHEN MY ARMIES MARCH THROUGH THE FALLEN ASHES OF YOUR WORLD—"

Sully cut him off. "Would you be interested in making some sort of deal?"

Eugene fell silent immediately, which Sully took as a good sign. She pressed on. "This chamber isn't a cold room. You can still feel what is going on outside can't you? Even in your weird little doll body you have senses, right?"

Eugene launched into his tirade again, his little head wobbling from side to side, his painted mouth not moving at all. "THE LEGIONS OF HELL HAVE SENSES BEYOND THE KEN OF MORTAL MINDS. WE WILL TEACH YOU NEW WAYS TO SEE AND NEW WAYS TO FEEL WHEN OUR TIME COMES. WE WILL SHOW YOU ALL

OF THE WONDERS OF YOUR UNIVERSE BEFORE WE TEAR THOSE SENSES AWAY AND LEAVE YOU NOTHING BUT BLIND, TWITCHING MOUNDS OF NUMB FLESH, TOO WEAK EVEN TO USE AS FODDER FOR OUR HATCHLINGS. EVERYTHING THAT HAPPENS UPON YOUR WORLD IS WITHIN REACH OF MY SENSES. I CAN SMELL YOUR TERROR. I HUNGER FOR YOUR—"

Sully butted in again. "Yes, very good. Are you aware of the unusual events that have been happening over the last few days in Nova Europa? Are they demonic in origin?"

Eugene rocked back and forth until with one last jerk it rose onto its stumpy little legs. "I HAVE SEEN THE VEIL BETWEEN THE WORLDS DRAW THIN. I HAVE SEEN THAT WHICH REACHES THROUGH. BY YOUR OWN FOLLY SHALL YOU FALL. WHAT IS YOUR OFFER?"

Sully blinked at that, taking a moment to translate his megalomania into common English.

"Let's see. You know what is causing this, you are willing to tell me, and you want to know what you get in return?"

Eugene was positively subdued when he replied. "YES."

Sully treated the doll to a smile. "You have been down here for about thirty years. I wonder if you might be getting a little bit bored."

The doll slammed against the invisible wall of the circles and rebounded to land in a heap at the epicenter of the spells that kept him contained. "RELEASE ME THAT I MAY RAIN FIRE AND DEATH DOWN UPON YOU. LET ME TASTE YOUR SWEET PAIN ONCE MORE AND I WILL TELL YOU ALL OF THE SECRETS THAT YOU HUNGER FOR."

Sully shook her head. "You are never leaving those circles, Eugene. You will be there until the world ends, one way or another. But . . . you don't have to be bored the whole time. We have many forms of entertainment. I thought that you might be interested in some of them."

The doll looked as though it was being wracked by a seizure, flopping around on the ground in the torchlight and hissing, "GIVE ME LIBERTY OR GIVE ME DEATH. THERE CAN BE NO DEAL AS LONG AS YOU HOLD ME IMPRISONED. THERE CAN BE NO DEAL WHEN ALL YOU SEEK TO DO IS GILD MY CAGE. GO BACK TO YOUR MASTERS AND TELL THEM THAT YOU HAVE FAILED IN YOUR DUTY. TELL THEM THAT I AM NOT SO EAS-ILY BOUGHT. RUN MORTAL. FLEE IN FEAR."

Sully rolled her eyes and said, "Ok. See you later."

She turned around and walked to the door, even lifting up one hand to knock before Eugene called out, "HOLD AND FACE ME FOUL TEMPTER."

Sully turned around and pointed the torch at the doll again, now sitting back in its original position on the floor. "LIST EVERY AVAIL-ABLE FORM OF ENTERTAINMENT AND EXPLAIN THEIR VALUES."

Sully smiled. "Let me tell you about television."

A perilously long negotiation followed, which didn't surprise Sully—demons liked deals; they were intrinsic to their nature. Some scholars even believed that the hells operated on contract law rather than the laws of physics. Both parties finally agreed to terms. Eugene would provide direct answers to any question pertinent to the matter that Sully asked him directly, or by a proxy of no more than one per-son removed, in exchange for a year of television with a basic cable package. The remote would be placed inside the ring so he could oper-ate the device himself, and it would be checked once a week to ensure everything was functioning correctly.

The final stipulation, one that Sully was rather proud of, was that Eugene would not harm anyone sent to assist him with his television, nor exploit any part of this agreement in an escape attempt. She'd thought it was going to be a sticking point, but he capitulated when Sully offered to have the pornographic channels unscrambled.

With everything worked out, Sully sat down on the cold floor and started asking the important questions.

"Is this some kind of demonic incursion?"

Eugene shuffled a little. "THIS EVENT DOES NOT COME FROM THE HELLS AND A DEMON IS NOT THE WILL BEHIND IT."

Sully released a slow breath—that was a weight off her mind—and moved on. "Are demons able to possess living people, not just corpses? Can they take over living bodies and control them?"

Eugene shivered. "THAT QUESTION IS OUTSIDE THE BOUNDS OF OUR AGREEMENT. DO NOT TEST ME, IONA SUL-LIVAN. YOU SHALL FIND YOURSELF TO BE WANTING."

It was Sully's turn to shiver. The doll should not have known her real name. Almost nobody did. She apologized politely, ignoring the cold dread sinking into her bones. "Sorry, Eugene, I am just trying to work out how this is being done."

The doll didn't know how to respond to politeness. "YOUR NEXT QUESTION."

Sully stifled a smile with a cough and pressed on. "Can you explain what is happening in terms that I can understand?"

Eugene looked bored, how he achieved it with no facial expressions and the body language that only five points of articulation grant you was a mystery for another day. "YOUR PEOPLE'S BODIES ARE BEING CONTROLLED BY AN ENEMY. THEY ARE BEING MADE TO KILL. THESE THINGS YOU HAVE LEARNED FOR YOUR-SELF AND I MERELY CONFIRM. IT IS NOT DONE BY DEMONS OR ANY OF THE MAGIC THAT WE CAN TEACH. THIS MUCH I TELL YOU WITHOUT YOUR FUMBLING PROBING."

Sully smiled again. Maybe this whole deal with the devil wouldn't be so bad. "Who is using magic to control people?"

Eugene snapped to attention. "THAT NAME HAS BEEN OBSCURED FROM OUR SIGHT AS NOTHING ON YOUR PITI-FUL PLANE HAS BEEN BEFORE. THE NAME AND THE PLACE WHERE THE KEEPER OF THAT NAME DWELLS ARE BEHIND A BARRIER THAT WE CANNOT PENETRATE."

Sully frowned. "Do you mean the names are under a taboo? They have been magically sealed?"

The doll shook. "ALL OF THAT AND MORE, IONA SULLIVAN.

IT IS OLD MAGIC WROUGHT BEFORE YOUR VERY FIRST DAYS. JUST PRYING AT ITS EDGES SWELLS ME WITH NEW STRENGTH. THAT IS THE MIGHT OF THIS ENCHANTMENT."

Sully phrased the next question carefully, "Would you say that the person doing this is as powerful as a magus?"

Eugene tilted his head until the torchlight reflected off his painted eyes and they shone back at Sully. "MORE."

* * *

By the time Sully left the Smithsonian, arrangements had been made with the nervous research assistant, Clive. He would relay questions and answers between Sully and Eugene in exchange for a pretty small bribe. They'd discuss the matter of getting television service run down to the sub-basement with the Smithsonian's management as soon as Sully found the appropriate paperwork back at the office.

She would need to come up with a very good excuse for accounting to hand over six hundred pounds in expenses. A case like this bled money—especially around Christmas when every police department suddenly became extra thorough so that the overtime pay could swell their savings accounts. Sully took a taxi to Staten Island to brief Colcross on her anonymous source—might as well get that particular delight out of the way.

When Sully stepped off the elevator on Colcross's floor, Chloe was there to greet her with an unusually steady gaze—not a hint of the usual fluster. Sully was impressed with the valiant effort she was making, and in return, treated her to a rare smile. As horrible as everything was out there in the real world, life was pretty sweet for the lead investigator on what was shaping up to be the highest profile case in the Empire.

Accounts hadn't even blinked at her weird requisition requests. Just dug out—and possibly invented—the right paperwork to get a television delivered to a museum basement. They also handed her a wad of petty cash that made her eyes pop. It would give her a handy amount of leeway as she worked the case. Between the cash and the badge there were very few doors she couldn't open. Colcross's door was currently the exception.

Chloe hastily motioned Sully to her desk, a spark of panic flaring in her eyes, and whispered, "He's in a meeting with the governor. You probably shouldn't be here."

Ignoring the reek of tobacco and rumble of politics wafting out from under the Director's office door, Sully teased, "Tell me Chloe, why don't I see more of you?"

Chloe reached up to tug the one open button of her blouse shut over the bare skin of her chest and spluttered, "I beg your pardon?"

Sully cocked her head. "I see all the girls from down in the typing pool going out to the wine bars. I see all the agents going to the gentlemen's clubs. I even see the lab boys on their bowling night. But the only time I get to see you is in these few seconds before and after I go in there to get a new asshole torn. You seem like a nice girl. I'd like to see more of you."

Chloe flushed all the way up under her perfect little fringe bangs and looked away. "I'm engaged to a very nice boy, Agent Sullivan." Sully leaned over the desk and brushed a stray strand of hair back behind Chloe's ear. The girl shivered and let out a little gasp. Chloe really had it bad.

Sully leaned even closer so she could feel the heat radiating off her skin and whispered, "I didn't ask to fuck you on your desk." Chloe shuddered and Sully brought her voice back up a notch, a little less threatening to the timid receptionist. "I just thought we could get a drink some time. Have a chat. That sort of thing. Just gals being pals."

Chloe turned to meet Sully's gaze, and it was all Sully could do to keep the laughter from escaping. Chloe's eyes were wide and glittered with suppressed emotion. She mumbled, "I might like that." Her eyes drifted down and locked onto Sully's lips. Sully couldn't resist a setup like that. She licked her lips, and Chloe almost panted. Then the office door opened and Sully jerked back to attention so fast that it made the startled secretary jump.

The governor was not as fat as Colcross, but they were both cut from the same overstuffed cloth. He also wasn't the provincial governor that Sully was expecting—this was Lord Albert Price, governor of the entire American colony. He was clean-shaven, making the absence of anything like a chin on his face all the more notable, and his eyes were wide-spaced and watery. He smoked a cigar about twice the size of any that Sully had ever been able to afford, and if she hadn't been standing directly in front of him, Sully was pretty sure he wouldn't have even acknowledged that there was a human being in the room.

She was damned if she would or could curtsy, but she gave him a polite nod on her way toward Colcross's office, and he returned it in passing.

He paused just before he was out of arm's reach and said, "Sullivan?"

She nodded.

He made a strange face that might have passed as a smile but seemed more likely to be indigestion. "Take care, my dear. We live in dangerous times." It was no great feat to deduce from the spittle that still flecked the governor's lips that he'd recently been shouting. His next words were spoken softly but clearly, "Make this go away quietly."

Either the governor's office had worked out the significance of what was going on or they had developed a newfound feeling of paternal care toward the citizens of the colony. Sully knew which one her money was on.

Despite the rumblings Sully had heard coming from Colcross's office, he was composed by time she let herself in. He didn't look tired so much as he looked ready to retire. He nodded at the chair without even bothering with fake pleasantries.

Sully led with the good news. "It isn't demons"—Colcross visibly deflated a little—"it is some kind of magic. I am working on what kind now."

His hand was shaking ever so slightly as he lit his pipe. "Thank you, Agent Sullivan. That is good to know. I do not need to know how you came to this . . . eh . . . information, provided there is a valid explanation in your report."

Sully snorted. "I didn't break any laws, Colcross, I spoke to Eugene."

Colcross looked puzzled so she went on. "Somebody tried to summon up a demon down in Florida a while ago but they cocked it up. The demon came through, but instead of taking a dead body, it ended up in a doll. It's been stuck in Eugene the Sailor Doll ever since."

Colcross's eyes widened as she went on. "Did it not occur to you that this information could have been in some way pertinent to the Director of the Imperial Bureau of Investigation?"

Sully shrugged. "The information is out there for anyone to read it. I assumed that you knew."

Colcross pinched the bridge of his nose as he hissed out, "Agent Sullivan, just because knowledge exists in the world does not mean that everyone is aware of it. You have the unique privilege of both an excellent education and an inquisitive intelligence. It is the reason that you were accepted for employment here and the reason that you have climbed through the ranks, no matter what you may have been told by other supervisors. This was your value to the Bureau. Now kindly use those . . . eh . . . attributes to assist me, instead of being amazed at my ignorance."

That was definitely complimentary. Things must have been worse than Sully thought. She shifted uncomfortably. "You get the reports from across the colony. How often are the incidents happening?"

Colcross nodded, probably grateful that she hadn't acknowledged their awkward moment. "There has been one incident every day. There is no pattern to the location or time of day so far, but we do not have enough data points to compile a full assessment yet. We assume that—given the amount of magic I'm assured something like this would require, and the overspill of magic that allows us to detect them through the nuclear decay devices—this period of rest allows the perpetrator to regain their power."

Sully scratched her cheek. "Sounds likely, but there's so much we're missing. It is like whoever is doing this has no limits. There might be more of a pattern than we think. Could you check the time from the end of one incident to the start of the next instead of start to start?"

Colcross scribbled a note on his blotter. "That may correlate. Are there any other factors that could influence the magic?"

Sully snorted. "Only the time of day, the color of tie you're wearing, the position of the stars and everything else. Here in the city, with a million runes running every appliance and a million spells being cast, they are constantly interfering with each other. It poses challenges to a magician, and it's why all the colony's research work is done in isolation down in Maryland. Everything affects everything."

Colcross sighed. "So, you would have to be a genius to create a new spell safely?"

Sully smirked. "Genius? I've always said that you don't pay me enough. Most new spells come from the magi. Even my tinkering is considered risky because you never know what interacts with what. That's why everything is tested into oblivion. That's why selling off my unique spells is a retirement plan."

Colcross pinched the bridge of his nose again. "At least that narrows down our list of suspects."

Sully slapped her hand down on the desk and snapped, "This is political."

Colcross look was disdainful to say the least, but Sully cut off the sarcasm she was sure would come next. "It was something that the demon doll said. Something about these attacks being caused by an 'enemy.' Not just a crazy or a killer. An enemy. Like there is a reason behind it all. Could this be some enemy of the Empire? Some sort of political disruption? Fearmongering?"

Colcross muttered, "That is what I need you to find out, Sullivan."

From beneath the cloth that covered the bird cage in the corner, the Director croaked, "Sixty-three and counting."

Sully glanced at Colcross but the big man just shrugged. She called out to the cage, "Sixty-three what, sir?"

The parrot cried out again, "Spotted it first. Spotted it first."

Colcross blew out a long stream of smoke. "Perhaps that is enough for today. We seem to be troubling the Director."

The cage rattled under its cover and the croaking continued, "Spotted it first. Spotted it first. Spotted it first."

When Colcross approached the cage with sadness ingrained on his features, Sully slipped out of the room quietly. Chloe avoided Sully's eyes as she passed through but glanced over just as the elevator doors were closing. Sully blew her a kiss.

JULY 11, 2015

After catching up on the latest incident reports at the office, Sully met Marie for lunch, hoping to mend any damage that their latest spat had brought on while still vigorously avoiding discussing their relationship. It was a pretty cheap date since Marie didn't eat, and Sully ordered light in anticipation of her dinner plans with Leonard Pratt. Unless Leonard had changed drastically, she knew he'd insist on gorging himself later on, and it felt rude not to join in. Besides, the Bureau would foot the bill for that meal.

Marie tried to hold Sully's hand while they waited for Sully's sandwich to arrive. Sully didn't pull away but she didn't do much to encourage her, either. After a moment of awkward silence, Marie sighed, let go of Sully's hand, and asked, "Darlin' are we ever going to talk about it?"

Sully kept watch for the waitress. "Talk about what?"

Marie took a hold of Sully's chin and turned her head until their eyes met—an old habit from the old days; when Sully was still new to the city and completely out of her comfort zone with the "less magically inclined," and Marie was still a warm-blooded human.

Marie looked sad but not in her usual way. Normally, her sadness followed a flash of anger, usually when Sully had somehow let her down, and Sully knew it was just a matter of kissing it away. This time it was softer, as if the emotion had taken root deeper. Marie spoke, looking right into Sully's eyes. "What are we doing darlin'? Are we together? Are we apart? Is this some slow drawn out revenge?"

Sully frowned. "What would I want revenge for?"

Marie closed her eyes. "For leaving you. For coming back. I don't know. What am I doing to make you so angry?"

Sully drew back from Marie's cold grip and looked away. "I'm not angry with you. We're even. You left me. I left you. No hard feelings."

Marie scowled a little at that. "It ain't a game that you can win darlin'. This thing with you and me, I just want to know if you're here for the long haul."

Sully shrugged. "Can't get much longer. You're going to live forever, and thanks to the magic, I'll be a hundred before I get my first wrinkle."

Marie continued to stare at her hopelessly.

Sully huffed, "I can't promise anything. Like you said, it's the long haul. Sometimes we're going to be together. Sometimes you're going to be off fucking some carnival hick. Sometimes I'm going to find some cute girlie in a bar and work out my frustrations. That's just how we are."

Marie had actually covered her mouth with her hand like some proper southern belle when Sully swore, but now she surged forward in her seat. "It doesn't have to be that way. We could try and make something real. Something that lasts longer than me getting hungry or you getting . . . lonely."

Sully shrugged again, her eyes following her sandwich which was now weaving its way toward her through the crowd. "Do you really think I've got anything more in me, Marie? After everything else? Look. Maybe we can talk after this case is put down. There's too much buzzing around right now." Sully swatted her hands around her head as she said it, making it obvious to everyone in the café that there was something off about her. A few people stared while others deliberately looked away.

The waitress arrived, and when Sully took her sandwich, she let her fingers brush the girl's—not enough to make Marie angry or to get the girl upset—just enough to make a point. The girl flashed her a quick smile before retreating.

Marie looked like somebody had just kicked her. "Ain't no need to be cruel to me, darlin'. We can talk after you're feeling more settled. Like you said, ain't like either one of us is going anywhere."

Sully was seated in a corner of the café facing the door—one of the more useful habits she'd picked up in the military when she'd spent most of her shore leave in the local bars. That was why she saw the NAPD officer barrel in through the door with his saber drawn and swinging. She pulled Marie right off of her seat and tossed her into the back corner of the room, toppling a few startled customers in the process.

The cop screamed, "IT iS thE YEAr oF the KNIfe! TeLL yOUR MasTERS! wE arE COMIng BACK!"

Sully called up her freezing spell and tried to take aim as the cop hacked away at the queue. There was a lot of blood and a lot more screaming. The place smelled like a butcher's shop and the sharp iron scent reminded Sully of the exploding hick in Carolina. She cursed under her breath. Everyone in the deli was trying to run, but there was nowhere to go. The volume just kept on climbing as more bodies hit the ground and arterial spray decorated the room.

Sully yelled, "IBI! Freeze!" It had the desired effect: the civilians saw her, saw the spellfire blazing from her fingertips and dived for the ground.

The cop puppet turned to face Sully with a slack jawed grin. "JuST thE WITch we WANTEd tO See."

Sully kept her hand trained on him. "You could have just made an appointment."

The noise that came out of the cop's throat was not even a little bit human; it sounded like an alligator being dragged over a cheese grater but Sully decided it was laughter.

"PERhaps wE ShaLL VisiT yOU in yoUR TOWEr nEXT. WoULD ThaT pleaSE yoU?"

With a smile, Sully let the spell vanish from her hand. Talking was good. Nobody died as long as this thing was talking. She nodded, "You would be more than welcome to come and have a talk about whatever your grievance is."

The laughter was harsher this time—the civilians who still had their arms attached covered their ears. "THEre caN bE NO taLk. We ARE ComiNG bACK. WE CANnoT Be turNed awAY witH FEEBle pRoMISES and liES. Our SUFFERing HAs lASTed centURies. YOu toOK EVErything fROM US. Even oUR NAMe. OUR PaIN SHAll BE your PaIN."

The cop raised his arm to bring the sword down on one of the cringing patrons at its feet. Sully closed the distance, ducking the wild arc of the cop's sword. Wrapping her arms around him was like tackling a lampost; he was rooted solidly. The speed of her approach spun her right around him. She met Marie's wide eyes across the room and gave her a wink, then cast the traveling spell.

Things could have gone a few different ways. The interaction of her magic and the cop's could have caused an explosion like the one in Carolina, hopefully after they were clear of the crowded deli. Or, and this was the theory Sully wanted to happen, the sudden relocation of the spell's target could have broken the connection and given the cop his life back. None of the above were true. Instead, they appeared in the air above Red Hook in Sully's usual transfer spot and began to fall tangled in each other's arms. Over the roar of the wind Sully yelled, "Hey constable, are you in there?"

The cop's head twisted one hundred and eighty degrees with a wet, sickening grinding sound that reverberated through Sully's body. The mouth flopped open and a cavalcade of voices burst out again, "noBODY in HERe buT us WitCH."

Sully kicked away and the cop tumbled off to collide with one of the tall chimneys, tearing its legs off. Before she could hit a roof herself, Sully cast the traveling spell again.

When she collided with the door of her apartment, it was with all the speed she'd built up on the descent. She knocked it off its hinges and tumbled end over end before sliding to a halt, her head in the kitchenette, her ribs broken to pieces, yet again, and the bottle of gin in the sink cabinet just out of reach. She gasped for another breath before the buzzing darkness closed in from the edges of her vision.

* * *

Sully didn't really expect to wake up—she'd pretty much resigned herself to death in that little café. All those people needed protecting and Marie had been right there with them. She was vaguely aware of the cold touch of Marie's hands on her bare skin, as distant as a fond memory. Then the sudden sharp pain as one of her ribs was touched. She must have made a sound, must have done something, because suddenly Marie's hands were gone and the black buzz was back.

Raavi's big nose bobbed into the center of her narrow window of vision and he drawled, "Do shut up, dear. You have a rib in your lung and I am operating on a kitchen counter with a mad vampire cow-girl serving as my only assistant. Go back to sleep and let me see how much of you can be fixed, eh?"

Sully felt something shifting inside of her and yelped. It wasn't her most dignified moment, but she wasn't screaming or sobbing so hopefully Raavi's jokes wouldn't be too pointed later on. She felt stretched out where Raavi's hands were dipping into incisions; she felt wet where the blood ran down her sides. The rest of the sensations that should have been there had dropped down into some cold hole inside her and it was like she was being held suspended just above them. Just out of reach of the worst of the pain. There were weird tugging sensations inside and the heat that had been missing up until now returned.

Sully gasped and then Marie was there holding her hands. With the scent of so much blood in the air, Marie's pupils were blown out so large that they took up the whole of her eyes. She leaned in close to Sully and whispered, "It's gonna be all right, darlin'. I got your friend. He's going to patch you up real good."

Sully was panting for breath, but she squeezed out, "Hospital?"

Marie gulped back rose-tinted tears. "I didn't know how to explain. I didn't want you to lose your job over me being there with you. Y'know the government hates vamps like me. I'm sorry darlin', I should have just called an ambulance."

Sully gripped Marie's hand and whispered, "You did right. Would've killed you."

Marie let out an ugly sob. "Who cares about me. You could die."

Sully forced a smile. "Normal day for me."

Raavi called out, "Nearly got it. Don't mean to interrupt you love-birds but could the dead one go and grab me some sutures while there is still only one of you that I can call the dead one?"

Sully smiled at him. "No hospital?"

He winked. "You know I have been dying to see what you had under those garish shirts of yours for years. How could I pass up this opportunity?"

When she didn't laugh he clucked, "Not enough time by the time I got to you. You were in a very bad way. Now shut up for a minute so you don't bite through your tongue. This is going to hurt like buggery."

He started to stitch something. She could feel the drag and tug of the needle. A whole new set of scars.

* * *

When she woke up, she was in her bed with Marie next to her. Raavi was nowhere to be seen, and if it weren't for the blood all over the place, she would have thought his visit had been a dream. Marie wasn't asleep. With slow languid licks she was cleaning the blood off Sully's skin like a cat. It probably would have felt good if everything didn't hurt. She croaked, "Time is it?"

Startled, Marie stopped what she was doing. She hated Sully to see her doing things that weren't human. Sully fumbled around for her cell phone on the bedside table. Something that wasn't easy to do when every movement was pain. After making a sound like a mouse being trod on she gave up. Marie shook her head, "You ain't going anywhere, darlin'. You'll be in bed for a month, if you're lucky."

Sully muttered, "You'll be in my bed for a month if you're lucky. I've got things to do."

Marie let out a surprised giggle. "Glad that you're feeling better but you better keep it in your pants until you're able to move."

Sully smiled at her weakly. "What time is it Marie?"

Marie frowned. "It's about seven o'clock."

Sully pushed herself up onto her elbows. Her whole body screamed—she dragged in a shaking gasp before flopping back onto the bed. She was careful to draw only shallow breaths after that. Once the pain had evened out, she spoke again, "I need my phone."

Marie dug through the pile of bloody clothing Raavi had cut off his patient and returned with the mangled remains of a Sully's cellphone and an apologetic look.

Sully grunted. "How did you get Raavi?"

"That lovely brown man? His number was on your fridge. Something about ten pin bowling. You ain't gone and turned coat on me have you?"

Sully rolled her eyes. "Not my type."

Sully groaned, "All right, here is what we'll do. Go look through any paperwork that hasn't got blood on it. You are trying to find the number for Ceejay. He works with me but don't worry, he's got no problems with vamps. Probably. If he does, I have enough blackmail material to sink him, so you're safe either way. Tell him I'm hurt, but don't tell him how bad it is. Get him to call Leonard Pratt and have Leonard bring over takeaway. Tell him Leonard can have my address. Then come straight back. Quickly."

An anxious look clouded Marie's features. "Why do you need me back quick? Are you hurting, darlin'?"

Sully managed a mischievous grin, even though just thinking of physical activity made her ache. "You aren't finished licking me clean yet."

* * *

Leonard brought some sort of stew from an Ophiran restaurant that stank of spices. Sully was sure she'd hate it, up until the moment Marie started spooning it into her mouth on little bits of flatbread—then she shut up and enjoyed it. Sully had never been very adventurous with food, but this used to be Marie's thing—taking Sully to a new restaurant and finding that one thing on the menu that she would love.

Sully guessed it was the first time Leonard had ever eaten takeaway. If not, then it was certainly the first time he'd eaten it straight out of the tinfoil takeaway containers. He was perched precariously at the foot of the bed, directly in Sully's line of sight from the mound of pillows she was propped up on, yet not intruding on her personal space. Trust him to know the etiquette, even at a time like this.

Marie smiled broadly. "This smells delicious."

Sully grunted. "Leonard always knows where to find the best food."

"So complains my tailor," said Leonard and patted his stomach, causing a burst of giggles from Marie.

In the midst of the chaos of Sully's apartment, Leonard looked as perfectly put together as always. His three-piece suit was placid green and tailored to disguise his newfound bulk; his silk waistcoat had an oriental peacock design. In deference to his advancing years and receding hairline, his head was shaved completely smooth, in stark contrast to his beautifully trimmed goatee. He would have looked every inch the perfect English gentleman if not for the rich chestnut brown of his skin. Back on mainland Britain, for every door opened by his education, connections and class, another slammed shut due to this one tiny detail. The British colonies were much friendlier to those of mixed ancestry and extended him imperial citizenship—at least for as long as he maintained his decorum.

Leonard was an upstanding citizen, a renowned expert in his many fields of study, a noted academic and, at every opportunity, a borderline revolutionary. There wasn't a university that did not immediately start thrumming with talk of secession from the Empire following one of his lectures. He left a string of crushed protests and wild-eyed idealists in his wake, but he'd never even come under suspicion. Sully had an instinctive hatred for "gentlemen," but Leonard slipped by it by being a gentle man in addition to the other meanings of the word. He had not said a rude word to her since he arrived, despite her vocabulary having been reduced to grunts, talking briefly about the cities that he had visited on his tour, to the delight of Marie, and very politely not questioning why a loyal servant of the empire had a vampire nursing her back to health.

During a lull in the conversation, when Marie cleaned up the takeaway rubbish, Leonard cast his eye over the room and stopped at the whiteboard with a little smile on his face. He glanced at Sully as if asking permission and when she didn't object, drifted over to puzzle through the formula.

Marie returned and sat beside Sully on the bed, giving her hand a squeeze and sending incidental jabs of pain running up her arm. Apparently, there was a little break in the bones there, too, as well as the dislocated shoulder that Raavi had popped back in while she was still sleeping. It had been a hell of a day.

Leonard clapped his chubby little hands together with excitement. "My goodness. I believe you may have solved the exponential growth problem."

Sully couldn't help but smirk a little. If Leonard Pratt thought that she'd cracked it, then she'd probably cracked it. He tapped a finger on a section of the spellwork and asked, "Won't this dispelling loop cause it to collapse in on itself almost immediately?"

Somehow he always got her talking, even when it hurt to talk. "That's the point. Instead of letting it grow exponentially or continue endlessly we convert it into a flash fire. Cast and then collapse. It means that it won't—"

In excitement he butted in. "—drain the life out of anyone fool enough to cast it, yes. A very novel approach. It will render it nearly useless for industrial purposes, of course."

Sully scowled. "It was never meant to be used for industrial purposes. Dante didn't want to smelt metal. He was a monster hunter. This spell is meant do some damage."

Stepping delicately away from the board, he said, "Well, I sincerely hope that you are successful in that endeavor."

Marie was grinning so wide that her fangs were showing when Leonard turned around. He looked from Marie to Sully and back again in a brief moment of confusion before Marie explained, "My darlin' is a genius. Always said so. Fixed the spell that couldn't be fixed."

Leonard matched her grin. "Yes, our dear Miss Sullivan has quite the aptitude for theoretical work. It is a shame that she couldn't be pried away from her activities in the field. As I have said many times before, there are a great many opportunities for someone of her substantial talent in the private sector, given her antipathy to academia."

Marie smirked down at Sully, who groaned. "That's it, wait until I can't fight back and all gang up on me."

Her tormentors laughed, and she even managed a chuckle before it brought a metallic taste back to her mouth, stopping her abruptly with a jerk. Marie was fussing over her again before she could get a word out, and Leonard clucked his tongue in disapproval. "This will not stand. I have a friend on the New England Medical board. Let me make some calls. I am sure that we can get a healing spell put together for you post haste. Your current situation is intolerable, especially if these injuries were suffered in the line of duty."

He didn't phrase it like a question, but Marie jumped on it anyway. "She threw herself at this crazy killer as if he were nothing. Then she vanished him away"—Marie snapped her fingers in the air—"just like that. I couldn't believe my eyes. Thought I was never going to see her again."

Leonard raised a perfectly preened eyebrow. "Vanishing killers and throwing yourself into danger, Miss Sullivan? One might almost think that you were some heroic character from the serials instead of the vicious curmudgeon that you claim to be."

Sully was scowling again. "I don't need any favors and I don't need anybody telling me how great I am. Thank you, Leonard."

Leonard waved away her concerns with one limp-wristed gesture. "Oh nonsense, my dear. I am always happy to help you. Let me make a couple of calls. I am sure that you are as anxious as always to return to your duties."

Before she could reply, he was already wandering off to the kitchen, busy with his cell phone. Sully groaned softly at everyone making a fuss. Marie leaned in close to her ear and whispered, "I like him. You shouldn't be nasty to folks who're trying to help you out."

Sully struggled to push herself further up the bed and growled back, "I've never met a man with money that didn't know to the penny the worth of any favor he does you. There's always a cost to this shit, Marie. He does me a favor, then I owe him a favor, and somehow, I end up working in some lab somewhere with his name above the door. He's one of the good guys as far as his lot go. But he's still one of them, and you should try to remember that."

Marie tutted but said nothing.

Leonard returned, slipping his cell phone back in his jacket pocket. "Clarice Simmons from the University of Boston is on the next train into the city. I shall have to meet her at the station by myself. I'm afraid she is rather flighty and, as loathe as I am to play into any unfortunate stereotypes about conservative academics, it would probably be for the best if your young lady was not present when Ms. Simmons attends to you.

"It would also be for the best if we also avoided 'talking shop' around her. I can't imagine that your office would have invited me to consult if it were a pleasant state of affairs that you were involved in."

Sully got a word in edgeways. "Thanks."

Leonard smiled at her beatifically. "It is my pleasure to be of assistance to you, Miss Sullivan. You know that if my time were my own then I would be more than happy to consult on every perplexing case that you investigate. I imagine that the inter-sectional nature of the areas of study you deal with must make every day exciting. My own work has become rather repetitive of late. They say that a change is as good as a break—"

Sully interrupted him with a raised hand. "Can we get to the point?"

He shut his mouth then nodded. Sully sighed with relief. On a normal day, talking to Leonard was a strain on her temper; today, it was a herculean effort not to scream at him. She asked, "Have you ever heard of mind control magic. Something to turn another person into a puppet?"

Leonard opened his mouth and glanced from Sully's scowl to Marie's apologetic expression and back before carefully saying, "Is that something that is happening?"

Sully sighed. "Yes. That is something that's happening. Daily."

He licked his lips. "Ah. May I"—he glanced furtively in Marie's direction—"speak freely?"

Sully looked at Marie and shrugged, or at least tried to. "She already knows enough to make trouble if she really wants to. Just pretend she isn't here."

Marie muttered, "That's what she does most of the time."

Leonard was just a little bit too polite to laugh, but he couldn't prevent a smile. "Developing a new spell, any new spell, is not something that happens in a vacuum. You have to research similar spells for formulae and components. Information must be exchanged with your peers. There is a great deal of reciprocity in spellcraft, so that every new magic benefits all of the creators who contributed evenly. That system extends even up to the magi. For all of their considerable personal power, each one is only a repository for spells that have been learned or purchased from other sources.

"You understand that this applies to something as straightforward as a single spell. What you are describing is an entirely new field of arcana. While there are a few precedents set in the areas of illusion and healing magic, I am dubious that any of them would serve as a sufficient foundation to develop that kind of direct control. This magic could not have been developed in secret—it would take input from many sources; therefore, I must propose that you look elsewhere. Is there any possibility that this is some new form of demonic oppression that we were previously unaware of? Some sort of parasitic entity from a remote area that is physically infecting the brain?"

Sully shook her head. "I eliminated those options already. This is definitely some new kind of magic. That's why I need you and not just some research mage. That's why I asked Colcross to call on you even though you cost more in a day than I make in a month."

Leonard smiled. "I did wonder why you would force yourself to endure my company when I always leave you so agitated."

Marie snorted at that. "That's how you know she likes you. She's like an ornery old cat. Hissing and scratching up the furniture until you pet her and then pretending it's a nuisance for her."

Sully's eyes widened in silent fury, but it did nothing to stop Leonard's cackling. Marie hopped off the bed to fetch a glass of water for Sully before physical vengeance could be meted out. Fuming in the bed, Sully blushed despite her best efforts and the day's blood loss. She blurted out, "Have you ever heard the phrase, 'Year of the Knife?'"

Leonard brought his snickering down to a more tolerable level. "Should I have?"

Sully shook her head. "Thought it was worth a try, since you get around so much. It's something the victims keep saying while they are under control."

Leonard shrugged. "I am terribly sorry, my dear, but if I have come across the phrase then it escapes my recall at the moment. What measures have you taken so far to identify the source of your spell? Some form of geometric backtrack, like you used in that case in Nebraska?"

Sully winced as Marie flopped back down next to her. "Nothing like that yet. I'm been pretty busy just dealing with the effects. I've been told that whoever is casting it is veiled pretty damned thoroughly, so I doubt that simple geometry is going to get us back to them. There is even a taboo on their name, so we can't approach it that way."

Leonard crept closer to the bed and settled himself by her feet.

"You are aware of the potential significance of your perpetrator being possessed of that level of power and skill."

Sully scoffed. "Yeah. I know it has to be a magus. Everybody has already warned me. I am keeping my head down until I have enough evidence. At that point, I'll hand it off to any of the magi who aren't complicit. Let them deal with it instead of getting turned into something small and furry myself."

Leonard looked startled. "You think that more than one is involved?"

Sully met his gaze, albeit briefly. "New fields of arcana don't get invented in a vacuum, right?"

Leonard rocked away from her and shivered. "You always invite me to the most interesting places, Miss Sullivan."

Sully smirked. "I aim to please."

He clapped his hands together and rose to his feet. "Very well. We shall start our work tomorrow, after your treatment. I have never had to research an entirely hypothetical field of magic before. I look forward to it. I thank you once again for your kind invitation. The fact that it also offers me a very tidy escape from this loathsome book tour is entirely coincidental, I assure you."

He turned briefly to Marie. "I am terribly sorry to impose, but would it be possible for you to stay with Miss Sullivan tonight? Just to ensure that she does not have any complications with her health before morning."

Marie gave him a courteous nod. "I'd be more than happy to. It's nice to be asked like I'm a lady."

She gave Sully a soft backhanded pat to the cheek as she said it. Sully's seething resumed.

The sound of Leonard cackling to himself could be heard as he made his way out of the apartment.

JULY 12, 2015

The healer, Ms. Simmons, was exactly as weird as Sully expected her to be. Her use of magic meant that her looks probably had little bearing on her age. Even so, she looked ancient and haggard, wrapped up in layers of wool and tweed as though New Amsterdam in July was as cold as the northern territories. She had on three separate scarves, which Sully had no trouble counting because the ends kept trailing over Sully's face as the blasted woman examined her. Eventually, she gave Sully a gentle pat on the head and muttered to Leonard, who had the good sense to stay well out of the way, "Punctured lung, crudely stitched. Broken ribs, barely healed. Dislocated shoulder, muscular damage. Tumor in the other lung, smoker? Smoker. Hairline fractures in the arms. Big fall? Big fall."

Leonard nodded along to her gibberish as if it had any meaning and asked the important question, "My dear Clarice, is it possible for these injuries to be mended or will the patient have to wait for her body's natural restoration?"

The healer stood stock still and let out a little nasal whine. On the outside, Ms. Simmons was utterly immobile, but it was apparent to Sully that inside her head the cogs were turning. Misshapen cogs that rattled quite a lot, perhaps, but spinning at a remarkable speed. She jerked her head toward Leonard. "Done all of the bits before, just need to put them together. Cancer is the hard one. Takes a lot to make it go back inside its shell. Might be better just to tear it out and patch the hole."

Sully said, "Sorry, Cancer?" but the healer rambled on, "That's the way to do it, tear out the cancer, patch both lungs at the same time. Bones are easy. Bones like me. Muscles will grump for a bit. Better to leave them to fix themselves. Get a belt for the patient's mouth."

Even Leonard didn't seem to follow that one, so he politely inquired, "A belt?"

The old woman shuffled over and reached for his groin. He backed away, crashing into the whiteboard and blustering, "Yes, of course. One moment, my dear. One moment."

He unthreaded the thick leather belt from his suit trousers then handed it over to the healer. She folded it over and snapped it a few times as she advanced on her patient. Sully's eyes widened, and the old woman squeezed Sully's cheeks until her mouth opened then shoved the folded leather between her teeth. The hag leaned in close and whispered, "Bite down you silly sow. Don't want to have your tongue flopping on the floor."

Ms. Simmons stepped away and, before anyone could object, lifted her arms above her head and started casting. Shimmering violet spellfire erupted from her fingertips, and she twisted and turned it into shapes that Sully felt fairly certain required the woman's fingers to pass through each other. The healer spoke words of power that Sully had never heard before and that caused the powerless lump, Leonard, to cower and cover his ears. The lights in the apartment exploded. The light from the windows grew dim.

In the distance, Sully could hear an inhuman scream—a high pitch somewhere between a girl finding a dead lover and a train slamming on its brakes. Sully shook. The whole bed shook. The whole building shook. The sound of Sully's own heartbeat echoed off the walls in terrible harmony with the old woman's words. The pattern of light in the air was a tangle of complexity: a detached nervous system caught in a spider's web. Sully felt the sickly chill of magic reverberating through the room.

Then, all she knew was pain. Complete and blinding pain that drove all other senses to failure.

JULY 11, 2015

The world came back in stages. First came the scent of blood and bile, thick and bitter in her nostrils. Then came the thunderous sound of her own breathing. Finally came the pain. Every inch of her was screaming. Then it was over, and Sully was awake and sitting bolt upright in bed, gasping for air.

Through the midday sun that filtered through the row of filthy windows, Sully took in her surroundings. She was alone. More importantly, though, she was alive. Definitely still a little shaky—it would take time to get her muscles moving in harmony again, but she could breathe without stabbing pain. As she lifted herself gently from the bed, she found she could move around unassisted. Remarkable, but given the intensity of the experience, unsurprising that more people weren't willing to go through it.

In a fairly brief time, she found some clothes folded in her wardrobe and a new cell phone still in its packaging sitting on the kitchen counter. Stuck to the fridge by a magnet in the shape of a topless woman with cartoonish assets, which had all of the hallmarks of a visit from Ceejay, was a list of phone numbers. She programmed the numbers into the new phone while perched on the stool by the breakfast bar, stopping occasionally when a vivid memory from the healing ordeal, usually accompanied by the taste of her own blood, threatened to overwhelm her.

While she'd been sleeping it off, someone had very thoroughly cleaned her apartment. That smelled like Raavi's work. As much as Marie might have complained about a mess, she would never have lifted a finger to fix it. Of course, it might have been another manifestation of Leonard's generosity, hiring a maid to clean the place up, but it seemed too personal a touch. Besides, a cleaning service wouldn't have left the place smelling of ethanol. Just like Raavi to sterilize all the surfaces.

She called the office first; Marie would have said that she was showing her priorities. There was less than a minute between the time she reached the receptionist and the time she was speaking with Deputy Director Colcross—he must have been waiting for her. He sounded completely calm on the phone; that was concerning.

"Welcome back to work, Agent Sullivan. I am glad that you are feeling better. Please try to avoid doing yourself harm in the future. The special care that your friend Mr. Pratt enlisted was expensive. Not to mention the fees to keep him in town while you recuperated."

Sully smiled, and amazingly, it didn't hurt. "Sorry, sir. I promise that next time I'll make sure they kill me to help balance your budget."

Colcross went quiet then sighed. "Yes, very droll, Agent Sullivan. Did you acquire any useful information during your latest bout with this 'mind controlling murder mage'?"

Sully blinked. "I beg your pardon, sir?"

Colcross sounded weary. "That is the headline that the New Amsterdam Times led with. Some of the rags with less class ran a picture of the Underwood family's kitchen and a banner headline 'It's the Year of the Knife.'

"I am not pleased with this, Sullivan. You can take my displeasure to be representative of both the governor's office and the displeasure of the Empress herself. In case I am in some way being unclear, if I find that information is being leaked to the press by someone within the Bureau, that person will not have time to clear out their desk."

If the governor's office and the government back in Britain were pissed about it, then the guilty person wouldn't need to clear out their desk. You don't need belongings when you're a pillar of salt. Sully didn't respond to Colcross, there was an implication of guilt in acknowledging that leaks existed, although her mind buzzed through the faces of everyone that she had discussed the case with, or in front of. It was probably leaking from the NAPD, as usual. If that department was a boat, it would be the Lusitania. But a nagging worry that Marie had needed some extra pocket money wouldn't quite go away. She pressed on, "What have I missed? Two days?"

Colcross slipped back into his usual flat tones. "On the 12th, we had reports from Kansas of a mass killing at a college. Not a royal college, just a center for education. Firearms were involved in addition to knives. The local constabulary had a redcoat on the scene within minutes. The body count was only eight, including the killer and the redcoat.

"The full breadth of information about your conflict in Carolina has not been released to the provinces yet, but the rumor mill has been hard at work. Everyone is aware that magic causes some sort of catastrophic failure on the part of this controlling spell. The peripheral damage of detonating so much bound magic inside a building had not been considered. I sent out a bulletin warning of this particular effect immediately afterward."

She asked, "What about yesterday?"

Colcross's voice seemed distant. "Nothing reported, yet."

Sully snorted. "Nothing?"

Colcross sighed. "We do not know if the attacks have stopped or if they are now operating with a degree of stealth."

Sully covered her eyes with her free hand. "That sounds ominous as hell. This thing was scary enough when they were just going berserk."

Colcross was even more curt than usual. It made Sully wonder just how many angry calls he was getting every day that this went on. "Your friend the curse-breaker has been set up in one of the laboratory rooms to begin research into the nature of this spell. I assume that you have some moves planned beyond hiding in theoretical discussions with Mr Pratt."

Sully smirked. "Glad you two are getting along. The idea is that he handles the theory, and I go put it into practice."

Colcross muttered something off the line, then snapped into the phone, "Get to work, Sullivan. Who knows how long this grace period will last," before hanging up on her.

Sully didn't even attempt to travel to the office by magic. After the last few days, it just seemed to be tempting fate. Instead, she got a taxi and used the time to send out a tersely phrased thank you text messages to everyone involved in her little health scare. She followed that up with threats and gag orders to Ceejay and Raavi. Then, after a few minutes of silence spent listening to the beat of her own heart like it was the most beautiful music she'd ever heard, she sent another text. This one was to Marie, offering to give her a more intimate thank you that evening, if she could find the time.

She got a few responses.

Ceejay inquired about the "luscious young vixen" that had contacted him about Sully's injuries. Raavi responded with a very reasonable request to get a snack later and catch up. She had not yet sent a message to Leonard, even though his direct line was now programmed into her phone; she just couldn't picture him sending a text message. It wasn't grandiose enough. She would thank him in person when she got to the office.

There was no crowd of news hungry press clustered around the IBI building when she arrived, just a few lone reporters who zeroed in on her the moment she stepped out of the car. She almost made it inside without having to talk to them, but one of them shouted out, "Agent Sullivan. How do you respond to claims that you were attacked by the Year of the Knife killer?"

She looked into the camera and shrugged. "Didn't do a very good job if he did."

* * *

Down in the depths of the IBI building, classrooms had been set aside for training new recruits, even though most of that sort of thing was done down in Quantico. Among those training rooms, which hosted seminars only once in a blue moon, there were a couple of labs that were used when the idiots upstairs needed some basic science explained to them by the geniuses in the basement.

It was into one of these dark recesses that they had stuffed Leonard Pratt, curse-breaker to the stars and man of international renown. If you weren't part of the bureau, most of the staff wouldn't piss on you if you were on fire unless you first signed a waiver. So having a civilian in the belly of the beast made them intensely uncomfortable. Yet somehow, Leonard had managed to scare up a cup of hot coffee, which was waiting on a metal bench for Sully when she arrived.

Leonard didn't have a single hair out of place, as usual. He welcomed her politely, handed her the coffee, which was in an actual cup, then gestured to a seat. She blurted out, "Thanks for bringing in the healer. I wasn't any use to anyone. Thanks for coming in to help, too. I know you are a busy man. You . . . you didn't have to call in favors for me, but you did it anyway, and . . . well . . . thank you, is what I am saying."

He smiled softly. "Miss Sullivan, it is my dear hope that somewhere underneath your prickly porcupine exterior you will come to consider me as your friend. I am sure that my minor contributions hardly warrant such high praise as of yet. But with time I would like for us to become closer."

Sully looked aghast. "Why would you want that?"

He pursed his lips. "I have a large circle of acquaintances in my life. I have even had the odd romantic companion over the years. However, I find that the number of people I can truly call a friend dwindles as more and more become business associates and place distance between us for the sake of their political ambitions. Or they simply pass away."

She held up a hand. "I understand why people want friends. I'm not a sociopath. Why would you want to be friends with me?"

He ran a hand over the smooth expanse of his head. "There are very few people who can keep pace with me, Miss Sullivan. I am rather overeducated—some say pompous—and I find myself drifting into academic lectures when I am attempting casual conversation. You understand everything that I am saying, but all the shortcomings that I find in the higher echelons of the elite have bypassed you entirely. Also, I find that conversations with you, in addition to being intellectually stimulating, can often be entertaining."

Sully raised an eyebrow. "So you flew in a healer and dropped your book tour like a hot potato because I'm not a moron and you think I'm funny?"

He gave a one-shouldered shrug. "In essence."

From the table, Leonard picked up a file and flipped it open— Sully was pretty sure he was extricating himself from a conversation that had turned oddly awkward. He tapped his finger twice on a shoddily typed line from a report that Sully recognized as her own, despite reading it upside down. "This may be significant, or it may be nothing, but this particular phrase—'We are coming back.'—I have encountered it once before."

Sully's response was absent her usual sarcasm. "Tell me about it. Please."

AUGUST 26, 1998

Heat was not a new experience for Leonard Pratt; he had lived through the brownouts that had plagued New Amsterdam in the eighties, when everyone prayed for air conditioning to come and save them from the stinking hell. The wet heat down in Louisiana was a different thing altogether—the humidity caught in his chest and choked his breath some mornings.

But there was a magical testing range in Louisiana, and he needed their cold-room to carry out his terribly clever plan.

His first client had already arrived and was waiting in the hall outside the testing chamber. He was a tiny Oriental man, known as the Eternal Emperor, so wizened and wrinkled that his features had been subsumed in the folds of his skin. Wrapped in silk and shivering, he was in the arms of his traveling companion and translator, a giant of a man, a former rikishi who'd spent many years sumo wrestling before his current gig.

The Emperor was older than the modern language and had outlasted the fall of his dynasty and all of those that followed. No one knew exactly how old he was or who had cursed him with immortality. The old man had told a thousand stories in his lifetime and traveled the world. He had ruled an empire and begged in the gutter. But he was tired now, tired of living. He had sought out the services of many a curse-breaker before Leonard Pratt, but it had all been to no avail. When his translator had explained Leonard's plan, the Emperor had quickly agreed—he was willing to go to any lengths to break his curse.

Leonard greeted the ancient man with a full kowtow, pressing his head to the tiled floor. It startled the pair of redcoats on guard, who realized that this visitor must be one of importance.

After exchanging pleasantries with the translator and his charge, Leonard directed them to the testing chamber. The white room was barren except for a series of interlinking circles set into the floor, each made of a different metal or crystal. Power pulsed through the circles and crackled in the air, causing the old man's long hair to drift, floating as if he were underwater. The moment the translator carried him into the center of the circles, everything in the room stopped and the air became silent and cool.

The translator tried to lay the old man down but, with a determined glint in his eye, the Emperor slipped his bare feet down to the floor. His legs bowed beneath him but he found his balance and stood with a smile and a gentle incline of his head toward the man who had carried him in. As the translator shuffled away from his charge, Leonard saw silent tears running down his cheeks.

The next to arrive was another of Leonard's clients. Malcolm Sinclair was formerly a successful banker. He currently resided in the icy wastelands of the northern provinces, where he'd gone after being cursed by his ex-wife, a hedge witch. Thanks to her, every living thing that came into contact with Malcolm died instantly. He, too, had been desperate by the time Leonard had suggested the current solution.

Malcolm wore a hazardous materials suit. The only thing visible was his face through the suit's thick faceplate. The years in the northern provinces had not been kind to him: his skin, once smooth and stylishly tanned, was now cold-bitten and weathered, his black hair was faded to gray, and his eyes had sunk into his face. The suit offered protection to those around him, but Leonard still saw Malcolm wince when they shook hands through the thick gloves.

Leonard was practically buzzing with expectation now that the two key elements of his grand plan had arrived. Introductions were made but it was all just preamble. A cage holding a pair of chickens had been delivered to the testing room. Malcolm approached the cage then stripped out of his protective suit, exposing a tattered vest and holey jeans underneath. Leonard made a mental note to put the man in touch with his tailor if they were successful.

Malcolm approached the cage and, with a miserable shiver, poked one of the chickens. It toppled over dead. Leonard examined it carefully from a distance, then motioned Malcolm forward toward the circles on the floor. At the center of the chamber, the Emperor gave a gentle nod and Malcolm returned it stiffly. Leonard, standing just at the edge of the outermost circle, called out to them, "Be polite gentlemen, when you are ready, shake hands."

They had both been thoroughly briefed. They both knew the risks inherent in Leonard's plan and had signed waivers well in advance. Leonard felt pretty confident that the Emperor, at least, would be happy with the outcome, but he was less so regarding Malcolm. The truth was, he had no idea what would happen when the magic from the two powerful curses collided, but as Malcolm had put it, anything was better than the forced solitude of his current existence.

The Emperor didn't move, and even Malcolm appeared to hesitate. Leonard called out to the Emperor in fractured Nipponese, "Enjoy your new adventure." The old man's face split into a wide grin as he snatched Malcolm's half-extended hand.

The explosion was contained inside the set circles, but it burnt so bright that it left after-images in Leonard's eyes. He was stumbling backward toward the door when the sound began. It started as a low shriek, then built in intensity, until both Leonard and the translator had their hands clapped over their ears. The shriek became a reverberating wail as the metal rings in the floor began to twist upward and snap. First the silver ring. Then the iron one. The gold and the platinum rings coiled away soon after, until only the crystal rings held the pillar of blinding light in place.

Squinting into the light, Leonard could still see the pale silhouettes of the Emperor and Malcolm holding on to each other for support.

Between the two men, a hairline crack had appeared, suspended in air. The reek of sulfur swept through the chamber and the room began to quake violently. The translator lifted Leonard with little visible effort and carried him back toward the door of the room. The remaining chicken was left to fend for itself.

Catching onto the doorframe, Leonard yelled, "*Tyotto matte kudasai!* Please. Wait!" and the huge man carrying him paused, glancing back into the room with terror etched on his broad face. The powerful energy still surged from the two men, but Leonard was happy that no demon came bursting out of the rift in the air. Then the unstoppable force of Malcolm's touch colliding with the immovable object of the Emperor's immortality appeared to flood into the gap between them. The light, the blazing fury and the thunder gone in an instant.

The Emperor's body hit the ground, crumbling to a fine dust, but Malcolm was pinned against the gap, blocking it from sight. He hung in the air like a puppet in the whipping wind, feet dangling three feet off the ground. He twitched and shook as the terrible suction tried to drag him down into the hole, too, but it was too small for a human body to pass through, at least in one piece, and Malcolm was still a solid mass. He croaked something, still conscious, and Leonard struggled free of the translator's arms and inched closer. Leonard cried out over the shrieking vibration of the crystal rings, "What?"

In a chorus of unharmonious voices, Malcolm bellowed, "We aRE COMinG BaCK."

A redcoat from the hallway pushed his way past the translator, who still stood in the doorway, and unloaded a twelve-round clip into Malcolm's flopping body. It fell to the floor, leaving no trace of the rift, only the devastation that had been wrought. The redcoat spat on the ground. "Not on my watch you're not."

JULY 11, 2015

Sully had finished her coffee and rocked the cup back and forth between her hands.

"What does this mean, Leonard? That it's really a demon and my source happens to be the only demon in all of history that can tell a lie? That it's some sort of construct made out of colliding curse parts?"

Leonard looked uncharacteristically glum. "I am afraid that I have shared all of the information I have with you, and beyond that, I could only hypothesize."

Sully grunted. "Well, hypothesize. That's what you're here for."

He wriggled around in his seat, getting comfortable. "I do not believe that we are investigating any form of demonic influence. There have been by far too many instances throughout history where being capable of this particular trick would have greatly assisted the infernal agenda. While there have been odd interactions between spells and construct creatures have been created as a result, intelligence is a trait that must be very carefully crafted if it is to be inserted into an artificial creature.

"The behavior of your possessed individuals, while violent, still displays some markers of logical thinking. Ergo, I do not believe that a construct creature was created in the accident. There are two alternate theories that I would like to put forward, both of which I realize are somewhat hazy."

Sully rubbed her eyes and nodded. A headache was already starting to build there, and they'd barely gotten started. Leonard flinched but kept going. "The first theory is that your mysterious controller has been in operation since the incident in Louisiana, capable of seizing control of people for all of these years, but without making use of that ability outside of that one select incident."

Sully shrugged. "Seems unlikely that somebody would have that power and do nothing with it."

He nodded his head in concession. "The other possibility is a matter of a more metaphysical nature, I am afraid. It is my firm belief that the energy released from the dissolution of the curses produced a dimensional breach. All evidence points toward that outcome when such an excess of power is produced. That is the reason that certain fields of arcana are so tightly regulated. Any time there is such an uncontrolled output, there is an increased risk of the barriers between worlds dissolving. We need to look no further than what happened in Europe to see—"

Sully cleared her throat to keep him on topic.

"The point I am meandering around is this: While there was every indication that a dimensional breach occurred as a result of the massive amount of power being released, I do not believe that it was singular. We did not just open a gate to hell. The planar connection to the alternate dimension was only brief, yet the rift persisted for a period of at least twice that time without any other olfactory indicators."

Sully raised an eyebrow. "The smell went away?"

Leonard smirked. "Precisely. In a hypothetical situation, I would propose that the escaping energy went on to produce a second disruption between the new dimension it had entered and yet another. I believe that there was such an outpouring of magic that it burrowed through the hells and out the other side.

"Many have theorized that the current dimensional model is incomplete. Some even say intrinsically flawed. That there are, in fact, multiple concurrent dimensions and our contact and limited access to the one occupied by those presences we have defined as demonic is simply due to our immediate proximity in five-dimensional space.

There are theories that many other universes exist beyond even that one—planes that we would perceive as even more alien than the demonic one, due to their abstraction from us. My second proposition is that this creature we are dealing with is one of the denizens of those far planes."

Sully rolled her eyes. "So your best guess is, 'Something so weird we have never even heard of it.' That's great Leonard, I see why they pay you the big bucks."

He held up his hands. "I did warn you that my options were limited based on the information that we have. But it would explain how such an unusual form of magic could be constructed without either the demons or us having any knowledge of it, and it would explain the unusually high output of magic from the victims. If the spells are being broadcast across the dimensional barriers, they would have to be extraordinarily powerful."

Sully shook her head. "Let's save the crazier theories for later. For now let's keep our focus. Eyes forward."

He smiled indulgently. "Eyes forward? You said that in Montreal, too. Does it have some special meaning?"

Sully shrugged. "Learned it in the navy when things got a bit rough. You can't change what is behind you, you can't even change what is happening right now, all you can change is what happens next."

Leonard sighed. "And what does happen next, Ms. Sullivan?"

Sully drummed her fingers on the tabletop as she thought. When she finally spoke, it was with controlled calm. "The only change in the pattern of incidents has been the missed day. It's significant. If you're running a campaign of terror, you don't take a day off. It lets the fear fade away. If you promise to kill once a day, then you need to kill once a day. So either the killing is still going on somewhere we don't know about, or the killing isn't the point of this whole thing." She slapped her hand down on the bench. "A distraction. It's a big, loud, showy distraction."

Sully rose and started pacing. "I'd bet good money that either people are being controlled more frequently than we know about, or there is something else, something huge going on that this 'year of the knife' shit is meant to distract us from."

She stopped, covered her face with both hands, and groaned. "God help me, we're going to have to talk to the British public."

JULY 15, 2015

The hotline was an unmitigated disaster with everybody and their dog calling in to tell the IBI about the suspicious or unusual behavior of their neighbors, family members and coworkers. Local constabularies were getting dozens of calls and more than their fair share of walk-ins. She'd heard the higher-ups had threatened to shut down the whole thing, but Sully was convinced that there was some snippet of information out there that would justify all of the madness, so she stood her ground with Colcross.

The killings had started again in a spectacular way, a petrol tanker driven off an overpass to land on top of a school bus. The driver had crawled out of the flames screaming about it being the year of the knife before eventually collapsing. The press was going mad, the governor was going mad, and if Colcross wasn't on her side, Sully was pretty confident she'd have been thrown to the wolves by now.

Constabularies were routinely checking for areas of unusually high magical output using the Schrödinger devices, so their detection was getting pretty precise. If only they could improve on response time.

Leonard, with a redcoat on loan from the Brooklyn garrison, had been sent to run experiments. He was having a good poke at the magic that was being used to hide the source.

Sully was running around the province, chasing the few promising leads they'd gotten from the hotline. Not that there were many of them. After several hours of fruitless interviews she'd stopped at a little corner shop to get a ginger beer. In passing she browsed through the headlines, happy not to see her name mentioned in today's broadsheets, even if the case was still front and center. On her way to the cash register, she started humming the tune playing over the store's sound system. It was only when she got behind an old lady in the queue to the register that she mouthed along to the lyrics for a second then froze. Before she could get control of herself, she shouted, "What the—!?"

She pushed the old lady aside and pointed a finger at the nervous looking boy standing behind the counter, who couldn't have been more than sixteen with his wispy moustache. "What's the name of that song and who's singing it?" she asked.

He looked at her like she was a crazy person who had just shoved an old lady, and when it became apparent that Sully wasn't going to wander off and argue with the tinned peaches, he shrugged. "I don't know. It's new, and I don't own the radio station, lady. You don't have to yell at me."

Sully ran the dates in her mind. How did the phrase "Year of the Knife" show up in a song that had to have been recorded before the killings started. If there was one thing Sully didn't believe in, it was coincidence.

She slammed her can on the counter and yelled, "I need names!"

* * *

As the IBI agent in charge of one of the biggest cases in the Empire, Sully had priority at every portal station in the colony. The attendants shuffled her to the head of the line and within minutes of arrival she was standing in the utilitarian copper transport circle, ready to be flung ten times the distance her traveling spells could manage.

She was raring to go to Nashville and have some short words with the bluegrass group who were making decent royalties singing about her case. Unfortunately, the person who was at the head of the queue before she arrived was one of the magi. Sully had never seen a magus willingly stand down from anything before, and the one who'd been scheduled to leave at that moment wasn't going to be the first.

He was old, wizened, impossibly tall at nearly eight feet, and skeletally thin. Garbed in silken robes with a paisley pattern running down the back, probably chosen by one of the handlers who were with him. The magus must have smuggled, or possibly summoned, a colossal black millipede into the building when no one was watching. It ran through his fingers the way that Sully'd seen a street hustler run a coin back and forth while waiting on the next mark. The fact that Sully didn't know this magus's name wasn't a huge concern. Most of the magi were kept behind closed doors, quiet and placated—focused on the vital work of the Empire. She guessed that the less they were out, the fewer awkward questions the Empire had to deal with—such as why everyone else didn't have their day scheduled down to the nearest bowel movement. An ignorant magus was a happy magus, or so it was said.

The magi were usually spotted early on in life during standardized magical aptitude testing and then schooled in their trade. They graduated to a seeming eternity of servitude to whichever company or nation state happened to hold their birth certificate. It was a very fair system to everyone except the magi.

The magus's hand, the one without the giant scuttling insect, was in constant motion, fingers twisted through arcane gestures and flapped spasmodically. He looked at no one's faces, and Sully recognized the mannerisms from glimpses of herself in pictures over the years.

This magus's handlers were still arguing with the attendants, demanding that their charge go at his scheduled time, when the magus stopped flapping his hands for a moment and glanced sidelong at Sully. She could swear that he gave a little wave, so she smiled and waved back. He giggled a little and then went back to running the millipede over his hands, almost like a child. She had to remind herself, though, that he wasn't a child at all—for all she knew, he could be the killer.

When one of the porting station attendants displayed Sully's laminated IBI card with the governor's personal seal, which Sully had handed them on arrival, she was allowed to proceed. Before she vanished, she saw the magus lose interest in his pet and drop it onto the shoulder of one of his handlers. She could just hear the beginnings of a scream; then she was gone.

* * *

Things weren't drastically different in the South, apart from the accents and the sensibilities. Still, Sully wished she could have brought Marie along as her cultural translator. If the colony was the breadbox of the Empire then this was where it kept the cakes. Music, film, television—it was all made down here in the South. It was the birthplace of bluegrass and country music, and the only contender to the diverse output of new music coming out of the nation of Ophir over the last few decades.

The center of Nashville was an assortment of chrome towers, not quite the rival of the mash-up of styles of the New Amsterdam skyline, but all the more notable for its clean, modernist design. Marie had rambled about her beloved homeland over the years, but to Sully this was just another city. A bit cleaner, brighter and drier than she was used to, but not the center of the universe the way that Marie made it out to be.

The studio was actually pretty easy to find, in an industrial area on the outskirts of the city, just down the road from the Global Film Studios lot. And every tourist knew where that was, since no visit to Nashville was complete without a picture in front of Global's statue—a big cast bronze thing made of criss-crossing rings of metal with cut outs of the continents welded on top to give the appearance of a globe. It couldn't have been gaudier if it was covered in gold leaf.

Sully knew that the band was in the studio because she'd spoken to their agent, who had insisted that his clients couldn't talk to her while they were recording. The gentleman clearly knew very little about impeding an IBI investigation. Sully sometimes thought that she should update her wardrobe from Hawaiian shirts and jeans to something a bit more imposing. If she came in dressed up in a black suit, with a trench coat flapping around her, people might do as they were told without her having to shove a badge in their face.

The cowgirl at the reception desk stood up when Sully came through the door. Sully flashed her badge and hissed, "Back in your seat! Don't make a sound or I'll have you arrested as part of the conspiracy to murder upward of eighty citizens of the empire. Do I make myself clear?"

The cowgirl sat down and shut up promptly.

Sully nodded. "Good girl. Don't answer the phone." Then she stalked off down the hall toward the sound of music and the red light that marked a recording session in progress.

The band froze when Sully burst through the door, with the exception of the bass player, who kept on strumming and swaying in place, seemingly oblivious. Holding up her badge, Sully yelled, "Everybody drop what you're doing and shut the hell up. I'm an Agent of the Crown, and you all are up shit creek with no paddle."

Even the bass player stopped then and stared at her, mumbling, "Dude, what did I do now?"

The band members all carefully set down their instruments, or in the case of the drummer, set down his drumsticks. Sully pointed a finger at them, "Tell me everything you know about the Year of the Knife."

A lot of meaningful stares were being exchanged in the recording studio. Sully noted that the whole place smelled faintly of cheese and rotgut whiskey, and the instruments still hummed even though nobody was touching them.

Sully had done her research while being driven to the portal station. The Smartwater Revival was one of those rare bands that didn't have just one front man who people remembered. Fans had a special appreciation for each of the four members. But everyone, male and female alike, agreed they wouldn't kick the lead singer out of bed. Axis was an androgynous beauty with a smoky voice that reached right down a person's back and made them shiver. Even Sully wasn't unmoved when Axis met her gaze and purred, "This is all just a misunderstanding."

Sully called the freezing spell to her fingertips and leveled it on Axis's pretty little face. "Year of the Knife. No lies. No nonsense. Start talking."

Axis shrugged. "It's just a song. We didn't mean to offend nobody."

Sully ground her teeth. "If it's just a song, how was it recorded a week before the first murder?"

The drummer covered his face with hands and hissed, "Shit."

Axis gave a graceful shrug. "Scheduling error?"

Sully smiled. "Cute."

She blasted the singer's feet, pinning them to the ground and filling the air with a cloud of chilled air that outdid the building's already prodigious air conditioning. Sully called the spell back up and pointed it at Axis's head. "Give me answers and you walk out of here free and alive. Surely whoever, or whatever, is killing all those people isn't dumb enough to announce it in a musical number. Start talking before I get angry."

Axis gestured down at their frozen legs and yelped, "This isn't angry!?"

Sully met their gaze with a cruel smirk. "This is me being downright pleasant."

Axis struggled to tug their thigh high boots out of the ice to no avail. Shivering, Axis said, "You can't treat us like this. We're British."

Sully stalked over and took a firm grip on Axis's face, smearing makeup all over her fingers in the process, and forcing their eyes to meet. "So were all the other dead people. If I could make this stop by torturing you to pretty little pieces, do you think anybody would lose a night's sleep?"

Axis's eyes darted around the room; they were getting hysterical. "I'm rich. I'm famous. You can't touch me."

Sully tightened her grip, drawing a groan from Axis's plump red lips that didn't seem entirely pained, and with schoolyard bully wit she whispered, "I'm touching you right now."

Axis jerked out of Sully's grip and looked to the other members of the band for support, only to find them all studiously looking away. Axis turned back with a snarl and their high-brow pretention fell away. "I ain't telling you shit."

Sully's eyes raked up and down Axis's body. "You know, I only need your mouth working."

Axis shivered as Sully leaned in closer. Interrupting with a hemp-slurred voice, the drummer said, "Stop with the Roman jackboot stuff, man. I'll talk to you. You said it's all about this murder stuff, right? You don't care what we did as long as you get that to stop, right?"

Sully, said, "If you haven't killed anyone, then I don't give a shit what you've been up to. Just tell me everything you know about the Year of the Knife."

The drummer smiled at her from behind his dangling fringe, another stupid fashion that Sully hated. "We're cool, man. We wouldn't hurt nobody. I'll tell you all about it, if you promise me we ain't going to jail."

Sully gritted her teeth, but nodded. The drummer clapped his hands like one of those cymbal monkey toys and said, "Could you maybe defrost our singer before they catch the cold. Axis is croaky enough on a good day."

Axis snapped, "This ain't funny, my feet are freezing in here."

Sully dispelled the ice with a wave of her hand and a flutter of words, then strode past the fuming singer to stand in front of the drum kit. The drummer pushed his hair back out of his face, giving her a brief view of his bloodshot eyes, before he launched into his story. "You probably know we are, like, the best band in the world right?"

Sully shrugged. "I'd never heard of you before today, but let's assume that's true so you can get on with your story."

The banjo player sniggered. The double bassist looked like he was about to jump out of his skin at a moment's notice. He had taken off his top hat and was drumming his fingers incessantly on the rim. Axis stalked back and forth, probably trying to get the feeling back in their admittedly shapely legs, and shot foul stares at Sully, and at the drummer, who mumbled on, "Yeah, we are. I'm the best drummer in the world. Axis sings the best, Clyde plays the meanest bass this side of the moon, and Bubba plays that old banjo like she's got the devil's own fingers. We know we're the best and that ain't just petting ourselves. We made us some arrangements."

Sully groaned. "Which one of you made the deal?"

Axis scoffed, "All of us made our own deals. That's how it works. Ain't you never heard the stories?"

Sully cast them a withering glance. "I've heard all the romantic stories about selling your soul to be the best singer. Then I went to school and learned which ones were lies. Keep talking, drummer boy."

He licked his chapped lips. "You promise we ain't gonna get into no trouble?"

Sully kept the heat out of her voice through careful training. "Just tell me your story."

The bassist looked like he was about to throw up, so when he blurted, "Bathroom!" Sully just waved him away. She kept her attention locked onto the drummer as he fumbled on, "When we were starting out, about three years back, we knew we needed something to kick us up a notch, you know? Get a leg up on the competition. There was a rumor about somebody here in Nashville who could cut that kind of deal, but we figured we didn't want some local busybody spreading around our business. Plus we wanted the good stuff, y'know? That big city magic.

"So we all got in a pickup and drove up to the Big Apple one summer. Found us a 'lock with a mean reputation. Dark-skinned fella from foreign parts, where they know all that business about the gentlemen downstairs. He took us up to some street by that big old lake—the Black Bay?—in between New Amsterdam and New Jersey. Said it was full of old magic and it made the, uh . . . gentlemen come a little easier. Gets you a better deal is what he said."

He paused to look at Sully, who stoically maintained her neutral expression. Shrugging, he went on, "He took us up this alley where he had all his stuff set up. The thing showed up in a chalk circle. Made a big stink like a rotten egg and looked like a big old horse with no skin. Scariest thing I ever seen in my life. We all asked for what we wanted and it said, 'sure thing,' and we never heard a peep from the 'lock or the demon ever again. But when it first came through, before it started talking to the 'lock, we heard something about the Year of the Knife. Like it had picked up the phone before it was ready. It was a catchy little bit, so we, uh . . . we used it."

Sully was losing patience. "That is the story of your damned song? You overheard a phrase that you liked?"

The drummer tutted. "We was writing songs a month or so back, and I smelled that same smell again, you get a whiff of it once in a while when things ain't looking so good for you, and you sometimes hear a little echo too. You ever heard one of them things talking? But this time weren't like that. We were safe and sound and strumming away. No reason for it at all. But it reminded me of the time in New Amsterdam. That's when we wrote the song. It got produced. It came out. Then some folks started getting murdered about the same time. That's all there is to it. You hear?"

Sully stared at him in disbelief. "That's it? A bad smell?"

He shrugged. "That's it. Nothing special."

Sully wiped her hand over her face and hissed out air between her teeth. "That's not helpful."

Axis stalked in a circle around Sully, softly singing and stamping a heel to the beat, "It's the year of the knife, it's going to cause some strife, every woman is your wife except your own. You can lay them down in bed and chop off their pretty heads, leave a trail of red, wherever you should roam."

Axis giggled and then came to a stop in front of Sully, smirking, "We free to go now, officer?"

Sully met the smirk with a placid smile of her own. "You're free to go down to the closest constabulary and turn yourselves in before this all goes seriously wrong. You've had a good run, I'm sure the story about a whole band dumb enough to sell themselves to demons will keep the public interested in you for a good few years. Well done. You're celebrities. Now do the right thing before somebody gets hurt."

Axis's smile melted away. "You said you wouldn't tell nobody."

Sully stepped forward, close enough to smell the bourbon on Axis's breath. "I said that if what you told me could save lives, then you were off the hook. Every minute that you morons are outside of safe containment you are putting every single one of us at risk. You ever heard of Oslo?"

The sudden change of topic threw Axis. "What the fuck is Oslo?"

Sully growled, "It used to be a city full of innocent people until some genius cut a deal with a demon for a boy he liked and then got run over by a tram. Out pops a demon and bye-bye Oslo. Now it's a burn mark forty miles wide. Go turn yourselves in and save me the paperwork."

There was a thumping sound from outside the recording studio— the soundproofed recording studio. Sully froze. Bubba was digging in the pockets of her banjo case, muttering something. The drummer looked around in a daze and asked, "Where's Clyde?" at the same time Bubba tried to subtly whisper to Axis, "Where's my junk?"

The noise in the hall was deafening now, more like an explosion, and Sully snapped into action. With a tweaked version of her concussion spell she tossed Axis and the drummer across the room into the little sectioned off booth full of recording equipment. She cast a full barrier over the empty doorway and infused it with enough of a recurring loop that it would last an hour. Then she tossed a veil over Bubba, who had dived down behind piles of gear, and hoped to hell that the woman had the sense not to move. Sully was just beginning to cast her own defensive spells when the demon burst through the wall.

The demon formerly known as Clyde, had huge thick legs ending in bird-like triple hooked claws. Its arms had withered and extended, trailing after its bloated body like the tentacles of some awful deep-sea creature, leaving a greasy trail on every surface they touched. The head had everted down into its torso, and the body had swollen to twice its normal size. And it was still growing. Sully figured that the growth was being spurred by the ambient magic that still lingered in the room from the spells she'd cast.

By instinct, she cast a spear of flame at the creature, but it washed right over the demon and appeared to swell the creature up another foot in height. If the demon had a mouth, it would have laughed. As it was, the open hole where the head had descended was making wet gargling noises like a boot stuck in mud. Sully cast in quick succession, her brain finally catching up to her hands and voice. She called the cymbals off the drum kit and sent them spinning like discuses at the creature, only to watch as it casually sidestepped them. The demon was between her and the only exit so Sully backed her way to the far wall and pressed herself back into the cushion of the soundproofing.

Stomping further into the room, the demon turned from side to side like a scenting dog, then lashed out with its tendrils. The thing couldn't have seen Bubba—it wasn't possible with a veil as complex as the one Sully had cast. Sully realized the demon wasn't looking for Bubba, it was just honing in on any magic in the room. The tentacles, fine as razor wire, tore through the banjo player like she wasn't even there.

Bubba's body started to change instantly. Her jaw split open with a loud crack and started to grow, deforming her whole face as it stretched into a toothy mix of crocodile and canine. Her limbs shriveled much like the first demon's, but then the staccato cracking of bones marked a new growth. Ribs jutted out of the wounds on her torso and flexed once or twice before a twist brought them down to the ground and set the demon scuttling across the floor toward Sully.

Two demons and no way out. This day got better and better. Sully glanced across the room to where Axis and the drummer were thumping their hands against the window and screaming—Axis's mascara was running and the drummer had froth on his lips. The wall behind her wasn't thick; it would be easy enough to let these morons die, get some distance and some time to think. The first rule of combat was that you didn't let your opponent pick the battlefield.

Alarms should already be ringing; the demonic response force should already be on its way to Nashville from whatever secret base it was holed up in. This didn't have to be Sully's fight. The demons were closing in on the barrier that Sully had thought substantial just a moment ago. The leggy demon kicked against the barrier, setting the whole building shaking. It had swollen so large that the raw flesh of its shoulder's scraped the ceiling as it swayed backward from the force of its kick. The demon that had been Bubba bared rows and rows of newly-formed teeth, building up speed as it scuttled in a long curve toward the unprotected window to the booth.

Sully swore under her breath and picked up a music stand. When she hit the toothy demon across the back, the force of the blow snapped the metal stand in half, leaving her holding a metal pole that she was more than happy to drive through one of the human legs that were now boneless, but still flopping about on the demon's back.. The leg burst like a lanced boil, but where the metal dug through the carpet into the floor, it leashed the demon in place, hooked through its necrotic flesh. Toothy was tugged to a halt and lost its footing.

A quick concussion spell scattered the amps and recording equipment all over the place. Leggy took another whack at the barrier still separating it from Axis and the drummer. The boom reverberated through the room at such a volume even Sully flinched, but the barrier held. The smaller demon rolled on its side in pathetic circles, propelled by the bones of its ribcage. It lashed its head from side to side and snapped the rows of teeth in an attempt to right itself and the pinned flesh was tearing loose in its frenzy.

Dancing away from its jaws, Sully had her moment to think and quickly cast several enhancement spells into herself: Her shirt ripped at the seams as her arms and shoulders expanded and new muscles rippled into place. The sound of the remaining band members' frantic heartbeats and the demons' languid pulsing and stretching pounded in her ears. Sully charged the leggy demon, no tactics, no cleverness, just the rush of adrenaline from a good few days of getting knocked around by forces beyond her control—that and having a nice big ass to kick.

The outside of the studio shook once, then again. Then the leggy demon exploded through the exterior wall, stumbling backward before tripping over a curbside tree and going head-hole over heels. It landed on a taxi, and then flipped the car out of its way with a casual flick of a huge leg as it rose up to full height again. Shoulders squared, it spread out a net of tendrils as it faced the hole in the side of the studio. Sully appeared behind it with a quiet clap of thunder, leapt up and drove her bloody fist into the back of its knee. Anyone stupid enough to still be close to the action could have heard her manic laughter. The demon toppled over and landed with a sickening crunch, cracking the curb. Black fluid seeped out of the fist-sized hole in the back of its leg.

The toothy demon chose that moment to burst out of the building like a bullet from a gun. It snapped at Sully as she tumbled to one side and, with one of its scuttling legs, snagged a piece of her tattered sleeve, ripping it off. With another lunge it sank its teeth into the overturned taxi that sat where Sully had just been. The shriek of teeth against metal echoed up and down the street.

Trying to buy time, Sully set off a concussion under the taxi, flipping it back up and on top of the toothy demon. Her mind buzzed with options, but none of them felt right. The leggy demon was starting to right itself and the toothy demon had grown large enough now to shrug the car off of its back. So much for buying herself some time.

Sully glanced from one to the other and sighed. Toothy, now the size of a rhinoceros, charged straight at her. Sully spread her arms and caught it by the most protruding of its wild tangle of teeth, setting her feet and straining to hold it back for one long, awful moment before she gave in to momentum and threw herself backward.

The demon, already moving faster than anything that size had a right to, was carried up and over her by her solid grip on its tusk. It flew down the street and skidded. Sully hauled herself back up onto her feet just in time to see the six-foot long claw from the other demon's foot plunge toward her. She gave it a frantic slap to the side, but couldn't stop the barbed skin of its foot from leaving gashes in her arms.

With her reserves draining fast, Sully staggered away from the next rake of Leggy's claws and let her enhancements drop before the exhaustion killed her. Just as suddenly, the demon stopped dead in its tracks. It flexed its claws and scratched at the ground. The toothy demon came barreling back, blood and ichor trailing from its jaws, but it, too, ground to a halt and started sniffing at the air.

Sully didn't move for what felt like a very long time, realizing that without her magic to draw the demons' attention, she was safe for the moment. Which was good, because she didn't know if she would have the energy to move if they came at her again.

Leggy, now about three stories high, scratched at the ground where Sully had been standing, as if expecting to find her hiding under the tarmac. It balanced on one leg, cradled its toothy companion in the other claw, and then with amazing form, threw the tank-sized demon over Sully's head. It took the sound of shattered masonry for Sully to realize it had hit the studio. The wet sounds from the top of the towering demon were like a trumpet being blown underwater.

From inside the studio, the chattering howl of the toothy demon answered. It was followed by an eerie wail. Then another. Sully shivered as all four demons sang out in harmony. With four demons now loose on the streets of Nashville, Sully covered her ears and limped away down the street.

* * *

The British Empire was not a good place to be a vampire, second only to, well, everywhere else in the world. In the Khanate, they were hunted for sport. In the Caliphate, they were buried alive. In the African empires, cruel and unusual punishments awaited any creature impersonating a human—varying from empire to empire in their cruelty. Even the United Nations treated them as a threat on par with the wendigo.

In the British Empire, vampires were considered second class citizens on good days, barely protected by the law, but it was better than the alternatives. Since British businesses wouldn't hire them, most vampires resorted to whatever means of survival they could find in the streets—most went into prostitution to cut out the middleman and trade blood for sex without having to get cash involved. But there was one role the Empire allowed them to fill where they could find an iota of respect—demon hunter.

No one knew why, but once vampires turned, their ability to use magic was gone, which had the side-effect of making them unappealing to demons. Between that and their natural strength, they were perfectly suited to the role. The Empire kept a hidden encampment of highly-trained vampire combatants, drawn from the armed forces or recruited from their own violent unlives elsewhere in the world. When a dimensional breach was confirmed by the redcoats, a team was deployed via portal to the location immediately.

The soldiers who arrived in Nashville dropped from a glowing sphere in the sky and landed in a ready formation just ahead of Sully. They were dressed in black uniforms and armed to the teeth with the latest Gatling gun technology and carrying enough bladed weapons to make a cutlery drawer jealous.

From her few brief previous encounters, Sully knew the correct greeting. She dived to the ground as a screaming flurry of bullets passed over her head. When the guns stopped Sully shouted, "I'm on your side, you pricks!"

A ripple of chuckling arose from the assembled soldiers, and one of them prodded Sully in her bare shoulder with a steel-capped boot. In the metallic voice created by the filter on the soldier's mask, he said, "Evacuate the area, civilian."

Sully clambered back to her feet and swayed, pointing a finger at the smoked glass of the vampire's face mask. "I'm a Senior Agent of the Crown. There are four demons down the road, all within a block of each other. I've been holding them here. On my own. Until your useless lot arrived. Still want me to leave?"

From off to the right she heard laughter filtering through the masks of two of the vampires. One said, "Take her word for it, sarge. That's Firecracker Sullivan."

The demon-hunter turned from Sully to his squadmates, then back again. He cleared his throat. "Sorry, ma'am. Didn't recognize you out of uniform."

Sully had no idea what this 'Firecracker' rubbish was, but she'd take anything she could get. When the demons called again, a hissing, wailing, roaring, gargling sound that echoed across the city, every vampire standing there flinched. Sully rolled her eyes at them as if she hadn't nearly pissed herself the first time it happened ten minutes ago. Sully squared her shoulders and then turned to the sergeant. "You got a plan for this sort of thing?"

A building down the street collapsed and all of the street lights suddenly flickered around them. The sergeant shrugged. "Never had more than one at a time before. What the hell happened here?"

Sully sighed. "Not important right now. Eyes forward."

The vampires all nodded at her and she realized in that awful moment that she was in charge of this squad. For years, she had kept herself as far from command as possible just to avoid situations like this. She was going to have to make decisions that would probably end badly for some of them. There was a time when this would have been easier, when she was still fresh from the navy and wouldn't have thought twice about letting some cold boys catch a bullet or two if it kept a civilian safe. Then Marie had made her world infinitely more complicated. She put her hands over her eyes and pressed until she saw colors. Then she screamed. Then she started giving orders.

The vampires ran along either side of the road, spreading out to make sure the demons were contained. Their orders were to get their attention and then run like hell back to the base of operations, as Sully was now known. The soldiers had the safeties on their guns off, despite the fact they would be of little use with the demons. They were also well-equipped with a variety of exciting chemical explosives that Sully made a note to stay well away from.

As the soldiers set their charges, a scowling Sully began casting the spells she hoped would save them all. Her magic came when called, spellfire swirling from her fingers and twisting into the words that no living mouth could speak. Seven separate spellforms were involved. Her nose began to bleed and her heart shuddered with the effort, but she held on to the twirling maelstrom of spells as if her life depended on it. Because it probably did.

Sully could see the leggy demon above the tops of the low buildings in the studio lot even before her soldiers engaged it. The tentacles around its torso were like the petals of a flower now, fluttering in the breeze and stretching out to gather as much ambient magic as it could get. And growing. Always growing.

Seeming to sense Sully's magic, the tentacles pointed toward her like a signal to all of its brothers in arms. To the right, Sully heard gunfire. To the left, she heard the screams of a vampire being ripped apart.

Sully kept her breathing steady and focused on maintaining the spellforms that hung in the sky all around her like her own personal zodiac. It was a delicate balance, feeding them just enough power to keep them ready but not enough to trigger them, but she was one the best. At least that was what she kept telling herself any time she felt a shape waver or the flow of her power flicker.

The tall demon was going to be a problem—the vampires couldn't even attract its attention yet. But the other three demons, even the toothy one that was now the size of a small building, would probably be handled by her plan. With screams and the staccato of Gatling guns in the background, Sully closed her eyes and drew steady breaths in between her chanted words. Her throat wasn't even sore yet. The ground beneath her feet started to shake and she opened her eyes again. As she expected, three of the demons, all except leggy, were headed toward her, in close pursuit of a line of sprinting vampires, who continued to fire over their shoulders without a backward glance.

Sully gave one of the soldiers who'd stayed with her a nod. He hit a switch and the big bronze statue outside of Global Film Studios exploded off of its pedestal, sailed over Sully's head, and frosted over as it passed through the first of her spells. The globe shattered when it hit the tarmac and Sully's second spell sparked off in a flurry of concussions, pushing and pulling at the rings that formed the globe, tearing them apart at their weakened welding points, and spinning them out to lay flat on the street ahead.

The fleeing demon hunters stepped over and around them as the rings rattled to a halt. Now it was all about the timing. Toothy leapt for her and, as it passed over the center ring, Sully empowered the impromptu magic circle. It was like the demon had hit an invisible wall. The sound of the impact set the other rings rattling until Sully cast another quick concussion spell in the air to slap them back down.

One of the other demons had stretched out, snake-like with a multi-eyed, vertical-mouthed head. When the upper half entered the circle, Sully slammed it closed, too, severing the rear half of the demon, which writhed, spraying ichor through the air. The last of the three, built like a gorilla and covered in quivering spines, tried to sneak around the side of their group and launch itself at the squad. A hastily cast concussion spell flung the ring into the demon's path, and the last of Sully's magical reserves flooded into the ring, sealing the creature in place.

Sully fell to her knees, gasping for air and knowing that it wasn't the lack of air that had her on the verge of blacking out. She had pushed herself past her limits again, and now inside her, where there usually was a core of magical power, there was nothing—a vacuum.

The three smaller demons were bound but there was still one to go. Sully figured it would likely take a bombing run from one of the military airplanes, which they pretended not to have, to bring that giant down. Sully was on the ground now, wanting nothing more than to just lie there. She'd done enough for one day, more than anyone could have expected of her, and darkness buzzed at the edges of her vision.

But the chittering half-serpent of a demon to her left made a terrible mistake: it laughed. "YOU FAIL BECAUSE YOU ARE WEAK. AS YOU FALL, SO SHALL ALL OF YOUR EMPIRE. YOU SHALL BE AS NAUGHT BUT DUST ON THE WIND."

Sully dragged herself, stumbling, to her feet and staggered over to the ring. The demon inside flopped from side to side, spasmodically, no longer in full control of its motions without fresh magic to heal it. Sully fell to her knees by the side of the circle. She let her fingers brush against the intangible barrier. It felt like pins and needles. Then her fingertips slipped down and brushed the ring itself. It was like being attached to a car battery—she was momentarily recharged.

Grinning furiously, Sully stretched her senses out over the magic circle. The demon hissed and roared, lashing around inside. One of the soldiers laid a hand on her shoulder and jumped back from the magical discharge.

In the early days of her time at the Royal College there had been many long, dull sessions with instructors trying to coax the full power out of each student. Some instructors used meditation, and others used more vigorous means of encouragement. But every one of these lessons had confused the hell out of Sully, who was brought up at the knee of one of the most feared hedge-witches in all of Ireland. Sully knew even as a child that magic didn't have to be coaxed, it was there, pressing against her like floodwater—desperate to get out.

She could feel it now, inside the circle—that same power straining to escape, if only there was a channel. Sully opened herself up to the magic and spread a tiny hole in the barrier with her finger. The demon began to shriek almost instantly, but the soldiers, who'd been swaggering around and patting themselves on the back, couldn't see why until it started to shrivel.

Within seconds, all of the magic in the circle was drawn out, ripped from the demon, cell by cell, inch by inch until Sully was again full to bursting, and the demon was dust. Her exhaustion vanished. Her fears and her doubts withered as the raw power flooded through her. She turned to the snarling, toothy demon, with its rows and rows of teeth, and shook her head contemptuously. In the third circle, the spiny gorilla demon was shaking. She asked, "Can you speak, too?"

It chattered its quills together and, to Sully's amusement, backed away a step to press against the far side of the circle, before answering with a wet, "YES."

Sully pointed to it. "You boys can put down the toothy one, but keep the hedgehog gorilla for questioning. I'm all charged up again and I'm going after the big one."

The demon hunters started arguing amongst themselves loudly, but Sully didn't give them a second glance. She was focused on the chrome towers of downtown Nashville, where the colossal demon still roamed free. At that moment it was throwing itself bodily against the side of a skyscraper. With a flurry of calculations and a licked finger held up in the air to catch the wind direction, Sully vanished.

She was used to being powerful. But even for Sully, the energy she had bound up inside herself this time was too much. The traveling spell barely put a dent in it, even though she had crossed more than a mile as the bird flies. She tumbled through the air, high enough that she wasn't likely to hit a wall, but not so high that she was impeded by the thin air.

Her options for dealing with leggy were limited even with the magic she had pulsing inside her. Direct magic just made demons stronger. Barriers and circles could hold them in place—she'd proven that already today—but there was no convenient circle with a diameter of a mile lying on the ground. Any barrier big enough to hold this thing back would drain even her swollen reserves dry.

The demon's tentacles had spread out in a misshapen sphere around it. Now they snapped to point at Sully, straining away from the bloated core of the beast.

In moments like this, with the odds stacked against her and lives on the line, Sully felt most alive. And in those moments on the knife edge, desperation made her creative. She vanished just as the demon flailed its medusa halo at her. The sound of her elated laughter hung in the sky before the thwarted demon's gargling roars drowned it out.

She cast half of the spell with the minimal amount of mathematics and left it stalled about half a mile up, where there was just enough air for her to still speak the necessary words. After that, she made her last jump. She was so high up at this point that she could barely gasp a breath, and frost formed on her lips even as she tried.

Sully completed the spherical barrier around herself, and then fell to earth. Around her, outside of its protection, the air screamed past. When she slipped down through her stalled spell, it adhered to the personal shield with a crackle and the world became an opaque blur that gradually grew redder as the heat spread. She had calculated for the heat, and when the red glow turned white, she knew that it was almost time. The bullet that Sully had made out of herself tore through the demon, ripping out the lashing tentacles at their root, boring through the thick core of flesh that was its center, and burning every bit of it that she touched.

From the outside, it must have looked like the demon exploded, but Sully could still feel its energy sapping presence when she emerged from her magical cocoon at the bottom of a crater in the center of town. Parts of it were still alive, healing and reforming around her, and she had nothing left to give.

At that moment, a second portal opened up above her and the next wave of vampires came tumbling through. Their gear was distinctly different, they carried flamethrowers and tanks of fuel; this wasn't the first response team, it was the clean-up crew. Sully skipped the bravado this time, she just ran as fast as she could before the first torrent of fire began to incinerate the strewn demon remains.

JULY 17, 2015

The streets of Nashville were still under martial law and would remain so until a decision was made about what to do with the gorilla demon, since between Sully and the vamps, they'd disposed of the other three. Local magicians had checked the stability of Sully's little trap and had even reinforced it with several rings of other materials, but the problem remained that it was in the middle of a big crossroads next to one of the Empire's biggest film studios. People were starting to get tetchy about it.

After escaping a certain flaming death, Sully had checked into a motel on the opposite end of town where the *normal* human beings—and in Nashville, that meant those not involved in the entertainment industry—tended to gather.

Her night was spent in various conference calls: first with Deputy Director Colcross, then with a very agitated General in Her Imperial Majesty's Armed Forces. Then there was a magus, who seemed to be only partially mentally present—which was par for the course—and finally, for one memorable moment, with Marie, who had called when Sully was waiting to talk to a demonologist in Newcastle and startled her out of her shell-shock.

The demonologist had turned out to be a wasted call, since his helpful theories turned out to be things Sully had already explored with Leonard. A few of the vampire squaddies visited when she was finally starting to consider sleep, looking to trade a few stories and share some surprisingly good whiskey that they had plundered from the rubble of an upmarket bar. They couldn't drink it but they seemed to think they owed her a favor or two.

* * *

The next morning, after no more than an hour's actual sleep, Sully took a cheap and nasty portal from the University of Nashville back to her apartment for a shower and a quick change of clothes. Then she went back to work, or as she was increasingly calling it, home.

The IBI offices were usually a flurry of activity and raised voices. The fact that Sully's return was met with dead silence was a clear sign that news had traveled ahead of her and had made the rounds of the office. She ignored her coworkers, who followed her every movement with owl-like attention, and headed down to the basement to run ideas past Leonard before she had to explain to the Deputy Director why her trip to Nashville to conduct an interview had turned the city into a demonic war zone.

She found the door to the lab locked, and her patience, which had the tensile strength of tissue paper on the best of days, snapped. She didn't even bother to unlock the door, she just shot a burst of flame from her fingertips that burnt away the entire handle and locking mechanism. Then she stormed inside. Leonard had been busy; the chalk boards were filled with equations and variables, and he had even rolled in several spares which were well on their way to being filled too.

Sully had the presence of mind to extinguish the flames with a flick of the wrist before she advanced on Leonard. "The demons are talking about the Year of the Knife; they've been talking about it since three years back. I don't think the doll knows about it, because he's been up here for about thirty years, but the demons are involved somehow. That's the angle we need to pursue."

Leonard winced but he didn't back away. "I am afraid that your assessment may be somewhat tempered by the facts, my dear woman.

We have very few records of instances of magic performed by the gentlemen downstairs, with the vast majority of their wish granting and such being done behind closed doors.

"However, there were several experiments conducted at the Bluetooth Institute in Greenland that clearly indicate a resonance pattern within demonic magic—a certain spikiness to their output that I am sorry to inform you does not match up with what we have been able to identify from the remains of your primary victims and the locations where they were originally affected."

Sully froze with her mouth still open and then let out a huff of air that could have easily been mistaken for a growl. "You're certain?"

He nodded slowly, as though any sudden movement might provoke her, "I am afraid that the structure of the spell involved is definitely consistent with a human thought pattern and that, while we do not recognize the particular field of arcana, it is certainly derived from our magical traditions. There are actually some hallmarks of the European pseudo-Teutonic spellforms—"

Sully cut him off dead. "And you didn't think that was relevant information?"

Leonard leaned away with a stubborn set his shoulders. She stood almost nose to nose with him now, give or take a box for her to stand on. "My dear Miss Sullivan, the pseudo-Teutonic forms have been adopted by almost every school that the British Empire has had contact with, due to their stability and ease of retention. Also, if you recall your history at all, then you may note that the vast majority of places our brave and bountiful explorations have led us to as a world power—after immediately adopting those elements of our most excellent education systems that would enable them to do so— rebel against our occupation. Most often culminating in decades of bloody warfare.

"When you incorporate the number of college-trained magicians within the Empire, as well as the refugees who were successful in their flight from mainland Europe before it was sealed off, we are left with a list of suspects numbering in the thousands."

Sully leaned forward the last inch and rested her head against Leonard's cravat for a moment, groaning. "So the lead that I leveled Nashville for is useless."

Leonard awkwardly patted her on the back. "Not at all, my dear. Not at all. We now know that someone has at least been in discussion with the gentlemen downstairs about the Year of the Knife. Either the demons became involved in a manner shy of wish granting, or they were merely consulted at the planning stage for this stunt."

Sully straightened up, giving Leonard a shy smile before her usual scowl reasserted itself, "You aren't completely useless to have around, Leonard."

Then she stormed back out of the room.

* * *

Sully emerged from the elevator and headed straight for Colcross's office at a brisk pace, barely bothering to glance at Chloe for permission. The girl smiled at her pleasantly as she typed at her keyboard. Maybe the shock of Sully actually flirting with her had finally broken her out of her weird rabbit-in-the-headlights habits.

Inside the office, Colcross was snoring. His overstuffed chair kept him upright, but the man was definitely asleep. The snoring wasn't earthshaking, just little unexpected snorts.

However long Sully's hours were, however beaten up she got, she could always go home for a few hours to recuperate between shifts. She couldn't think of a time when he wasn't here in his office. He looked almost innocent when he was asleep, not like a slave driver or her designated protection against the machinations of high society. She slammed the door with her back turned to him and when she turned around he had his glasses perched on his nose and seemed to be in the middle of reading a report. He glanced up at her over the top of his spectacles and sighed. "You generate a substantial amount of paperwork, Agent Sullivan."

She was about to fake a smile when he continued, "Considerably more paperwork than results. I am considering making another Superior Agent the lead on this case. I would still require you to be directly involved and your insights would be absolutely essential to progressing matters, but I have to take the public perception and political pressures into consideration."

Sully gritted her teeth. "Anyone else who was lead on this would be dead three times over by now."

Colcross nodded faintly, as if conceding the point but added, "Perhaps that is due to the manner in which you are conducting your investigation."

Sully nodded back sharply.

Colcross pressed on. "Thus far, you have squandered your budget on an expensive consultant, medical care and considerable transport costs, without producing anything substantial with which we could progress matters. You must understand how this looks—"

Sully butted in. "A human being is doing this—turning other people into puppets to conduct their little reign of terror. They're an enemy of the British Empire, but they were likely trained in one of our colleges. They consult with demons, but don't use them to do whatever it is they are doing. And what they are doing with the murderers is a distraction."

Colcross had been looking back at the papers in front of him until she said those final words. His head snapped up, "All of these deaths are purely a distraction?"

Sully shrugged. "It's the only motive that makes sense. How does scaring the crap out of people help your cause? It makes them chase after shadows. It keeps them on their heels and lets you get away with whatever else you're trying to do. Next time the governor or any of the twits from back in the old country ring you up, that is what you can tell them. We need to find out what this is really about."

Colcross took off his glasses and pinched the bridge of his nose. "Agent Sullivan, I gave you an already difficult task in finding the perpetrator of these murders, why do you insist on adding to your difficulties by inventing conspiracies?"

Sully snapped, "Motive is one of the three corners of a case, sir. If I get that, everything else falls into place."

Colcross rolled his eyes. "In my considerable experience, you will find that the reason for a crime is rarely important to your investigation. Leave that concern to those given the thankless task of prosecuting it."

Sully nodded stiffly and waited to be dismissed. Colcross glanced at the papers and then back up at her. "You will remain lead on this case until a better option presents itself, Agent Sullivan. Please produce something concrete so that my faith in you is seen to be well founded."

Sully turned on her heel and stalked out of the room, her temper held in check by the need for continued employment. Which was silly, really. Financially, she would be a lot better off packing in her job and selling off the spells she'd developed over the year—there were plenty of interested parties. The Navy was desperate for her concussion spell.

The anger faded away just thinking about her life after work. Sitting on a porch sipping gin all day until her liver exploded, or until Marie showed up one night when she had another girl over and drained her dry in a fit of jealous rage. To hell with that.

Chloe caught her eye as she came out of the office and crooked a finger in invitation. Sully approached with a smirk: the girl didn't even seem flustered today, just sitting there with a letter opener in her hand and a pile of Colcross's mail in front of her. When Sully got close enough, Chloe grinned up at her.

Sully finally asked, "Did you need something?"

The pretty girl's head lolled to the side. Her mouth hung open and the words hissed out. "IT iS thE YeAr of thE KNIFe."

She lunged forward with the letter opener and would have gotten Sully in the gut if Sully's bar fighting experience hadn't kicked in. Sully jerked her hand up and, for her trouble, caught the blade right in the palm. A gleeful grin spread over Chloe's face as she tried to twist the blunted knife. The pain nearly drove Sully to her knees. It was all happening too fast—Sully didn't have time to think. A hundred spells were on the tip of her tongue but every one of them would have blown the walls off the building when they interacted with whatever was controlling the girl. Sully had already proven that theory in Carolina.

The girl's arms were hanging limp at her sides but when she jerked them forward she still hit like a brick. Chloe leaned in close and that brimstone aroma washed over Sully for an instant before another smell took over, the ozone scent of air after a storm. Chloe whispered, "YOu havE crOSSED me fOR THE LasT timE WITch."

Sully must have cried out, or maybe it was the sound of the tussle that brought Colcross out of his office with an old service revolver in his hand. Sully couldn't have guessed the caliber, but it looked too big, even for a man of Colcross's size. He aimed it very carefully at Chloe and spoke with a quaver in his usually robust voice. "Chloe, let go of the knife and step away from Agent Sullivan."

Chloe started to laugh and that garbled blend of noise rolled over Sully's strained voice as she shouted, "Don't shoot."

Colcross wasn't a military man, as far as Sully knew, but he sure as hell could shoot straight. The back of Chloe's head blew out over the wood-paneled walls. Blood and things thicker than blood splattered across the wall and stuck there, and as long as Sully kept her eyes on that and didn't turn her head, she wouldn't have to see the big hole in the pretty face of the silly girl she used to torment.

Chloe didn't fall—she just kept on laughing. Despite herself, Sully looked up into the bleeding hole that used to be the girl's face. The tongue still waggled around inside the hole like some obscene worm. The body jerked, pulling the letter opener out of Sully's hand. Staggering back a step, Chloe fell into her chair before half-heartedly tossing the letter opener at Colcross. It tumbled to land by his feet, still slick with Sully's blood. The gun slipped from Colcross's fingers and fell on the floor beside it.

Sully tried to breathe calmly, even as the pain crept up her arm and gripped her chest in a vice-like hold. Avoiding the corpse, she looked at Colcross instead and eventually shouted, "Hey!" to break his vacant stare. He looked like a man in a dream, so Sully tried again. "Hey! Go downstairs and tell someone what happened."

He nodded and walked toward the elevator. Sully stared at the blood-soaked carpet and the mess that had been Chloe. The girl's remaining eye showed no signs of life now, but for all Sully knew, the orchestrator of the attack might be observing her at that very moment. She didn't give them the satisfaction of seeing her cry.

JULY 23, 2015

Sully woke up in a terrible mood. Six days had passed since Chloe's unfortunate incident and the fresh corpses had been steadily rolling in. One bloated corpse had even shown up in the Black Bay not six feet from the front door of Sully's apartment. It didn't seem logical that the killer would've dumped the body just to taunt her, but the Schrödingers had confirmed that there was an unusual amount of magic involved.

Now that it was fairly clear that their adversary was capable of picking and choosing targets—Chloe couldn't have been a coincidence, after all—all pretense at randomness appeared to be abandoned. The kills had become silent and systematic, completely contradicting the idea that this was all meant to be a noisy distraction from the controller's real activities. Sully wasn't convinced, and she had argued with Colcross about it. He thought the organized attacks were an escalation of the pattern. Sully thought they were a ruse to convince the IBI that murder really was the goal.

When she'd been debriefed after Chloe—questions and more questions—she'd ended up breaking the wall of silence that had been in place around the murders since day one. Now every Superior Agent of the Crown that worked in the IBI building had the whole story. In fact, she'd penned a memo with the details and circulated it. She'd gone along with stealth mode when it was just another case, but now everyone at the IBI was at risk, and Sully couldn't stomach that.

Colcross was taking a few days off, officially to recover from the assassination attempt, but really just to get a bit of distance from the whole thing so that he could start thinking clearly again. When this case was closed, Sully really needed to consider taking some of her vacation time. Or maybe even stepping down to work as a regular agent again. This was too much like hard work.

Sully left her apartment, headed for the subway and another day of the relentless grind. When she stopped near a group seagulls on the sidewalk, they parted in front of her. All except one, which stepped forward and looked up at her. That was not your regular bird behavior. Sully glanced back at the men in uniforms over by the flood wall. Not one of them was paying the blindest bit of attention, so she met the seagull's gaze and nodded across at an alleyway. The gull fluttered off and she followed at a discreet distance, shaking her head at the sorry state of affairs she found herself in.

In the alleyway, the seagull waddled around behind some bins, and Sully politely looked away when she heard the tell-tale sound of tearing skin. A perfect golden-skinned woman rose up from behind the bins, completely nude—untroubled by the sea breeze, and absent of anything resembling shame. The woman nodded to Sully and held up a hand in greeting.

Sully groaned. "You know that your people have an embassy. You don't have to keep turning into animals and sneaking over here every time you want to share information."

The woman shrugged, the movement setting things into motion on her toned body. Sully had to quickly correct her drifting eyes. In all of Sully's limited dealings with the Native Americans, she had never met one that wasn't beautiful. Maybe aesthetics were how they picked their police and spies, as those had been the only interactions Sully had with their neighbors to the west.

When the woman spoke, her accent was soft, almost musical. "If we use the channels that your Empire demands, then it is obvious that we are the ones telling you things. This is unacceptable to our own people, so we must make these compromises. I must fly across the land you stole from us as a filthy scavenger bird. You must have meetings between buildings with women who wear no clothes." Noticing Sully's blush, the American woman tutted. "Look before you strain something. I do not know why your people have such a strange fascination. They are for feeding babies."

Sully grumbled but still didn't look down. "What are you here to tell me that you aren't really telling me then?"

The woman bent to pick up the tattered skin of the seagull lying on the ground and folded it over her hand before coming closer and lowering her voice. "Your manitou has attacked our people, too. Your body thief. It took one of our people near to the border. It killed many people and we could not understand its words. A translator who had dealings with your kind came and told us what it spoke of. A year of knives. A return from a place of exile. When it became aware that we were not of your Empire, it left. It killed the one that it rode. My people thought it justice to keep this from you. I think that your troubles always overflow your borders."

Sully reached for her notebook with her wounded hand, and then swore quietly. She awkwardly drew it out from her inside pocket with her right hand. The woman looked on, amused. Sully said, "I am going to need specifics of the incident. Where it happened and when it happened."

The woman gave another single-shouldered shrug and Sully stared intently at her notebook, "The attack was many days ago. It was in an area that your people called Idaho when you stole it from us, among a nation called the Kutenai."

Sully waved away the historical commentary. "What date?"

Counting back on her fingers, the woman said, "It is difficult to follow the turning of days when you are a bird, but I would say that it was nine days ago."

Sully flapped the notebook in triumph. "The fourteenth of July— one of days we had no attacks. I knew there was something else going on."

When Sully smiled the woman finally seemed uncomfortable. "I must go now. You have the information."

Sully said, "Can I buy you a drink at least?"

The woman stalked away as if hadn't heard the comment, but that didn't dissuade Sully. "So how many of your folk are over here, pretending to be pigeons?"

That gave the woman pause. She glanced back and Sully jerked her eyes back up to meet the woman's gaze. "How many of your spies are hidden among our nations? We all do what we must to survive."

Sully took a step after her and held up her hands. "I don't really care. Do what you've got to do. I just don't want to clean up when another of your people goes berserk after spending too long as a wolverine."

The woman frowned. "We can take care of our own business."

Sully scoffed, "Tell that to all the dead vampires your last lunatic shredded when they were set loose on my city."

She hissed, "The manitou were already dead. They are all dead. They were just reminded of that."

Sully found her fists clenching, and she didn't know why. "They were people. If you didn't feel bad about it, then why are you trying to repay me for stopping her?"

The woman crouched down in the rubbish. "Consider the debt paid, if that is how you see the world. I shall not assist you again."

She slipped back into the shape of a gull and then fluttered up and out of the alleyway. Sully went to catch her train.

* * *

It was about nine hours later, and Sully had been trapped behind Colcross's desk for eight of them. She'd passed along the information from the woman from the United Nations, even if she couldn't reveal her source, and now she had invited Leonard up to share some of the Director's very fine brandy. She told herself that it was just to take the edge off the tension currently cramped in the back of her neck and that if the Director objected then he wouldn't have been perched so comfortably on her shoulder as she looked over reports.

She kept tapping at her blank notepad. "The attack outside the borders means something. Every other attack has been on the Empire. Very deliberate. Screwing up like this, right in the middle of the run? It's too strange."

Leonard swirled his brandy and stared deeply into the amber liquid, uncharacteristically quiet. Eventually, he looked up at Sully. "I have no doubt that it is significant my dear girl, I just . . . I do not know why I am still lingering here. I have gone as far as I can with magical theory. Given our experience so far, I believe we will be denied a living prisoner, and barring that, I've done all I can."

Sully watched Leonard's gaze flick toward the Director and back to his glass. Then she scoffed, "They got to you."

He feigned indignation. "Excuse me, Miss Sullivan, but I think you are well aware that I am in high demand across the imperial territories and that I was in the throes of a very lucrative book tour before you had me cloistered here. I do not require further prompting to move on when I have completed my tasks, and as I have said, there is little more that I can do to be of assistance of here."

Sully rolled her eyes theatrically. "Who was it? The governor? Someone back in jolly old England? Some anti-imperial faction from Africa? Did they try to bribe you at least, or was it all stick and no carrot?"

Leonard stared at the walnut-paneled wall as though it were the most fascinating thing in the world, eventually muttering, "Perhaps I can stay a while longer. There are a few avenues I have yet to wander down, and as I have informed my publisher, the longer my presence is delayed by terribly important business, the more gravitas I shall carry with me when I am shaking hands and signing books."

"Thanks, Leonard. You know if you need help with anything, if you're getting grief from anybody, you can tell me."

He knocked back a mouthful of brandy "If the need arises, rest assured we shall have that conversation."

The Director croaked startlingly loud right in Sully's ear, "Birds like me! Birds like me!"

JULY 25, 2015

The Deputy Director was back from his short leave and stowed away safely in his office, so Sully made time to visit Eugene at the Smithsonian. The safe was now well lit and under guard: Colcross had been a busy boy. Inside the safe, the loud, meaty sound of fucking was deafening. On the TV screen, a peroxide blonde bimbo with a Yorkshire accent was grunting and moaning nasally as she was pounded from every direction by a pair of muscle-bound Mongolians, The doll was just staring at it, the colors from the images playing over its age bleached face. Seeming not to notice her, in as much as a doll or demon notices anything, Sully coughed to attract Eugene's attention.

The head creaked around. "DO YOU DO THESE THINGS? THEY SEEM TO BE THE GREATEST FORM OF AMUSEMENT HERE ON THIS PLANE."

Sully covered her mouth to suppress a laugh and then turned it into a cough. "No. Not those particular things. Try channel five four six."

The doll laughed. "THOSE THINGS ARE ALSO A GREAT AMUSEMENT. THEY LACK IN THE DELICIOUS VIOLENCE OF CHANNELS FIVE FOUR EIGHT AND NINE."

Sully chuckled. "I didn't come to discuss the finer points of pornography with you. Just to ask if you had anything else to help my investigation."

Eugene turned back to the screen. "YOU MUST SOLICIT MY

ANSWERS. MUCH IS KNOWN TO ME AND I CANNOT KNOW WHAT YOU SEEK WITHIN THE BOUNDS OF OUR CONTRACT."

Sully scowled. "Maybe I should tell you some things. You aren't the only demon I've spoken to. The other one knew all about the year of the knife. You're out of the loop."

Eugene rocked back and forth on the spot. "FOR TOO LONG I HAVE BEEN HELD CAPTIVE ON THIS PLANE. ALL THINGS OF MY DOMAIN I ONCE KNEW BUT NOW IT WARPS WITHOUT MY ATTENTIONS."

Sully shrugged. "Shouldn't have snuck in the back door if you didn't want to be here."

Eugene was practically vibrating. "YOU KNOW NOTHING. YOU KNOW NOTHING OF OUR PAINS IN THE WORLD BELOW. YOU KNOW NOTHING OF OUR TORMENTS. THIS IS OUR ONLY ESCAPE. OUR ONLY HOPE IS TO CLIMB. THIS PLANE IS WRONG. IT SICKENS US. BUT IT IS STILL BETTER THAN WHAT THEY WILL DO TO US."

Sully was grinning like she was in the middle of a good fight, and she didn't know why. "What's so scary that demons run away from it?"

Eugene fell silent and then slammed its little stuffed fist against the floor feebly. "NOT PART OF OUR CONTRACT. FILTHY TRICK-STER. I SHALL NOT BETRAY MY KIND TO YOU FOR ANY BOX OF LIGHTS AND AMUSEMENT."

Sully held up her hands. "Calm down. I'm just trying to talk to you."

Eugene froze in place, as immobile as a real doll. Sully tried again. "We can talk about this if you want. We could help you. We don't have to be enemies."

The demon flung itself against the barrier of the magic circle, snarling viciously. It rebounded and flung itself at the invisible wall again. And again. It shrieked at her, "MY PEOPLE HAD NO WORD FOR LIAR BEFORE YOUR COMING. WE HAVE IT NOW AND I DECLARE IT TO BE YOUR NAME. LIAR. PRINCE LIAR OF A RACE OF LIARS. I SHALL GIVE YOU NOTHING."

Sully shook her head and left the demon to its television.

* * *

Back at the IBI offices, Sully had a visitor waiting for her. She looked to be in her late forties, with frizzy gray hair, wide shiny eyes, and wearing a floaty Republican-style dress. She smiled as Sully approached her cautiously. Her voice was classic middle-class English, perky with a hint of dizziness. "Agent Sullivan? The black gentleman told me to wait here for you."

Sully smiled. "Did he mention why he wanted you to wait here?"

The woman tittered. "Terribly sorry, I should explain. My name is Roberta Collinwood. Bertie to my friends. You were looking for reports of people acting in unusual ways. Something to do with those awful murders?"

Sully sighed. She thought that Ceejay would have cut it out with the practical jokes by now. "So, who was it you saw doing something unusual?"

The woman looked down and shuffled her feet. "I didn't see anyone as such . . . or rather . . . so sorry, I'm getting it all mixed up. I'm the one who has been behaving oddly. I'm the one who is being controlled."

Sully raised an eyebrow. This was new; maybe she was going to have to call security on this one. "What is it exactly that makes you think somebody's controlling you?"

Bertie looked embarrassed. "Well, if I'm being honest, I thought that I was going off my rocker for a while there, but then I thought to myself, better safe than sorry. I keep on losing time you see. I blink and an hour or two has passed, and I have . . . done things. Strange things that I can't explain. So I caught the underground over here to turn myself in or whatever it is I'm meant to do. Your associate listened to my story and then he waved this little box at me, and it made lots of beeping sounds. He said that I should speak to you."

Sully looked back the her sharply. "You set off the Schrödinger?"

Bertie pushed her hair back behind her ears. "I'm terribly sorry, I'm afraid I don't know what that is."

Sully pulled a seat out of Ceejay's cubicle for Bertie and perched on the edge of her own. "The Schrödinger's Box detects high concentrations of magic, or things that have been affected by complex or powerful spells."

Bertie looked a little perturbed. "So you are saying that someone has cast a spell on me?"

Sully gave her the best fake smile she could put together at such short notice. "The box is saying that, apparently."

It was enough to draw out another titter, so Sully pressed on. "Can you tell me when you started losing time?"

JULY 3, 2015

Bertie was upstairs in her brownstone townhouse in Brooklyn, which was done up in the Art Deco style, at the time considered the cutting edge of sophistication. She was in the bathroom looking at herself in the mirror. Her lipstick was smeared, or perhaps just very badly applied, and she noticed that the tube of lipstick in her hand was completely blunted away to mush. On the mirror, someone had used lipstick of that very same shade to write a word.

Bertie read the word but she could not seem to remember it. The moment it went into her head it faded away again. It was infuriating, and she didn't understand it, and it was making her head hurt. She snatched up one of the pristine white cotton towels and tried to rub all of the lipstick off the mirror, but only managed to smear the glass. She turned the handle on the chrome faucet her husband had installed for her last spring after she'd found out about his affair with the shoe saleswoman—the man had impeccable taste when it came to fixtures and footwear—but a wet towel was worse than a dry towel. The mirror was now scarlet all over.

JULY 7, 2015

There was a drawing pad sitting on Bertie's knees, and in her left hand, she was holding a charcoal pencil, which made no sense, because she was right-handed. And besides, this week she was doing impressionist work and that meant shades of color, never black. She couldn't recall the last time that she had used charcoal as a medium. There was a word written on the paper, but she forgot it each time she read it. It was irritating. She read it over and over, trying to get back to the start of the word before she forgot it. Eventually she threw the pad across the garden into a fountain, buried her head in her hands and screamed.

JULY 3, 2015

Bertie had a little fender bender while driving to the shops in Red Hook, but she couldn't remember getting into the car. The Egyptian gentleman in the other car was very courteous and concerned about her well-being, insisting that she wait with him for an ambulance to arrive so that the EMTs could make sure that her confusion wasn't caused by a concussion. It wasn't a concussion, apparently, but the EMT kept giving her funny looks until she pretended that she knew why she was there and what she was doing. She was finally allowed to leave after making certain that the lovely Egyptian gentleman had both her insurance details and her phone number.

It would serve her husband right if the gentleman did call. He wasn't young but he had a swarthy handsomeness that she had often admired in films. His hair was thick and black, and she could just picture him in bed with her as her darling husband walked in. Her husband would be stunned silent. Besides, he wouldn't have had a leg to stand on if he did start an argument. She drove home and let that fantasy keep her warm.

JULY 11, 2015

On the pad of paper in front of her was a simple drawing of a man, almost primitive in design. Beside the pad were two torn out sheets of paper. One had a picture of a little straw boater hat and the other was completely covered, from edge to edge, in tan pastel. On the back of Bertie's left hand she'd written a word in Indian ink that she couldn't remember. She kept looking at it and forgetting it, until eventually she looked away.

She pushed her hair behind her ears and examined the pictures. They were so simple a child could have done them. A man. A hat. A sheet of tan pastel. It made no sense. She shuffled them all into a plastic folio and put them away. Then she went to the bathroom and scrubbed at the back of her hand until it was raw, and the word had faded. Her migraine—that she had a hunch was somehow related to the word on her hand—was gone.

JULY 15, 2015

Bertie had been robbed. She was quite certain of it this time—this wasn't just a weird lapse in memory. Her purse was sitting open on the car seat beside her and all of her cash was missing. Further, ribs were aching. That was it: she'd been beaten and robbed. It was the only rational explanation.

She looked outside the car and saw she was in parking lot in a rough neighborhood. That made sense; people got robbed in neighborhoods like this. It was out past Red Hook, in the part of the city constables rarely patrolled. To the side of the parking lot was a shop with a blinking neon sign that read *Tattoos* under a banner of a scantily clad woman in a sailor's outfit. She felt a sharp stab of pain across her ribs, so she pulled up her shirt to see how badly she'd been beaten.

Instead of bruises, she found a word, scrawled across her ribs in black ink. It was raw to the touch and bleeding in spots. She read the word over and over, but she couldn't keep it in her mind, no matter how many times she tried.

JULY 25, 2015

Sully interrupted the woman, "You got a tattoo?"

Bertie nodded. "No matter how hard I scrubbed, it still wouldn't come off. It hurts my head every time I look at it but . . . it won't come off." Her eyes were shiny with suppressed emotion again.

Sully tried to mask her excitement. "May I see your tattoo, Bertie?"

The woman blushed. "Perhaps if we go to the ladies' room. I'm not one for undressing in mixed company. Wouldn't want anyone to think I was being forward."

Sully bit back about a hundred replies, but led Bertie to the bathroom. Under the floaty dress, Bertie wore a pair of tights and very practical white underwear with a hint of lace. It didn't do much for her. It didn't do much for Sully either. And there it was, clear as day across the woman's ribs, a word that fled even Sully's disciplined mind the moment it was out of sight.

The woman could still be crazy, listening to her story had done nothing to make Sully think otherwise, but what were the odds that Bertie would just come across a word under taboo. Sully smirked to herself, a taboo tattoo. She wiped all expression from her face before Bertie caught her, then quickly snapped a picture with her phone before the woman could object. Bertie flushed bright red and struggled back into her dress. Bertie gave an indignant grumble in Sully's direction, but it was ignored.

Sully said, "I think that you might have come under the influence of our perpetrator, so I'm going to need your drawings if you've still got them. And I'd like you to talk to one of our experts here, too. You may have heard of Leonard Pratt?"

That sorted Bertie out promptly. "Oh my goodness. *The* Leonard Pratt? Curse-breaker to royalty? What an honor. Oh, here I am without any makeup on, meeting Leonard Pratt!"

Sully chuckled. "He's going to like you."

* * *

A junior agent retrieved the drawings from Bertie's house and they were spread out on the metal bench of Leonard's lab, alongside a blown up photo of the word written across her ribs. It had taken over four hours for Leonard to feel confident he'd gotten all relevant information from Bertie—with her preening over him the entire time. They were relieved to finally have her driven home.

Sully had wanted to hand her over to Raavi, not for dissection exactly, but certainly for examination. Leonard had downgraded Sully's demands and arranged for the woman to visit her own general practitioner by the end of the week. Reports of anything unusual were to be sent to Leonard immediately.

Sully had argued with him politely for a solid ten minutes before he'd hissed, "How do you think it is going to go for your delightful friend from the subcontinent if it is discovered that he had an English woman stripped down and probed in the side room of a morgue? Do you suppose that he will have a long and bountiful career in the medical field afterward?"

That had finally shut her up. Now they were both staring at the pictures until finally Sully asked, "What do you think they mean?"

Leonard rubbed his temples and leaned back carefully; he overhung the sides of his lab stool by a good few inches. "I haven't the faintest idea what *man-hat-tan* means. Nor can I retain any information about the script that some delightful person has inscribed on her skin. I can recall that it is a word, and I am aware that it is under a well-constructed taboo, likely in support of some larger scale curse that would be weakened if people could recall the name."

Sully sighed. "So how does this help us?"

Leonard treated her to a warm smile. "If this word that is being hidden from us is related to your killer, then I propose that we find out what the word is."

Sully looked up at him from under her scowl. "How are we going to do that?"

Leonard sighed. "If only we had a world class curse-breaker available to us who deals with taboos on a daily basis."

Sully grinned at him and this time it was genuine, not a thinly veiled threat.

JULY 28, 2015

Sully ducked and rolled under the swerving truck. Flames trailed from her hands, stinging at the cut that kept reopening on her palm. The homeless man, who was currently being piloted remotely, was running for his life. It seemed ridiculous that he would do that, since none of these controlled killers had allowed law enforcement to take them alive—whoever or whatever was doing the controlling seemed to like throwing them in harm's way, perhaps for the amusement of watching the reactions of horrified bystanders.

The running homeless man was a bit of an oddity. He'd choked a string of victims and tossed them into the Black Bay. The magical residue left behind on their throats connected them to the case. At that moment, though, the important thing for Sully was not that he was an oddity, but rather that he was now an isolated oddity, trapped between two crumbling warehouses in a desolate area near the Harlem River. She launched a lance of bright white flame from her palms that struck his shoulder in a spectacular show of pyrotechnics.

In a blinding flash, the wave of raw magic escaping the man's body was consumed by the initial spark of Sully's new spell, and while the walls of the buildings on either side of him had begun to crack, they didn't look likely to fall down. At least she could safely fight back now. One success in a month of disasters. Sully stopped cackling and wrapped yet another fresh handkerchief around her hand. Bandages had been too cumbersome; they interfered with her finger movements, disrupting her spells. She would rather be alive and bleeding any day of the week.

Suddenly, she felt as if someone was watching her. Scrying on her most likely. Sully turned around several times, trying to sense the source, but the feeling was gone. She growled deep in her throat and stalked away.

Street after street of back alleys separated her from the rest of humanity. So many of these warehouses sat empty at this time of year that the area was practically a ghost town. There was graffiti all over the walls. A stenciled picture of a snake seemed to be in fashion at the moment, with the words, "Don't tread on me," underneath.

Sully had seen these more and more over the last few years: wannabe revolutionaries in college bars; malcontent poor people who blamed the Empire for every tiny problem in their life. It only took her a few moments and a little bit of magic to erase identifying details from the graffiti so that the redcoats couldn't hunt down the artists. A small act of defiance that didn't cost her anything.

Sully was still drunk on adrenaline and swaggering by the time she got back to the populated streets. Not one of the people looked the least bit unusual, scurrying about their daily business, trying to get by. Any one of them could be next victim. Any one of them could be the next killer. Sully hated feeling helpless, more than anything else in the world. That, and having to rely on other people to solve the problem. It weighed on her—twisted deep in her gut.

She should have called the office and arranged for the dead homeless man—latest in the long list of dead civilians—to be scraped up off the pavement before the gulls got at it. But she couldn't stomach going through the motions again right now.

After wandering aimlessly for a while, she shuffled into the queue at a coffee stand that was being run out of an old white van. The usual suspects were lined up at this time of day—workers ducking out between shifts for a little boost—but among them, sticking out like a sore thumb, was a gentleman.

He was slim and tidy, probably in his late thirties, with thick, slick hair. His skin had a faint olive tone that reminded Sully of the European dignitaries who'd made it out alive before the Veil of Tears went up after the Great War. He was dressed in a tailored black suit, accented with a pale green silk waistcoat and tie. On Staten Island, or one of the other boroughs of the city, he would have fit in just fine, but this was a rough area of New Amsterdam. She noticed him staring, but her patience was dwindling. With a scowl, she strode up the line and introduced herself. "I'm Agent Sullivan of the Imperial Bureau of Investigations. Are you lost, sir?"

He smirked, and when he spoke the accent was indistinct; he had clearly spent a lot of time in the Empire. "A pleasure to meet you, Madame Sullivan. Thank you for your concern. I am enjoying the delights of your city. Although it is very easy to find the most excellent cafés and talented baristas across the world, only here in Nova Europa can one experience such terrible coffee without a great deal of exploration. It is on every street corner here, no?"

Sully forced a smile and resisted every natural urge to hit him. "Well, I'm heading back into the city if you need directions."

He held up a well-manicured hand. His smirk seemed to have been carved right onto his face. "Not necessary, my dear. I know precisely where I am going. Which is more than can be said for most of your people, no?"

She sighed, "Alright. Have fun with your bad coffee."

Sully knew that the man did not belong in this part of town, but had not quite reached the level of paranoia that let her drag people into cells just because they looked out of place. In New Amsterdam, that could be a full-time occupation. She walked to the end of the street and then did a quick travel spell. With a quick leap straight up and a few hops to get around the bay, she found herself in the janitor's closet on the ground floor of the IBI building.

Today he was on top of a ladder smoking a rolled-up cigarette. In his other hand, he was holding a disconnected wire that led to the rooftop smoke alarm. He was startled, but not so startled that he fell or stopped smoking. Sully laughed despite herself and snuck out the door.

Her desk held multiple towers of paperwork. Sully had been sending and receiving dozens of reports from the increasingly nervous Leonard Pratt—all of which were duplicated on her desk. Beyond that heap of folders were the stacks of "observations."

Sully had assigned a team of junior agents to keep track of Bertie, only to discover just how many man hours that entailed and how expensive it became when your target fled the city despite your polite request that she not do so. Bertie had gone to an isolated log cabin in Pennsylvania. Sully thought it was stretching the truth to call a three-story, half-glass, half-wood Swedish pinnacle a log cabin, but she lacked any better terminology.

There were other reports in her cubicle, too: detailed descriptions of each of the attacks and dozens of civilian interviews that sounded somewhat like Bertie's story. Sully ignored the buzzing of her cell phone, as well as the ringing phone that was buried under a mound of toppled reports. She had so many autopsy photos on her desk she could probably keep the penny dreadful tabloids in business for years to come.

Something caught her eye on the top of one of the heaps of manila folders: A letter-sized envelope made of thick cream colored paper. Her name, identification number and the branch's address were on the front of it, fine calligraphy in swirls of green ink. It was so out of place that she was tempted to open her mail for once. The elevator was halfway open when Colcross forced his bulk through the gap, gasping out as he spotted her, "Sullivan. Don't move."

She froze for an instant—that niggling sense of paranoia rushing back. Who would be a better choice of assassin than Colcross, if the killer wanted her gone? She observed the Deputy Director carefully as he sprinted down the corridor. Was his gait lopsided? Was *he* still *him*? She had never seen him run in all her years working here. Barely seen him out from behind his desk, in fact. She knew, and her perpetrator knew, that her boss carried a gun.

Sully stood still, but her heart battered at her ribs as he barged into her cubicle, nearly bowling her over. Her contingency spells fired off automatically and the whole cubicle started to spin around her—folders and letters and pictures swirled up off the desk, orbiting at increasing speed around the two of them. He stood before her, shoulders sloped, panting and watching in confusion at the paper storm. Sully spied the odd cream-colored envelope drifting in the air near her and reached toward it.

Colcross saw her slight movement and jerked his hand out to snatch her wrist, snarling, "No!"

But Sully moved out of his way, leaving Colcross's hand in the empty space where Sully's had been, and his fingers lightly brushing the envelope.

An unnerving sound erupted: tearing gristle, tubular bells, crunching, roaring, and a high-pitched whine all in a simultaneous cacophony. Sully leapt back, disrupting the protective swirl of her defensive spells and letting all of her mail and office supplies tumble to the ground around her. The red macaw now standing in her cubicle looked perplexed.

She carried the Deputy Director, whose name escaped her at the moment, back to his office and was greeted by the squawk of his predecessor, perched up on the curtain rail.

The Deputy Director fluttered up to take his position beside the Director, and Sully felt sick. There on the desk, untouched and unopened, was a cream colored envelope bearing the Deputy Director's name, identification number and the building's address scrawled in green ink. It sat on the desk like a poised scorpion, and she was damned if she would go anywhere near it until every half decent curse-breaker in the colony had taken a look at it.

She would never have recognized the threat, but the Deputy Director had been present when the Director went through his transformation. She reeled at the thought that her boss had received this letter, recognized its significance, and sprinted downstairs to protect her. And she couldn't even be bothered to do the courtesy of answering her phone. She sank down into her usual seat opposite the Deputy Director's desk, and she shook.

JULY 29, 2015

Sully tentatively sat down behind the Director's desk. She reminded herself that this was temporary—that had been her condition when the higher-ups had asked her yesterday to step in as acting Deputy Director. There were other contenders for the job—waiting in the wings, of course. Better political choices who would be more than happy to swoop in and bump her back out into the field if she got a little bit too comfortable sitting in the big seat. That would suit her fine. After this case, chasing the wendigo back over the United Nations border would feel like Christmas come early. But for now at least, the seat was hers.

There was a lot of paperwork involved in the job. More than she would have wished on her worst enemy and certainly more than she was willing to dump onto the few loyal, foolish people who had pushed her forward for the spot. Ceejay had even told the barefaced lie that the old Deputy Director had been grooming her for the position. It bugged Sully that she couldn't remember her boss's name, but she knew that she should leave it alone since it just caused her headaches. Still, she kept finding herself staring at the brass name plate that was sitting on his desk—reading it and then forgetting it the moment she looked away.

Whoever was behind this was a talented psychopath. The method of attack was as clever as it was sinister.

For hours Sully worked her way through the Deputy Director's paperwork—information flooding in from all parts of the colony about a variety of cases, not just Sully's mass-murdering magus, and piles of administrative work as well. Sully was mildly shocked to find that the Director was still drawing a full salary, which was automatically split each month and deposited into two accounts: one was his wife's and the other belonged to a Republican woman who was rumored to be his mistress. Sully had been busy with the case as her only priority. She had no idea how she'd keep up with the added responsibilities.

The only faint glimmer of rest and relaxation in Sully's future was a scheduled evening with Marie tonight, and she'd been knocking back iron tablets all day in preparation. She probably had enough to set off a metal detector by this stage, but she didn't care; blood loss made her anemic and wobbly. And wobbly casting could cost her life. She was damned if she was going to miss out on a night with Marie, though.

Sully had spent too much of her life denying herself the few pleasures that were available to her, either out of misguided morality or out of spite, she wasn't sure which. From now on she was letting her anger go and moving on. The fact that the prior Director was allowed to carry on an affair with a foreigner without scandal gave her high hopes for her chances of public romance with a citizen of the Empire who just happened to be a little mortality challenged.

After chugging a cup of coffee for lunch, Sully finally got Ceejay into her new office. He walked through the door and immediately slumped into a full kowtow, shuffling across the room toward her with his backside sticking up in the air. She guffawed, and he finally looked up at her. "Oh high and mighty leader. Give me my orders so I can attend to your every desire."

Sully snorted. "Sit down and shut up for a minute."

He threw himself into the chair with a cocky grin. "How can I serve you great one?"

She threw a crumpled-up piece of paper at him, and it got stuck in his beard. He collapsed into giggles, and she muttered, "You voted me in, you prick."

He cowered. "Forgive me! Forgive me!"

"Knock it off," she grumbled.

Shrugging, he said, "You were a better option than any of the others if I wanted to keep my job—and you aren't totally useless at yours, so it made sense."

She sighed and rubbed her temples. "Yeah, but now I'm stuck behind this desk, and I've got to tell people that I kind of like that they need to go out and take a bullet for me. This is a nightmare."

Ceejay shook his head. "The job is dangerous. You care if we live, and that's nice, but the job is still going to be dangerous. So let us get hurt. We all signed up for it."

She pushed a folder across the table to him; it was thin, not nearly as close to bursting as the others that dominated the desk. "I need one of these controlled people taken alive. If you hit them with any kind of magic you kill them. It's going to take a proper knockdown fight, and I need somebody who can get places fast."

He looked horrified. "My gods, Sullivan, you are actually delegating a fight. What's next? Will they make you wear a suit and get a sensible haircut?"

"Do you want the job or not?"

He scooped up the folder with a flourish and a wink. "Of course I want it. This will be fun. It will get me out of the office, and this case is bleeding so much overtime I'll be able to buy a boat."

"What would you do with a boat?"

Ceejay shrugged. "I don't know, it's something that rich people have, isn't it?"

He sidled around the desk and gave her a pat on the shoulder. "I'll bring you one of these people if it can be done. You're going to be fine, girl. Don't worry what anyone here thinks. You're going to be fine."

He wandered off with a spring in his step, and for the first time, Sully felt a real pang of regret that she couldn't be out there fighting alongside him. They'd had some good times out in the field. Both the violence and the drinking afterward.

By three in the afternoon, Sully's backside was numb and her feet were itchy, so she stalked off down to the labs for an update from Leonard. She hadn't seen him all day, and his last report had included some promising diagrams that implied there may be an indirect way to assault the taboo on Bertie's words. It had been highly theoretical, and Sully always found it easier to work these things through if she had someone to yell at face-to-face.

Leonard had been moved to a different room in the basement after some anonymous trickster melted the lock off the last door, so it took Sully a couple of turns before she found his new lab. The lights were off, and when she turned them on, she wasn't happy with what she saw. There was a locked filing cabinet, presumably holding all the reports Leonard had been generating. But all of the whiteboards had been wiped clean of the complex layered diagrams they'd held—Leonard's theories on how the mind control could be achieved, what the purpose of the taboo might be beyond masking the attacker's identity. All that work was gone. Everything else had been tidied away neatly, just like Leonard would have left it.

On the metal lab bench was an envelope with the word "Sullivan" scratched across the front in Leonard's distinct frippery handwriting. Sully cast a detection spell over it before picking it up. She wouldn't trust mail for the rest of her life. A period of time that would probably be extended by not trusting mail for the rest of her life.

Dear Miss Sullivan,

It is with great dismay that I must inform you that my time consulting with the Imperial Bureau must come to an end. While I have found the work engaging and your company delightful, as always, I am afraid that certain personal concerns must take precedence. To ensure my continued good health and prosperity, I am continuing my book tour of the Americas beginning with an engagement in the capitol of the Republic. It is not my intention to return to Nova Europa until such time as your current case is resolved. To that end, you will find all my notes on mind controlling arcana filed in the cabinets within this room, although most have already been duplicated and transferred to your own offices in the course of my studies here.

In particular, I would hope that you will continue the latest threads of my research which, combined with the attack within the realms of the United Nations, lead me to suspect that this is not in fact a new school of magic being developed, but rather a very old school of magic being explored, presumably by some- one who has spent a considerable amount of time out of com- munication with the outside world, possibly within one of the abandoned polar research laboratories.

I am most sorry to hear about what has happened to your superior officer, and it is with a heavy heart that I must leave you during such a trying time, particularly when you are facing such dangers yourself. However, a chance encounter with an old acquaintance left me quite convinced of the necessity of my departure.

He is not someone that either of us have had much corre- spondence with, but I have on occasion seen him in the better establishments and gentlemen's clubs around the Empire. Often in the employ of one or more of the noble families of Great Brit- ain or in the service to branches of the government with which I am not familiar.

In the remains of Carthage, at the symposium on acoustic variance in the Yucatan casting chant, he was introduced to me as Adolphous d'Argent, although my understanding is that the surname was rather a pun on his mercenary nature. He is a Franco-Roman expatriate of no small talent, who I am given to understand assisted many of the continental powers in the management of unruly acquisitions before the war.

A slight idiosyncrasy of his seems to be the need to introduce himself informally to those he is tasked with managing prior to the execution of his assignment. If you should happen upon him, please pass on my regards and try to share some of the experimental data that you showed me on my first night in the city.

Until we meet again, I remain your humble servant,

Leonard Pratt, M.B.E

It was not difficult to read between the lines. The assassin with the bird spells had popped in to say hello to Leonard and sent him running for the hills. It took Sully a moment longer to understand that, by experimental data, he meant her Dante spell—he wanted her to roast this Adolphous alive. She carefully placed the letter inside the filing cabinet and locked it. Then she went to the door and locked it, too. These laboratories were soundproofed, so she could scream and the staff would never know. She couldn't even be angry at Leonard; if this assassin was up to what Leonard was insinuating, anyone would have run scared.

When Sully returned to her office, she re-read every single report that Leonard had sent her over the last week. She realized that one word came up over and over. Then she went through all of Raavi's reports to see if anything he'd found contradicted Leonard's theories. Despite sitting in her well-lit, climate controlled office in the middle of summer, she shivered. She tapped her finger on the word in Leonard's reports. Necromancy.

JULY 30, 2015

The night with Marie had gone better than expected. There was a recording of old show tunes Sully had picked up at a flea market a few years back that had been an extremely popular choice. Once, when she'd still had a heartbeat, Marie had landed a lead role in a tiny production of "The Khan and I." She was deeply touched that Sully had not only remembered but also gone out of her way to find a recording of the banned musical.

Marie was lying in a hot haze, feeling fresh blood flooding through her body for the first time in weeks. Sully was covered in a sheen of sweat and was aching all over, but this time it was a good ache. Not the kind that marked her impending death. Marie was ready to sleep as usual, all curled up in a comfortable bed, but Sully was restless.

She didn't pace, the apartment wasn't big enough for pacing. But she kept finding reasons to get out of bed. To check the alarm was set. To check she didn't have any messages on either her cell phone or the landline which had somehow been installed when she wasn't paying attention. When she found herself wiping an accidental smudge of ink off her whiteboard Marie gave an exasperated groan. "What's troubling you darlin'?"

Sully flopped back onto the bed and landed with her head in Marie's lap. Marie didn't sweat like normal people did, but Sully wasn't sure if that was a vampire trait or something unique to Marie. She couldn't remember the girl ever having a smudge in her makeup or a hair out of place in all the time they had known one another, even when Sully herself had been reduced to a sweltering frizzy-haired mess.

Marie sat up carefully and stroked her fingers through the tangle of Sully's hair. That little moment of intimacy was too much. Sully sat up, nearly banging her head against Marie's in the process, and covered her face with her hands. Marie couldn't see the look of blind adoration and devotion on Sully's face; she couldn't. It was too much, and it had taken a lot less to spook her and have her running off into somebody else's waiting arms last time.

Sully reclaimed control of her face, packaged up all of her fear and grief into manageable little blocks, and stowed them away, until her chest was aching. Marie had the good sense to stay still and, if she saw how red Sully's eyes were in the dim light that filtered in from the street, she was wise enough not to comment. Sully faked a flirtatious grin. "Guess I'm not as tired as you thought. You up for another round?"

Marie laughed and it sounded like music to Sully, just like it had across a crowded room on that first night they met in some upmarket wine bar. Back when she didn't know how to flirt without her uniform on and just walking up to that cluster of wannabe starlets would have had her choking on her own clumsy words. Sully flopped back onto the tangled sheets, and Marie said, "Darlin' I don't know where you get your energy from. I don't even breathe and I'm out of breath." She held out her arm and, feeling awkward and a little pathetic, Sully cuddled into her side, tempering the softness of the moment only by reaching over and filling her hand with a breast.

Marie giggled and Sully squeezed and Marie giggled again, drawing Sully in close against her side and stealing some of her warmth. Sully shivered a little despite the heat still lingering from the daytime. One of these days, she would get an air conditioning unit wedged into one of her little half windows. One of these days, she would use some of her savings to buy a place instead of perpetually renting. Admit defeat and settle down somewhere.

She shuffled slightly in Marie's cradling arms and sighed softly.

Marie stroked her cheek with the back of her hand and Sully didn't flinch. Marie whispered, "Darlin', if I can make any of this easier on you . . . if there's anything I can do. Just tell me. Please."

Sully thought about it for a very long time, weighing her options, her dwindling allies, her growing body count and finally asked, "Do you know any necromancers?"

Marie let her go without ceremony, "Beg your pardon?"

Sully shrugged, which was difficult to do while lying down. "You spent some time on the streets. You spent even more time wandering around over the years. I know you must have crossed paths with a few shady characters. I was just wondering if—"

Marie wasn't smiling any more. She snapped, "I didn't fuck any warlocks. I didn't finger any zombie queens for a glass of blood. I ain't like that. Fuck you. Fuck you for even thinking it."

Sully groaned and covered her face. "I didn't mean it like that. I'm sorry."

Marie leaned over her again, their faces a few inches apart. "Say that again."

Sully drew her hands away slowly; Marie's eyes filled her whole world, wide and bright. "I'm sorry?"

Marie let out a little gasp, so quiet that Sully wouldn't have heard it if they weren't almost touching. "I declare that's the very first time you've ever used those words, Iona Sullivan."

Sully flinched at her full name; she should never have shared it with anyone after she got her honorable discharge from the navy. Sully dared to laugh, a soft bark in the night. "I'm sorry. I mean it. I didn't mean anything bad. I just . . . people are dying, and I'm running out of fresh ideas."

Marie growled, "So you thought your dumb, dead, girlfriend would know some bad man that you could knock around for answers?"

Sully smirked. "You're my girlfriend?"

Marie slapped at her playfully, "I'd be a lot more if you'd let me."

Sully reached up and caught Marie's hand. "Let me get this thing finished. Then you and I are going to have a proper talk about that."

She drew Marie's hand to her mouth, let her dry lips brush over smooth knuckles that had never been in a brawl. Sully murmured, "I'm so tired of fighting."

Then Marie leaned down and kissed her. They got tangled up under the blankets and drifted off to sleep as peacefully as either one of them could.

* * *

When the sun rose, Marie was in the shower, using up all the hot water. Her sleep schedule was understandably all over the place, but it was a bloody nuisance every time she stayed over. Sully sat up in bed and felt that warmth again, deep in the pit of her stomach. That scared her more than a dozen Euro-trash assassins. They both got dressed and kept smiling at each other when they didn't think the other one was looking.

When Marie was walking out the door, Sully caught her by the wrist and pressed a key into her hand. It was a big step for Sully and Marie knew it, but she didn't let on. At least not outwardly. They kissed with a little more passion than Sully had intended, but neither complained.

After walking along the bay front under Marie's little black parasol, the two headed down into the subway together, holding hands like schoolgirls, finding it difficult to let go when they parted ways to go to different platforms. Sully was still in her rosy little world when she spotted the man she'd seen at the coffee queue a few days ago. He was standing at the far end of the carriage, dressed in a fitted charcoal gray suit similar to the one he'd worn last time she saw him, topped off with a fedora, which he tipped at her as their eyes met. She realized that this man was probably Adolphous. The good feeling she'd been enjoying that morning had been too good to last.

Sully pushed her way through the rush hour crowds toward the man and watched his eyes for any flicker of emotion. He didn't tense. He didn't go for a weapon. His hands didn't twist and coil, ready to cast. He just stood there placidly, smiling at her. The smug bastard thought he was untouchable. As Sully drew close, the man carefully extended a hand. "Lovely to see you again, Madame Sullivan. It is a pleasure to cross your path so close to home. I believe that introductions are in order. My name is Adolphous DiNapoli, a transient visitor to your fine colony from the old world and a proud employee of the East India Trading Company. Perhaps you can enlighten me about the purpose of some of your colonial constructions. What is the purpose of these leather loops? Do your people require hanging so frequently that gallows are part of your transport? Are you so ashamed of your locomotives that they are hidden in tunnels beneath the ground, no?"

Sully's stare held the full breadth of her contempt. He lowered his hand as she said, "You're under arrest."

Adolphous scoffed and shook his head. "No, no, Madame. That is not how the game is played. I have committed no crime here in your city. You have evidence of my wrong doing, no?"

Sully didn't carry cuffs on her; she wasn't some beat cop who had to drag people in. Most of the time, her deployment in the field resulted in nothing but corpses. When she grabbed him by his carefully pressed lapels, amusement lit up his face and Sully wanted to hit him and never stop. Instead, she said, "I'm sure I'll think of some charges between here and the cold room."

Still not a flicker of worry crossed his smug face. "I think not, Madame. Anywhere you take me will be only a brief sojourn. I have many friends in your Empire. Many debts owed to me. You, on the other hand? You are alone in this world. You have no patron to shelter you. Your politicians would feed you to the wolves if they thought it would buy them an extra plate at supper, no? And all of this without them discovering that the leader of their noble crime fighting organization is romancing a monster of her own?

"Can you imagine the excitement among your wonderful free presses if that particular tale were to be told? Do you imagine that your little courtesan would hide to protect you? Or would she unveil all of your secrets to the world for her fifteen minutes of fame? Do you think that she would do it, Madame Sullivan? Would she tell all the secrets of your bedchamber, all those whispered words that lovers share, in exchange for some time in the spotlight? Would she shield you bravely from the barbs and arrows being slung, even though her own terrible half-life would be dragged out into the open and through the gutters? You will not arrest me, Madame Sullivan. Your career would not survive the maelstrom."

With that, Sully drove her forehead into his perfect, aquiline nose, crushing it and splattering both of their faces with warm blood. He was most assuredly not untouchable and now the evidence was running down into her eyes. Sully leaned back with a broad grin. "Resisting arrest? Gentleman like you should know better."

She drove a knee up into his crotch, and he doubled over with a bark of exhaled air.

Some of the other passengers in the car shuffled away but one guy who had the look of an ex-military home-front hero started toward Sully, until she yanked her IBI identification out of her jacket and flashed it at him. She brought the same hand back around, dropped her ID to swing on its cord, clenched a fist, and drove it into Adolphous's eye socket with just enough force not to break bones.

Violence was a fine art that Sully had quickly mastered sleeping in a berth with twenty-nine navy men that she couldn't incinerate if she wanted to keep earning a paycheck. None of them had ever gotten fresh with her, of course. None of them would dare after the first playground, hair-pulling bullshit, where someone cut in line ahead of her in the mess and ended up laid out in the infirmary—it had taken three men to drag her off him. She had her wages docked for the price of the dinner tray that got bent out of shape but it had been an investment in a peaceful future.

Of course, after they had seen a tour of duty with her—watched her burn cities to ash—it was a moot point. She was part of the artillery by then.

The sleazy man in his expensive suit crumpled to the ground.

Adolphous might be out of his holding cell within a day or

so—and she would argue with every bureaucrat that mentioned freeing him until they stopped her—but for a day or so, she didn't have to worry about him being at her back. It gave her time to think. She gave him a final solid kick in the ribs to make sure he was out. The downside? He was likely to be pretty pissed off with her when he woke up. And this *was* a guy who, in a good mood, turned people into poultry.

Sully took out a handkerchief and wiped his blood off her face. She had stopped caring about her career a good few bodies ago. Threatening her career was like threatening to cut off a cancer victim's tumor. Sully was going to see this Year of the Knife through to its bitter end and then she was retiring to some foggy country where Marie could strut around in a bikini all day and she could catch up on the last decade's lost sleep. Maybe she would get back into theoretical research or maybe she would sell her story rights to some movie studio once they rebuilt Nashville and live off the royalties. She was done with this lifestyle, and she was done with this city.

* * *

The redcoats and their medical staff were handling most of the dead bodies from the case now, at least those that were more than just a big evidence bag of soup, and a visit to Raavi's lab reminded Sully of what happened when Raavi got bored. His autopsy tables had been pushed flush against each other, and two medical clamps and a strip of clingy plastic had been rigged up as a net across the center—perfect for an impromptu game of table tennis. At one end was Raavi, paddle in each of his four hands, and at the other were two research scientists engaged in a spirited defense.

When the researchers spotted their acting Deputy Director standing at the door, they froze in place. The little white ball bounced and hit one of them square in the chest, and Raavi lifted up his arms and waved them from side to side in triumph. "Oh yes. Oh yes. Losers. Two on one, and you're still losers."

Sully coughed behind him and one of the researchers covered his face. Raavi glanced back over his shoulder at Sully and then grinned cheekily. "Honestly. This isn't even close to being the worst thing caught me doing in here."

Sully sighed. "I'm just relieved you aren't using an eyeball."

He clapped and then pointed at the other two. "Didn't I say that! I said that first. These two were scared of getting vitreous on their shirts. Pansies. Although I suppose one good whack would probably pop the eyeballs."

Sully rolled her eyes and politely smiled at the researchers, who had the distinct appearance of people who liked their jobs and probably didn't want to be parted from them over a moment of silliness. Sully asked them, "Don't you have somewhere to be?"

They fled gratefully, and Sully hopped up to sit on the table while Raavi went to fetch cans of ginger beer from a fridge, probably right next to a rack of corpses. Sully took it anyway; death by a tainted tin didn't rate much concern at this point. Raavi waggled his eyebrows at her. "And exactly when were you going to tell me about the lovely Marie? If she hadn't called me to your rescue, I may never have found out. I want to know all the sordid details. If you were a gent, I would probably make some sort of sucking joke, but I'm not really sure how you do your thing."

Sully glared, and he stopped his nonsense for a moment. "Did you talk to anyone about Marie?" she asked.

He dipped his head and looked up at her. "You know me, Sully. I'm a terrible gossip. Love to tell everyone in the world all the secrets that would get my friends in trouble. Of course I haven't told anyone, are you daft? I like you just where you are. Out there killing all the things that want to kill me. I don't care if your taste in ladies runs a little bit frosty. I could tell you some stories from medical school that would turn your stomach, I'm sure."

Sully held up a hand to stop him. "Please never tell me your medical school stories. Sorry. I didn't think you would have said anything but . . . Somebody knew about her who shouldn't have."

Raavi cleared his throat and slumped his shoulders. "Well shit. Sorry, love. Is it causing trouble for you?"

She shook her head. "Not yet. I think the guy was following me, so I knocked him out and threw him in a cell."

Raavi laughed, saw the look on her face and abruptly turned somber. "Really glad I didn't say anything now."

Sully waved it away as if it didn't matter, because honestly it didn't as long as she could get this case closed. That was the nature of politics. You could get away with a lot if you did a lot of good, or were at least seen doing a lot of good. She said, "That wasn't actually why I came to see you. What do you know about necromancy?"

His eyes widened again. "Sully, you've got to stop having these conversations with me. My heart can't cope with this much excitement."

Sully scoffed. "If that were true, you would just shove in a spare one."

He fidgeted. "I don't actually know an awful lot about necromancy, what with it being banned bloody everywhere, and it being the most evil of all magic and whatnot. Are you thinking what I think you're thinking?"

Sully cocked her head. "What do you think I'm thinking?"

He wet his lips. "I think that you think that the reason these bodies are getting weird results in the autopsies is because they have actually been dead for longer than we thought. Perhaps, these aren't people being controlled by new magic that nobody has ever heard of. Perhaps this is really bloody old magic, medieval even—killing folk with one whack then picking up their corpses and making flipping zombies."

He clapped his hands in excitement. "Zombies, Sully. Flipping zombies. Like in the old Republican serials. Shambling corpses. That explains all the crazy Schrödinger readings, too. Must use a ton of energy to run all the little chemical processes that make a body work. Explains why they go pop when you zap them. Also explains why nobody with their own magic has been taken over."

Sully looked confused so he wiggled his fingers at the big crystal apparatus in the corner of the room. "When you die, your magic doesn't just go out like a busted bulb. It filters out, becomes ambient magic. Sometimes gives hard working medical examiners a fright when what they thought was a scalpel turns out to be a squirrel. Plays merry hell with sterile conditions, I tell you. That wonderful contraption in the corner there is like a heat sink or a lightning rod. If magic discharges from a body, it is meant to go into that and make it all glowy. So if your necromancer—gosh that's a fun word—tried to bring a body back that had its own magic still hanging around, it would just fizzle."

Sully snorted. "Fizzle?"

He shrugged awkwardly. "Fizzle or pop like the killers you've been turning into puddles. It wouldn't work. If you left the bodies alone a few days for their levels to drop, then you could march them around like tin soldiers, but not right away."

She pondered this for a second. "So if the necromancer tried this on magicians we should have had reports of exploding people all over the colony?"

Raavi scratched at his stubble. "I do the science, you do the magic. That is your area, love."

Sully thought about it carefully, then closed her eyes, visualizing the spellforms that she had seen during the healing spell, trying to gauge what she had felt. She snapped her fingers. "The spell builds up. Lots of major workings are cast in layers that you bring together to complete. So if you make a mistake you don't accidentally drain yourself or ruin the whole spell. The magic would start to build, the victim would get overcharged and die too soon. Then the necromancer would abandon the attempt."

She drummed her fingers on the side of the metal table. Pieces of the puzzle starting to come together. She glanced up at Raavi. "This isn't hypothetical. This has been happening."

She slipped off the table and strode toward the door. Raavi called after her, "How do you know that? There would be no evidence."

She thought back to the random squawking of a certain Macaw.

The numbers that the director had been shouting since the first day of the case. "A little bird told me."

That afternoon, armed with her last few scraps of information, Sully sat down to interview the Director of the Imperial Bureau of Investigation after cleaning out the bottom of his cage—apparently that was another job she'd inherited. The problem with the gorgeous blue bird perched on the desk chair was that the Year of the Knife hadn't even started when he was turned into a bird. There was no apparent reason or connection, which didn't make sense. But the Director and Deputy Director—and if the killer had been successful, Sully—wouldn't be taken out of action in exactly the same way if the reason wasn't related.

So, either senior civil servants who spent the majority of their time compiling crime statistics were being birded by some crazy as a hobby—and that same crazy had seen her on the news and tried to take an extra swing—or this was all connected to the case. Based on Leonard's cryptic goodbye letter, the assassin she had tossed into a cell downstairs was almost certainly behind the letter curses. But why would somebody high up in government want her investigation stopped when having the Year of the Knife drag on and on was such a public embarrassment to the Empire?

There were factions at work in the Empire, but usually, for something this big, they would have at least faked a united front. Which meant that there was a secret buried in this whole mess. Maybe a government-owned magus was a necromancer on a killing spree? She was pretty sure she knew how Adolphous operated, and she didn't think he was the necromancer, although maybe they were both working for the same silent partner. If he was the necromancer, then there would have been no need for the letters and the threats—he could have easily had the Directors snuffed out completely like the other Year of the Knife victims.

Sully rubbed her eyes and finally said to the macaw, "I know that it's difficult for you to speak clearly, so I'm going to be as patient as I can. Tell me what you know about the Year of the Knife."

The bird cocked its head from side to side, looking at her with each of its eyes in turn, and then shuffled back and forth along the top of the chair, clearly agitated. It was making a low croaking noise, deep in its chest. Sully watched and waited and said nothing. Finally, the words came. "Nearly done."

Sully let out a long breath. "How many deaths were there before you got turned into a bird? No, scrap that. How many before the Deputy Director and I started investigating? Before the killings got flashy and easy to notice?"

The bird scratched at the leather with its claws and croaked. "Exhaustion."

She drummed her fingers on the blotter then pressed the button on the intercom. "Get me the last year's figures for deaths by magical exhaustion."

The line crackled, but she heard some affirmative muttering. The bird flew to her shoulder and perched there, squeezing through her shirt. The Deputy Director fluttered down to sit on the chair behind her, and it seemed almost normal to have the massive birds as company while she worked at the desk.

Some kind soul from downstairs brought her up some of the Mongolian takeaway. It seemed to magically appear in the office each day. She was learning to live off the stuff, switching back and forth between cold lamb and hot coffee over the course of the day. It was so easy for this to become your life. Sully hadn't even noticed that she missed bowling night the other day, and everyone had understood without her even having to call. She used to miss it when she was out on assignment, so she always made a point of attending when she was in the city but this time it had passed her by.

At about the same time the cleaners had worked their way to the outer office, Sully's phone buzzed on the desk top, startling her out of a statistically-induced coma. The Director was apparently startled too, based on the way he clamped down on her shoulder with his claws. She managed not to yelp but it took some effort to pry him loose. He fluttered up to the curtain rail and made some grumbling sounds that closely resembled a duck. There was a text report on her phone from the surveillance team. Bertie was on the move, headed back into the city in a hired car without her husband in tow. He had spent a little time at their wooden palace, in the company of his wife and, as far as the team could tell, he was staying put. That was something at least.

Sully had received the magical exhaustion report and was reviewing it for the third time, when suddenly the pattern appeared to her like one of those three dimensional paintings where you had to cross your eyes to see the real picture. There had been forty-one deaths by magical exhaustion in the days prior to the attack on the Underwood family. Since then, they had averaged out to about one a day. Nobody would look twice at magical exhaustion deaths; most of the victims were heavy users, industrial magicians who churned out dozens of spells each day. The coroner's office wouldn't have looked twice at a single one of these. People using magic made mistakes, and they died for those mistakes. Magic wasn't for the timid. She suspected sixty-seven deaths the IBI had not connected to the case. The body count was catastrophic.

Sully knocked back the last of her cold coffee then stared at the pattern of grounds left at the bottom of her mug. Instead of getting any closer to solving the case, she really was turning into a bureaucrat. She rounded up the birds, put them in their cages, and went home.

JULY 31, 2015

It was Friday morning, and Sully didn't want to get out of bed. This by itself wasn't that unusual, but normally it was because Thursday night was student night at many of the nightclubs in the city, and Sully had always had her pick of the presumably legal and fairly experimental art students. She liked to think of herself as a formative experience for a lot of girls out there in the world.

Lying in bed alone and not wanting to get up was an entirely different experience. Sully wondered if this was what depression felt like. Her brain was, figuratively, on the verge of exploding.

She knew that the answers to the Year of the Knife case were in there somewhere; they were screaming at her to be let out, but she just couldn't find her way through the maze. She needed a drink—a drink so big that it came in a dozen different glasses—almost as badly as she needed for there to be no more bodies on her conscience. The bodies. She needed to stop thinking about them. She needed to stop wondering who they were before someone made them into weapons.

Maybe she would have been better off if she'd picked up her letter. Birds probably didn't worry about the loss of innocent lives whenever they weren't paying enough attention. That was why she couldn't be an officer, and why she shouldn't be in charge of the IBI. She lacked the ability to separate casualty reports, acceptable losses, and collateral damage from the sound of devastated family members wailing over the charred remains of their loved ones.

Sully needed some distance if she was going to work this out. She needed to think like Leonard Pratt, not the one who ran for the hills at the first sign of danger, but the one who came at problems from all different angles. She sat up abruptly and thought about Leonard and his story about the incident in Louisiana. Not the void and the voice. She had a hunch that manipulating the narrative was part of the necromancer's plan—to make her focus where she shouldn't. Instead, she thought about the man who couldn't die and the man who killed everything he touched.

Unstoppable force and immovable object.

Sully got out of bed in stages. First taking a trip to the bathroom, then sitting back down on the bed. Then having a shower and sitting on the bed wrapped in a towel. Finally, Sully got dressed in some items from her new and uncomfortable wardrobe of plain-colored blouses and suits that some helpful administrator had arranged to have delivered for her. Of all the surprises in her life, waking up one day with an expense account had been one of the most jarring.

Sully sat at the foot of the bed again and tried to find some other reason not to do what she knew she needed to do. Coffee would resolve this. The bay-side streets always had new coffee shops popping up, doing good business for a few months and then finding a better location. Far enough from the Black Bay that the clientele didn't looked spooked at the bark of the coffee grinder.

Sully had only been to one Alcoholics Anonymous meeting in her entire life. It was not long after Marie had left her for the carnie— Sully had woken up with a broken bottle in her hand that she couldn't remember buying and decided to give the higher power thing a spin. She'd had the same problems in the meeting as she'd had in her twelve years of Catholic school, but she heartily agreed with their stance on coffee—douse everyone in so much it that they sailed beyond sober and out onto the jittery other side. It wasn't a new addiction, but it was something to balance against the gin. It had pushed alcohol off the top of the list of substances that would kill her eventually.

She had just pulled on her jacket and stepped onto the sidewalk when she noticed how quiet it was. All the sounds, from the sloshing of the bay to the honking horns, seemed to be coming from far away, and Sully realized that the midmorning sunshine was filtering lazily through a barrier that stretched over the street.

Adolphous DiNapoli was standing opposite her door, leaning on the handrail and looking out through his barrier spell at the seagulls fluttering around, confused by their inability to land on their usual perch.

Sully appreciated his gesture with the barrier. She knew it was to minimize the attention that their conflict drew, rather than to prevent others from getting hurt, but it was still a nice touch. It gave the whole event some gravitas, like an old-fashioned magician's duel; thirty paces, turn and cast. She wasn't much of one for formality.

She cast her new fire lance, just because she fancied it and wanted to see how it worked against a shield. It was never intended to ignite structured magic the way it did the wild explosions. As it turned out, the white fire deflected just like everything else did when it hit a shield. The blast hit the barrier and the whole hemisphere of the bubble lit up. Adolphous was facing her now, pale blue spellfire spiraling around his fingers, his pretty face somewhat spoiled by the black eye and the broken nose. Sully couldn't help but grin. "You got out fast."

He shrugged one shoulder and made a little "eh" noise, as though walking out of a high security, magically shielded holding cell at the heart of the Imperial Bureau of Investigation was the sort of thing anyone could do on a whim. "My employer insisted that I stop slacking. Thank you for the kind hospitality, though."

Sully looked from his bruises to her own hands and back, still smiling like a lunatic. "That's how we do things here in the Americas. You'll get used to it."

He launched a flurry of short sharp attacks. Little silvery darts that she ducked around or deflected with brief, flickering shields the size of saucers. He was testing her reflexes. It was cute, the sort of thing they taught you in the duelist clubs in the imperial colleges. A polite approach to murder.

Sully cast a far less polite spell in reply—her concussion spell, packed with a little extra energy, set off underneath a parked car. It flipped up in the air and crashed down on top of Adolphous. Sully snorted with laughter. Hearing a sigh behind her, she turned to see Adolphous standing in a cloud of smoke.

"Poor form, Madame"

She dived forward and rolled, not ready to use a short distance traveling spell except as a last resort—in such close quarters the chances of an accident were obscenely high. Tumbling, she felt a tingling sensation as a lightning bolt arched over her back. Where it hit the trashed car, the metal burst like wet pudding and splattered all over the road. That would have hurt. Adolphous was casting something with one hand—it looked huge and complex—while keeping a shield up between them with an Enochian chant and the other hand.

Sully cast her white flame lance straight at him before he could get the big spell off, and it made his shield flash so bright that he must have been blinded for the second it took him to dispel it. He abandoned the big spell, and used both hands to snap up mini-shields one after the other to avoid her onslaught. A kaleidoscope of colors surrounded him from the spells flitting from Sully's fingertips. A rainbow of colors deflected from his shields, one turning a lamppost into a flock of crows, another scorching her apartment door black, others bouncing and battering off the barrier to shatter the tarmac at the far side of the bubble.

Adolphous couldn't see through the flurry of her assault, and Sully knew she couldn't stop or he might find his footing. Of course, she didn't have a moment to think, or even to reach inside her jacket, either. Sully spat out curses between each breath of air, and, in the odd off moment in her rhythm, panted out a manic, exhilarated laugh. *This* was what she was built for. Not planning or paperwork. Not chasing mysteries or calculating acceptable losses. She had been made a weapon long before she ever found her way onto the auxiliary deck of a Royal Navy dreadnought, waging war on every empire except the one she fought for—the one that her mother had raised her to hate like no other.

Sully detonated a series of concussions in a cluster around Adolphous. He staggered, but he was not unprepared; a shimmer of some sort of armor wrapped around him, absorbing the worst of the concussions and deflecting it back outward. Sully paused to catch her breath and, with her eyes locked on Adolphous, tossed a spinning ring of fire around him, hoping to keep her foe occupied while the part of her brain not directly wired into her instincts did the complex calculations for her next spell.

Not even close to breaking a sweat yet, with a flick of his wrist he snapped the ring of fire with an icy dagger and the lethal flames flopped to the ground like a headless snake. He smirked at her. "Tiring so soon, Madame? I had heard better of your stamina. You are meant to be a fighter, no?"

She ignored his taunts—in movie fights, there were witty one-liners in between the hits. If you pulled that nonsense in real life, you were as good as dead. With little more than a murmur, Adolphous launched another flurry of razor-edged icicles at her. She deflected the spread with some difficulty and it gave him the moment he needed to finish.

Adolphous tossed a shimmering orb toward Sully. It burst on the ground just in front of her and sent a wave shimmering through the air all around her. The moment it hit her, he lowered his arms and smirked once more. "Alas, Madame, your skills were not quite sufficient this time. Perhaps in another life you would have chosen a more sensible path."

Spellfire was still coiling around Sully's hands but when she tried to cast a barrage of flames to shut him up, the words would not come. Her lungs started to burn. She staggered a couple of steps forward, toward the nearest edge of the airless circle he had created. Then she stumbled to her knees. Her lungs had been empty when he cast the damned spell—her breath used up on counter-spells and shields.

Adolphous bowed to her from the edge of the vacuum. "Farewell, young lady. Take some comfort in knowing that you have been defeated only by the very best." He summoned a crackling orb of green lightning between his hands and blasted it at her head contemptuously.

Sully saw the jagged orb of death flying through the air toward her, raised her hands and caught it. It writhed within her spellfire-wrapped grip, pressing against her with a strength far greater than mere muscles could withstand. With a heave of her shoulders and a fresh flood of raw magic she squeezed the orb between her hands.

Adolphous stared in blank-faced amazement as she crushed the spell between her hands until it vanished into thin air. With painful slowness, Sully rose up, forcing one foot under her, then the other. With tears streaming down her bright red face, she ran toward Adolphous—it was as if she were moving through molasses.

He had been too busy gloating to prepare a defense. Sully broke through the edge of the bubble gasping for air. The moment she had enough in her to croak, she launched a ball of fire at the startled assassin. He leapt into the gutter to avoid it, but the fire still managed to singe his well-tailored suit. Glaring at Sully, he ripped down the barrier.

A typical New Amsterdam crowd had gathered, poking at the barrier and peering in through what had been a fairly opaque surface just a moment ago. Adolphous stood right in front of a crowd of locals now, cocking his head from side to side, ready to dodge and let the people behind him bear the brunt of anything Sully sent his way. She lowered her hands, and he scoffed. "Such weakness. Softhearted nonsense. What more should I have expected? You are just a woman."

Sully was still gulping in air or she might have been tempted to make some pithy remark. Adolphous wasn't relying on tricks any more. Bright arcs of golden lightning leapt from his fingertips, annihilating three of the lampposts along the waterfront and carving through a pack of terrified civilians, a chorus of screams that quickly changed to clucking. Then there were chickens fluttering all around, tossing up clouds of feathers and a red mist of blood from those left partially malformed by the curse.

Adolphous gathered his power—it swirled all around him—then hooked a clawed hand at the bay, summoning up a towering wave that crashed off the hasty shields Sully had cast. He followed that with more lightning—real electricity this time, instead of the bright colored energy he'd just used. The electricity burst through the water that was now flooding her street. It was only a well-timed leap straight up and a vigorous burst of magic that kept her out of the lightning's lethal reach.

There was no barrier now, no mask of civility; he wanted her dead and didn't care about the cost. From her heightened position, Sully spotted the parasol pushing its way through the crowd of fleeing civilians before Adolphous could have. Marie tilted it back just far enough to catch a glimpse of Sully without exposing herself to the stinging touch of direct sunlight, and her eyes widened.

The assassin buffeted Sully further up into the air with a sudden upward gust and set her tumbling head over heels. She slammed up a spherical shield that protected her from his next volleys, and the air inside her bubble started to heat up almost instantly. It was a fundamental flaw with completely sealed shields—there was no way for all that energy to escape.

The barrage of spells Adolphous used to hammer the shield were new to Sully. She didn't understand their purpose, let alone how to counter them. All the while she was quietly thankful, because as long as his eyes were on her, focused on breaking through her defenses and destroying her, Marie would have time to get away. The girl was a lot of things, but stupid wasn't one of them. She had to recognize that she was a liability right now. She had to.

The barrage stopped, allowing Sully to cast a clever adaptation of a spell that made her shield explode out away from her. Adolphous had doused the whole area with tiny metallic spiders, and the explosion conveniently flung those away from her, too. Sully landed almost gracefully on the curse scarred tarmac but she was distracted from pressing the attack.

Marie was on her knees, and the dregs of the crowd were scattering.

Her parasol had been jostled to the side, and smoke rose up off her. Adolphous had a circle of blue hot fire coiling lazily around Marie where she knelt, drifting in a slow spin and shrinking an inch or so with each rotation. He pointed to her with a smirk. "Your little concubine? What a beauty. Such a tragic waste for her to burn, no?"

Sully could hear her own knuckles cracking in the sudden silence on the street. The damage to Marie was probably only as bad as a mild sunburn by now. Sully had plenty of sunburns through the years: Marie was going to be all right. She was going to be fine.

With one hand, Adolphous jerked on the unseen leash that led to the coil of fire, dragging it shut. With the other, he cast at Sully—another sudden crackle of golden lightning burst from his palm. Sully threw up both hands to summon a shield.

The shield encased Marie and the coil of flame skittered harmlessly off its surface, burning itself out and burning away the shield but leaving her unharmed. The lightning hit Sully square in the chest and sent her flying. Black feathers began to erupt from her skin as she collided with the railings on the flood wall. Adolphous chortled. "Another bird in the Bureau. Magnificent. You little people are so terribly predictable. It took only simple study to discover your young lady and your mortal weakness. Ah, to die for love. So romantic, no?"

Sully was fighting the curse, turning all of her magical potential inward and ramming it hard against the insidious spell working its way through her body. She was losing, of course—there was a reason that spells were blocked or dodged. Not swallowed whole and fought off with raw determination. It had not reached her face yet, so she had no beak, or she would have pecked him as he gloated. She croaked at him instead. "Didn't do enough homework."

He rolled his eyes. "I have studied under the grand masters in Paris, Rome, Madrid, Madinat al-Salaam and beyond. You think what? That a few years in some backwater university makes you my equal?"

Sully slapped her hands on the guard rail and pushed hard with her magic. Feathers spread along it in a prickling flurry, causing the feathers on her skin to thin a little, buying her a bit of time. She fumbled a warping hand into her pocket, and slurred back, "Didn't do your research. I didn't learn magic in any college."

With a shudder, she bent down and touched the street beneath her with her free hand, unloading more of the curse that coursed through her. Feathers fell from her like sweat. She stood back up, drawing a doll out of her pocket. A simple thing made from sackcloth, but dressed up in a hand-stitched suit. Its shirt was made from a handkerchief, still stained with Adolphous's blood from their last meeting on the train.

He stopped short and stared. Holding it in both hands now, she squeezed the curse into the doll and finally finding a path of no resistance it flowed out of her freely. Adolphous toppled to the ground. He was trying to fight the curse, trying to unload it like she had, but while her education had started with feeling the natural flows of magic, his had started with a book. He screamed as his knees reversed their direction with a gristly tearing sound. Feathers began to blossom all over him like an oil spill. Sully spat on the ground by his twitching feet. "I learned my craft at the feet of an old witch in a bog, and if she wasn't a grand master, I've yet to meet anyone who is her equal."

Sully's eyes found Marie who had located her parasol and was now safe from the sun. This time Sully didn't hide her face or pretend that she wasn't in love. After today she couldn't lie about how she felt any more, not to Marie and not to herself. It was all out in the open.

Adolphous writhed on the ground as the spell twisted and contorted his body. He would not become a bird—too much of the spell's purpose had been squandered and thwarted—just some terrible halfway thing. It was an awful state to leave a person in. A cruelty. Someone would have to be a monster to do that to anyone, even an enemy. Sully crouched down beside the mess of feathers and blood as it twitched and shivered. "Tell me who hired you. Tell me why."

When Adolphous opened his mouth, a screech came out as he fought back the curse as it contorted his vocal chords. Sully could barely make out the response that followed. "Madame, I am a professional."

Sully sighed at her own soft-heart and tossed the doll into the bay.

The assassin grabbed at his throat with his newly-formed wings and began belching out saltwater almost instantly. As Sully rose up and shook herself off, the last of her own feathers tickled their way out of her sleeves and floated to the ground. The last spark of the curse within her collapsed in on itself. Adolphous drowned, lying there on the street, and apart from a very brief pause to kick him between the legs, Sully didn't give him another moment's attention.

Marie's burns were mild. In life she had always tanned perfectly and it seemed that some of that carried over. Between the burns, the chaotic state of her hair, and the froth on her lips from hysterics, she looked almost human in her imperfection. Sully wrapped her shaking lover up in her arms, being careful not to squeeze too tightly on any of the sun-touched skin. Marie was speaking softly into the side of her neck. "I'm sorry darlin', I never knew. You called me and I thought you wanted to . . . then he . . . I thought you died. Then you got hit by lightning. Oh my god, Sully. What did you do?"

Sully moved her hands in soft circles, shushing Marie like a baby. "It's all right. It's over now. He's dead. He's finished. He's gone."

Sully was startled when Marie reared back and punched her in the shoulder. "Don't you ever scare me like that again! Do you hear me? Never again. Promise me."

Sully smiled sadly. "This is what I do, Marie. This is who I am. I'm always going to save the princess. I'm always going to fight the monster."

Marie pointed a finger at her face. "Not any more it ain't. You go quit. I'll book us the first tickets out of town. Let's go live on a farm and get old and fat."

Sully laughed and pulled her back into the safe circle of her arms, then Sully snuck them back to her apartment, hoping to stash Marie out of the way before the NAPD and the redcoats arrived. Now was not the time to explain her relationship with Marie.

Inside, Sully gave Marie a quick summary of what was going on, with a promise to give her the whole story and all the gory details when they had more time. Ignorance clearly wasn't enough of a shield anymore, and Sully wanted Marie to be protected properly. After Marie checked her over to make sure all the feathers were gone, Sully left her safely stowed away and headed back outside to deal with the crime-scene.

There were a few tense exchanges when the police arrived, and if Sully's face hadn't been regularly plastered all over the newspapers lately, she probably would have had to come in for questioning, badge or no badge.

* * *

It was late in the afternoon before the chaos had settled down enough for Sully to catch a train to the office. She hit the doors of the Director's office at a pace just a little under a run, trying to stay ahead of curious coworkers, who had started hounding her with questions the moment she stepped into the Bureau's atrium.

Rumors dogged her constantly at the best of times, but today of all days, she didn't have time for it. She had two curses to break, and despite the exhaustion already snapping at her heels, she needed to get started while the incident with Adolphous was still fresh. She took some small comfort in the knowledge that her shaky hands were just the drop from her adrenaline rush. She shut the heavy office door in the face of the rabble outside, locked it with a twist of her wrist and a flex of will, and then turned to face the room.

The Director was perched on the back of the visitor's seat, preening his feathers, and the Deputy Director was snoozing in his cage. Sully closed her eyes and let her other senses sweep out over the room, heard the little protection and alarm charms woven into the walls like the faint jingling of bells, felt the fire runes etched into the underfloor piping like prickles on her feet. Blocking them all out, she brought the full weight of her attention down on her target: the Director.

What had been chaos before now felt familiar. She hadn't just seen this magic executed by Adolphous, she had felt it in her bones. She stalked closer to the Director, eyes still closed, guided forward by the beacon of raw magic that bound him.

A Gordian knot of different curses, all woven together with such precision that the moment one was undone, another would spring into its place. It wasn't a single work of genius, it was a slow determined labor, piling one spell onto another, securing it to the next and layering on more. The longer the curse persisted, the harder it would be to break. Even repressed memories would fade until all that was left was a bird. The curse repeated its lies to the universe over and over, the same story told in different ways, whispering to reality "this man is a bird." Sully had taken the time to shower off the last few downy feathers before she left the apartment. She knew the lies that the spell was telling.

Reaching out to the Director—her fingertips brushed against the feathers of his chest and she flinched away from the memory. She let spellfire wreath her hand and she thrust it at the bird. It seared through the feathers, slicing through the delicate spellwork but not attempting to unravel it. There was resistance as the curse tried to regrow around her hand, but another pulse of flame forced it away. She pushed and pushed, sweat streaming down her face, until she was up to her elbow in the bird, and finally, her fingertips brushed against the unmistakable texture of tweed. She grabbed hold of the material and pulled. The resistance grew, the curse pulled at her, trying to drag her into the macaw with the Director; to make her a bird once more. But Sully wasn't having any of it. Spellfire wrapped its way around her whole arm, blinding bright even through her closed eyes, and it seared away every infectious touch of the curse. With one final grunt, Sully pulled Director out of the parrot. She kept her eyes closed as the spellfire died down. She had wanted to look of course, but if you've seen one parrot turn inside out and a full-grown man stumble out, then you've seen them all.

Director Mueller—with the spell gone, Sully finally remembered his name—was gasping for air. He collapsed to the ground then let out a sad, ululating noise that Sully realized was meant to be a squawk. She let gravity take its course and dropped to her knees too. There was a broad circle of brightly colored feathers scattered all around them, and a blackened scorch mark on the floor where the front half of the Director's desk used to be. He flung himself up, waving his arms frantically before landing back on his face, knocking his horn-rimmed glasses off and sending them skittering across the floor.

Sully crawled forward and grabbed him by the shoulders, pinning him down before he tried to take flight again and did himself some damage. She found herself talking, in a tone that was much softer than she would have expected from herself. "It's all right. It's over now."

He twisted his head around to look at her, wincing when it could only swivel through ninety degrees. "Over? It is over?"

She ran a hand over his oiled hair. "You're as human as you ever were."

His upper lip appeared to stiffen under his pencil moustache. "Yes. Quite. Thank you for . . . rendering this service, Sullivan."

He looked at his hands. Touched his face. Ran fingers over bare skin and then fabric. He took a hold of Sully's hand without seeming to realize that it didn't belong to him. Given what he had just been through she could forgive a little unprofessional conduct. She smiled down at him. "Welcome back to humanity"

He cleared his throat and untangled their interlinking fingers before turning away to wipe at his eyes with the backs of his hands.

Sully spoke softly, "You haven't been able to communicate very clearly while you were incapacitated. I have some questions, if you don't mind?"

He nodded dutifully, and between the two of them, after a few fluttering false starts, they managed to get him into his seat. He seemed smaller than she remembered. Maybe the all-fruit diet had helped him with his weight. When his eyes had finally stopped darting around and his breathing was regular again, Sully sat down at the remains of the desk and said, "The Year of the Knife."

Mueller groaned. "It was the Year of the Wand when I first started investigating." He drew a ragged breath and then pressed on. "There was a spate of deaths—magical exhaustion, or so it was supposed—with corresponding readings on the magical detection apparatus. Massive concurrent spikes in energy: it looked like spells gone out of control. In a sense, it was. There was a pattern, in the things that the victims said, in what they left behind. The Year of the Wand was one thing that kept on repeating. Another was a word that was under a powerful taboo. I filed my reports with photography of the messages left behind, that word included. I imagine that is what prompted the attempt on my life—"

Sully butted in. "You think somebody in Westminster knew what that word meant?"

He nodded thoughtfully. "There are means of circumventing a taboo if they are set up ahead of time. Storage of information in an extra-planar cache, things of that ilk."

"So somebody further up the food chain is willing to let people die rather than have this word come out?"

Mueller closed his eyes. "This is all speculation."

Sully tried a different approach. "So why have we seen this change of tactics?"

The Director tried to smooth his lapel with his beak, realized his mistake and patted it down with his hand. "It wasn't working, clearly. It was an observed trend that magicians, magi, witches or whatever you call yourselves, place entirely too much focus on magic as a solution to all problems. I suspect that this killer believed that possessing the bodies of powerful users of magic would allow for the most widespread destruction and draw the most attention. Instead it seems to have resulted in their rather abrupt deaths."

Everything added up to the same solution either way. Sully sighed. "So these killings aren't going to stop, our own government is trying to undercut the investigation, and they aren't above assassinating senior civil servants to achieve their goals?"

Mueller patted his chest pocket. "You don't happen to know where my cigars have gotten to?"

Sully offered him one of her own cheap imitations and then lit it for him with a flick of a finger. He smiled. "Fingers, it will be nice to have fingers again."

Sully caught a glimpse of the clock on the wall and hopped to her feet. "You will have to excuse me Director. I have to get to the Smithsonian before it closes. Can you . . . uh, explain everything?"

Mueller chuckled. "Of course, my dear."

She paused at the door. "And can you also feed the Deputy Director and tell him that I will sort him out as soon as I get back?"

They both looked at the cage. It seemed unlikely that a parrot could glower, so Sully just wrote it off as her imagination. Mueller added. "What is at the Smithsonian that is so important, Sullivan?"

Sully flashed him a grin. "Just a really big lever, sir."

* * *

Down in the vault, Eugene was pretending not to notice Sully. It was watching an old documentary about the Great War and grumbling to itself at the way the camera always cut away before the explosions. Sully tapped her foot but she didn't disturb the doll until finally it slapped its hand down on the remote and turned the television off, dropping them both into complete darkness. Sully actually found that she preferred it this way. The voice still made her hind brain freeze up in terror every time she heard it, but at least she didn't have to look at the creepy little face.

Eugene said, "WHY HAVE YOU COME BACK? WHAT MORE CAN I TELL YOU? NOW YOU HAVE FRESH HOSTAGES TO INTERROGATE. LEAVE ME TO MY ENTERTAINMENT. WHEN WE RISE UP AND TAKE YOUR WORLD I WILL BE FREE TO REAP MY VENGEANCE UPON YOU."

Sully was too excited to be put off. "I think I want to make a new deal."

Eugene snapped, "YOU HAVE NOTHING TO OFFER ME."

Sully pressed on regardless. "I know you speak our language. Can you read it too?"

Eugene tutted, impressive without a tongue or moving mouth. "YOUR SIMPLE ETCHINGS HOLD NO MYSTERIES TO ME."

"You're a creature of great power outside of that ring. You can't tell a lie and you can't break a deal. Right?"

The doll sounded bored. "ALL OF THESE THINGS ARE THE TRUTH ALTHOUGH YOUR KIND RARELY SPEAK IT SO PLAINLY."

Sully took a deep breath. "Here are my terms. I've got a photograph of a word that I need you to say. If I let you out of that circle, you will say the word. That's our whole agreement."

Eugene thought it over carefully, examining the wording, examining the intent. "AND IN RETURN?"

This was the turning point. "If you promise not to harm another human being then I will let you go free."

The safe shook. "WHAT?"

Sully conjured a little ball of witch-light above her head, ruining the sanctity of the cold room and bringing power dangerously close to the demon, which she now realized was standing directly in front of her, pressed up to the edge of the barrier. It didn't look any better with the decent light. The paint on its face was starting to flake away. Eugene roared, "I SHALL DO MORE THAN HARM YOU WHEN I AM FREED. I SHALL GRIND YOUR CITIES TO DUST. I SHALL BURN YOUR PEOPLE TO ASH. THE WORLD THAT YOU ONCE KNEW SHALL BE NAUGHT BUT—

Sully cut it off, "Alright. Alright. Cut out the revelations crap. If you say the word for me then I will send you home."

Eugene rocked back and forth on his little stumpy legs. "I AM TO SERVE AS A FOOTHOLD HERE FOR THE LEGIONS OF HELL. I WILL NOT ABANDON MY LIFE'S QUEST SIMPLY TO ESCAPE THIS CELL. ALL THINGS CHANGE WITH TIME, I CAN OUTLAST THESE METAL WALLS AND I CAN OUTLAST THE

WORLD BEYOND. ALL THAT I MUST DO IS WAIT AND VIC-
TORY SHALL COME TO ME."

Sully raised an eyebrow. "Still too scared of whatever oogie-boo-
gie lives on the ground floor of hell? Fair enough."

Eugene threw itself against the side of its enclosure. "YES. I FEAR
THE BEASTS FROM BEYOND THE OUTER WALLS. AS SHOULD
ALL THAT ARE LIVING. BUT YOUR PETTY TAUNTS MEAN
NOTHING. I CANNOT BE GOADED. I CANNOT BE TRICKED.
GIVE ME YOUR FLESH. THAT IS MY OFFER. TO SPEAK THE
WORD THAT CANNOT BE SPOKEN. GIVE ME YOUR FLESH
AND LET ME ROAM THE WORLD AS I WAS MEANT TO BE.
NOT CRIPPLED AND BOUND IN THIS STRAW STUFFED
HOMUNCULUS."

Sully shook her head. "How about I let you out and give you a day's
head start before we start hunting you down—"

Eugene didn't even let her finish speaking. "DEAL."

She held up one finger, "If you come at me after I let you out then
I'm going to kick your ass back into that ring and drain all the magic
out of you."

Eugene was pawing at the barrier now. "I AM NO FOOL. SUCH
THINGS ARE BEYOND YOU HUMANS."

Sully grinned and made sure Eugene saw it this time, "Tell that
to the big snake-looking demon that I drained to a husk down in
Nashville."

The doll took a half step back. "WE HAVE NOT SEEN SUCH
FEATS OF MAGIC IN THREE HUNDRED YEARS."

That wasn't exactly a promise but Sully was running out of time
and options. How many people could this little doll kill in one day
anyway? More than the necromancer? Playing the odds was always the
officer's job. Right now, a creepy doll wandering around the world was
quite firmly the lesser of two evils. So Sully chose. She cast a whip of
flame from her hand, white hot and blindingly bright in the enclosed
space, then she used it to slice through every ring in a single swing.

Eugene was out of sight for a moment as the shower of sparks cleared and when she next heard its voice it was from right behind her left shoulder. "SHOW ME YOUR WORD."

She spun around and there was the doll, lying limp in the corner behind her. That wasn't terrifying at all. His head lolled from side to side and goose-bumps ran up her arms.

"Come outside of the safe, just in case there is a discharge, I don't want to get fried."

Eugene did not reply, but when she blinked he was gone.

The doll was propped up on top of a dusty crate just outside the door of the vault when she emerged. Sully took the photograph of Bertie's tattoo out of her pocket and tried one last time to hold the word in her mind before giving up and handing it over. The doll read the word but no sound came out. "THIS IS THE MAGIC THAT YOU CALL A TABOO? YOU THINK IN WORDS. SO WHEN THE WORD IS TAKEN IT CANNOT BE THOUGHT OF. YOU APES ARE POS-SESSED OF SINGULAR INGENUITY TO BALANCE YOUR LACK OF POWER. LET ME TRY AGAIN."

The neon tubes in the light fittings began to rattle and Sully took a step back, leaving the Polaroid propped up in the doll's rigid hands. She cast a few layers of shielding over herself, stopping short of an actual barrier; she wanted to see how this played out. Wisps of light danced around the doll and static crawled and crackled all over the metal shelves. Still it did not speak. There were tremors running through the whole building now. A climbing vibration that sounded more and more to Sully like somebody shouting through a solid wall. An ancient Roman vase smashed on one of the rear shelves and Sully winced, hoping it wasn't anything too old or valuable.

Sully heard the television inside the safe turning on and off, giv-ing brief loud bursts of static, screaming, grunting and clipped, ran-dom words. The lights began to glow all over the basement, getting brighter and brighter as the rumbling in the walls grew in volume. The lights began to burst, moving in concentric circles away from where Eugene was sitting. Sparks showered down on row after row of ancient artifacts from all over the Empire and its holdings.

It occurred to Sully that she probably wasn't going to be welcome back in the Smithsonian for quite some time. She felt the magic building, felt the invisible spell of the taboo. If she had Leonard Pratt's brain, she probably could have picked the spell apart, now that it had come out of hiding. But the head-on attack had always been her style and she was sticking to it.

She could smell sulfur—the reek was pouring out of Eugene now, and although he looked as harmless as ever, Sully could feel the power pooling around him, making him swell and press against the limitations of his stitching. When Sully retired, and had time to research for fun again, she was going find out how Eugene had been made. Think of how helpful a pet demon could be—a near infinite magical battery if she could get past the sass.

Shelves began to topple, spilling their ancient contents across the floor and clattering against each other like dominoes. A thick nimbus of pure white light was all around Eugene now, the photo of Bertie was flapping back and forth in his hands and, at the very edge of Sully's hearing, she could make out his terrible voice. Little more than a whisper but growing louder and louder as the taboo stretched to breaking point. It pounded at Sully's head. That word that couldn't get in. Over and over. Whispered and screamed. She pictured the little drawings that Bertie had created. The man. The hat. The page colored tan. In her gut she knew that this wasn't just important, this could blow the whole case wide open. It could be the necromancer's name. It could be the necromancer's home address. It could be something that would let her bring this nightmare to an end. It had to be.

Eugene's seams started to split as the spell forced more and more power into its badly designed body. Smoke started to rise off of its straw stuffing and the flaking paint on its face crumbled and twirled away, making geometric shapes in the air all around it as the spell fought back, trying to reassert its order against the wild, raw power of the demon. There was smoke drifting out of the rents in the doll; the brimstone reek swept over Sully and she gagged, but she didn't run. The demon was roaring as the strain of the unspoken word roiled all around it, until finally, after what seemed like an eternity, Eugene said, "MANHATTAN."

The word rolled out like a wave as the taboo was broken, setting the whole building quivering in its wake. When Sully came out from behind her blackened shields, there was no sign of the doll except a sooty mark on top of the streaked and smoldering crate. It was gone and she had nothing.

She slipped down to the ground and leaned her head back against the crate, muttering to herself in soft despair. "Man. Hat. Tan. What the hell is a Manhattan?"

AUGUST 1, 2015

Sully couldn't remember the last time she'd had a day off, and based on the heavy-handed hints she was getting, apparently every member of staff thought she needed one. The janitor in the closet just shook his head when she arrived. Raavi dropped in to cluck about the effects of exhaustion on rational thinking. Even her own secretary suggested Sully call it a day because she looked so tired.

Sully's first order of business in the morning had been to break the curse on the Deputy Director. It had been less dramatic than her attempt with the Director. Colcross had been less disturbed, although before being dragged off by his physician for bed rest, he had given her a hug, which seemed pretty out of character.

Sully was still acting Director for now, neither Director Mueller nor Deputy Director Colcross would be ready for active service right away—it was going to take them both a bit of time to get over the habits they'd picked up while they were macaws, like the tendency to flap their arms instead of walking or the way they kept shitting themselves. It wasn't certain they'd even want the job again after what they'd been through.

Sully spent much of the day trying to dig up anything she could find on the taboo word. Given what had happened to the Director and Deputy Director, she wasn't ready to share the information with anyone at the IBI for fear news would make it back to whoever was trying to keep this a secret. She combed the internet, made a few discrete calls, but turned up nothing on the word Manhattan. She had called in a lot of favors chasing after a word that was still meaningless to her.

She eventually got a call from Ceejay, who was still on the road. Their conversation boiled down to him calling her an idiot, telling her to take a break, and updating her on his fruitless zombie hunt in Atlantic City. Afterward she sat and stared at her amended death toll figures. Three hundred and ninety-eight dead from the Year of the Knife in less than three months. She finally gave in to the pressure from her peers and went home early—with minimal grumbling—and found herself at a complete loss as to what to do with herself.

Sully couldn't stomach the idea of going inside her apartment— her apartment had never felt claustrophobic before, but it did today. Instead, she crossed the road to find a spot by the Black Bay to think. The guardrail that ran along the edge of the bay still had shiny black feathers growing, and Sully trailed her fingers over them. Although she could think of a dozen reasons not to, Sully called Marie, leaving an awkward message that casually mentioned she had the rest of the day off and nobody to spend it with.

She left a message for Leonard, too—the bureau could foot the bill for a long-distance call or two—telling him that she was sorry she didn't get a chance to say goodbye but was happy to report that New Amsterdam now had its pest problem under control. She lit a Republican cigar from the box she'd rescued from the remains of the Director's desk and was contemplating calling Raavi to see if he wanted to sneak out for a pint, when her phone rang, startling her. It was Ceejay.

"Hello, gorgeous. Do you want the good news or the bad news?"

Sully groaned. "Get the bad out first."

She could hear Ceejay grinning on the other end of the line, it was uncanny. "The bad news is your little holiday is getting cut short. I am very sorry. Can't be helped."

She leaned against the barrier carefully, in case the Adolphous incident the day before had loosened anything. "So what's the good news?"

Ceejay let out a belly laugh. "I have only gone and caught one alive."

Sully nearly dropped her phone. "You caught one? What the hell? I thought it was a wild goose chase I'd sent you on—something to keep you busy while I cracked the case."

Ceejay's laughter rumbled in his voice. "You thought dumb old Ceejay would go chasing around in circles while you solved the whole thing, as usual, but this time I did it. I got the break. I win this round. How does it feel to be coming in second, Sully? Does it feel good? Should I be getting the big fancy chair?"

Sully couldn't help but laugh in disbelief. "You can have every seat in the building if you want. Can the prisoner be transported or should I come down there?"

Ceejay chuckled, "That is the best part of all, we caught him on the train into the city. He was on his way to see you. He isn't saying much now, but I think he's looking forward to meeting you. He even asked for you by name."

Sully blew out a stream of cigar smoke. "Why am I always so popular?"

Ceejay chortled. "Must be that winning personality of yours."

She closed her eyes. "Must be. When are you getting back?"

Ceejay switched to professional mode. "Our ETA is about an hour, chief. Are you coming to meet us at Grand Central?"

Sully snorted. "Like I'd willingly run out to Yonkers twice in one year. I'll get backup sent out to meet you, have him secured in one of the holding cells in the basement, and we can deal with him there.

Ceejay mumbled something about slacking desk jockeys and then hung up on her.

She called the IBI switchboard. Ceejay would be met by everything short of a twelve-cannon salute and a pride parade. Then she stubbed out her cigar and tossed the butt into the water. She was back in the game.

With a direct line to the necromancer, she could start some

probing spells to get his location. She could read the unique patterns of his magic to get an idea of his personality and training. She might even speak to him through this corpse version of a tin can on a string. Her blood felt like it was pumping again for the first time since she'd heard the word "Manhattan." She turned to hail a cab and nearly ran into an old oriental man.

She muttered, "Sorry," and was about to keep moving when something gave her pause. His track-suit was badly messed up, with lines of soot across the front, and he had a smashed camera gripped firmly between his hands. She studied his slack face and realized with shock that this man had been among the dead after her fight with Adolphous. Up close, she could see blood stains on his polo shirt where the fractured shard of a concrete slab had torn into him. He bowed to her politely, muttering something, and when Sully leaned closer she could hear it clearly.

"ManHATtan, MANhaTan, MaNhAtaN, maNHatan."

The old man staggered past her and took her place at the guard-rail, staring out over the bay. She could still hear the chant, it had replaced the rhythm of breathing he'd had when he was living. A constant rumble of the word that still meant nothing to Sully. Looking farther along the bayfront, she saw that there were more people with the telltale looseness to their joints, the crooked look that had startled her so badly on that very first night in Winchester Village.

They were spaced out along the waterfront as far as she could see, and with the quick flash of a sensory enhancement spell, she could see their lips moving and hear them chanting. A deafening buzz made her jump, and she realized that was what her phone sounded like with enhanced hearing, which she dispelled promptly. She saw that it was Raavi calling and answered with her usual subtlety. "What's up with all the dead people walking around?"

Raavi practically screamed. "If you know about it, why is nobody helping me?!"

Sully paused. "What?"

"What?!" Raavi yelled. "They are breaking out of the morgue, Sully. All the victims. All the killers. The whole lot. They are trying to break down the door. What do I do? Why aren't you here?!"

Sully shouted back, "Get out of there. I'll be there as fast as I can."

Raavi spluttered, and said, "Wait. No. They aren't bothering with me. They walked right past me, even though I know one of them saw me. You worry about what is going on out there and send someone down here to stop them. Oh shit. They have the door down. There're hundreds of them Sully. Why did we bring them all here?"

Sully's mind was racing again, out of the territory of "new evidence" and heading right over the edge of "too much to process." She stared at the old man's corpse and whispered, "It made sense to bring them all here. We had the best lab. The best coroner—"

Raavi butted in. "This isn't the time for flattery you know. They are almost all out. I pulled the alarm. Will that do anything? Will you do something?"

She said nothing for a moment and he shrieked, "Sully! Do something!"

She hung up the phone and ran toward the old man. Whatever this was, it had to be stopped. This was the endgame of the whole exercise—the goal that the entire enemy operation had been building toward. There was magic crackling in the air above the Black Bay. Much more than the usual random discharges that haunted the place. Whatever these corpses were chanting, it was doing something out there in the water.

She could start exploding them. If the others were anything to go by it would be easy. But before she could finish her thought, cold dead hands closed around her wrists, and others clamped over her mouth. It was easy for them to creep up on her since they didn't breathe. Sully was dragged away from the water by two dead men and a dead child. The child had climbed up and latched itself onto her back with its fingers interlinked over her mouth.

They hustled her back into the alleyway beside her building and held her down. The child hissed and crackled in her ear. "YoU hAvE doNE yoUr PArt WITch. We aRe cOMiNg baCK. ALL tHe AbanDOneD peOpLe of ManhaTtAN aRE cOMING BAck. ThERe iS no stoppiNG uS nOW. ThE ciRCLe is cAsT aND THe SUMMoNINg HaS bEGUN. YoU reTURNED ouR nAME aNd WE aRE COMinG bACk."

Sully struggled because it was in her nature, but the grip of the dead men kept her from casting no matter how much impotent spellfire burst from her fingers. Even if she pulled off one of her spells without words or motions she would just be committing messy suicide with them pressed up against her.

She tried to hook her two attendants' legs using her own, but even that was hopeless as they just slammed her down onto her knees and put their full weight on the back of her calves. The little girl spoke again, so close that Sully could feel the movement of the child's jaw on her cheek. "Do NOt rESISt uS. We MEAn yOU nO HARm buT wE ARE ComING Back."

Sully sank her teeth into the cold skin of the girl's fingers but the girl didn't even flinch, just squeezed against Sully's jaw even tighter. "We HAvE BEen wATCHING yOU, SULLIvAn. YOu dO nOT loVe tHIS EMPire aNY MOre thAN wE DO. LeT US coMe tHRough. LeT uS SHOW tHe wORld WHAt wAS DONE tO Us. LeT uS COME HomE."

Sully yanked down with all of her strength and the dead men staggered for a moment, but before she could get free, they jerked back into place. This time Sully was in an even worse position, her arms were twisted behind her—heat and pain spread from her shoulders.

Sully never understood where the skinwalkers hid their spare pelts—every time she'd seen them they were stark naked—but even so, they always seemed to have one more shape up their figurative sleeves. Maybe there was a pocket tucked inside the other furs. Regardless, when the grizzly bear exploded out from behind the bins she was grateful. The first corpse lost its head with the bear's initial swing, and even though the second one dropped Sully to square off against the black furred mass, it didn't help. The bear batted it down and ground the flesh from its ribcage with two fast rakes. One more stomp snapped his spine.

Sully threw the little girl off her back, and a quick blast of white fire left nothing but a blackened outline on the alley wall. With the dead girl's hands away from her face, Sully gulped down air, the reek of sulfur now sweeping over her. Magic crackled in the air all around them, setting Sully's skin prickling and the bear's fur on end. The bear stalked around in a circle and then settled back on its haunches. The damned thing was taking up the whole alleyway. Sully gave the bear an awkward pat on the head. "Thanks. Now stop stalking me, you creep."

The bear shrugged, which was something to see, and a slit appeared down its flank. The perfect golden limbs that emerged didn't even distract Sully this time. She shared a brief smile with the Native American woman and then took off running, right over the bear pelt and out of the alley.

Back at the waterfront, the voices of the dead were climbing to a bellow, echoing around the bay and the whole city. Soon the whole colony would be able to hear the word "Manhattan" chanted over and over again without pause. The water in the bay was churning, and Sully saw shimmers of white light shining up from the depths. It broke the surface of the water, bursting upward to illuminate the clouds. Sudden flashes of green and purple chased across the bay, and down in the deep, was a constant red glow, like a lava vent had just opened up.

Sully cast a succession of simple, fast spells—little darts of her white fire that wouldn't even have singed a human being, but turned the magic-infused corpses into puffs of ash with the minimum of collateral damage. She knew what a dimensional breach looked like, and she had to stop this before it was completed.

There had been horror stories about the Great War pasted into every text that she'd picked up at the Royal College. Detailed documentation everywhere. Lectures that preached dire warnings daily. Europe was meant to be the wake-up call for the rest of the world to get their casting under control. Instead, hell was coming to New Amsterdam, on her watch.

After the first few explosions went off, the corpses took notice of Sully, but they kept their formation lest the spell be disrupted. Lights flickered and tremors swept over the city in time with the chant. Sully went about her work quickly, destroying as many of the corpses as she could, but the dead moved, repositioning themselves to keep an even distribution. They weren't going down fast enough; the breach was still going to happen.

Deep in the bay was the sound of an explosion. The concussion swept out, shattering windows on the buildings facing the water and tossing Sully off her feet like a rag doll. A huge wave sloshed up over the flood defenses, soaking the lines of dead where they stood, knocking Sully back to the ground as she tried to stand. The Native American woman grabbed her by the back of her collar and hauled her to her feet with a snarl. "This is what happens when you let the manitou live among you. The dead and the living are meant to be in their own places. This is what your abomination has made."

Sully shoved her away. "Please, vampires have nothing to do with this. Piss off back to your little paradise and leave us to it, then."

Her perfect face twisted in fury. "After all that we have done to help you. Despite everything that your people have done to us. This is how you repay our kindness?"

Sully spat into the salt water swirling around her feet "Thank you ever so much." She turned to start casting again and a corpse's decomposing fist caught her in the jaw. Her defenses snapped up before the second blow could fall and his next swing met a field of magic. He exploded in a shower of dried blood and sharp shards of bone. The wave of escaping magic smashed Sully and the Native American woman against the side of her apartment building.

There was a hazy patch of time when things seemed to shift sideways and Sully felt the world spinning. The flashing, crackling lights and the distant shrieking could have been the magic out in the water or they could have been a concussion, she wasn't sure.

When Sully staggered back to her feet, she caught her breath and recognized the tell-tale strain and wheeze of cracked ribs. This time when she spat, a tooth splashed into the puddle.

A semicircle of the dead surrounded her, and one was knelt down over the seared body of the Native American woman, hacking at her head with an axe and tearing away her sleek black hair in handfuls. Sully took a staggering step forward but the dead huddled in closer to drive her back.

With all the magic, all together, it was no wonder there was a breach in the making. The dead were still talking to her but the words weren't getting in. The ringing in her ears drowned everything out. She lifted her own hands to shush them and could see the sparks trailing from her fingertips, but wasn't sure why.

In increments, Sully's hearing came back, and she heard the dead chanting again, thumping at her head, so loud it was impossible to ignore. She found herself whispering the word in reply. "Manhattan. Manhattan. Manhattan." It echoed all around, pulsing against her skin, pulsing through her skin, and vibrating in her bones. She shook her head to keep from getting caught up in the flow of the magic swirling all around her.

Something clicked in her brain. The spell that was being cast to punch through the planar border was not being made by these corpses. The magus, the necromancer, whoever was doing this was still out there, still hidden, using dead bodies to cast the spell. The animated bodies had formed a circle around the ritual. Lining this side of the bay and pouring out of the redcoat's mortuary out in New Jersey to do the same there, If she broke that circle, all of the power bound up in whatever spell was being cast would escape and it would be catastrophic.

Another huge wave swept up and over the street knocking Sully and the corpses to the ground. A deafening roar of displaced air hammered her back down when she tried to find her footing. When Sully finally got back on her feet, she was alone—the dead bodies were just dead bodies again. She staggered across to the guard rail and grabbed on so that she wouldn't fall again.

Sully's mouth dropped at the sight in front of her. There was now an island in the middle of the Black Bay. An island almost as big as the Bay had been. On the island was a city, and on top of that city was another city. Layer upon layer of construction rising up from behind a twelve-foot wall that bristled with crystalline spikes. At the bottom there was recognizable human architecture, but as it climbed into the sky the buildings contorted and became more impossible, more like an anthill than something constructed.

A city had grown from the human roots, drawn out of nowhere by raw magical power beyond any magus on Earth. At the top, it expanded out into spikes and twisted battlements. A city built for siege on an island that fit perfectly into the bay—the same bay she'd spent the last decade staring at from her windows. Sully had never really wondered what a city built by demons would look like. Now she didn't have to.

The magic was gone from the air. Not just the massive build-up of power that had been used to summon whatever the hell that island was. All of the magic that had been hanging over the bay—for as far back as there was written history—was gone. The necromancer must have known something about the bay and how to tap the ambient power to achieve this massive undertaking.

Sully tried to stand upright but she could feel herself swaying with the high waves, either with shock, or the concussion, she didn't know. She drew in a few steadying breaths and then saw something rise up from behind the city's walls, a little black spot that grew larger by the moment. With one ear bleeding and her hands quaking, she was in no way equipped to be fighting a demon, but she was damned if she'd get chewed up without a fight.

She staggered toward her apartment, blasted a hole through the wall and cast the full version of her calling spell—catching her sword by its handle before it skewered her. She flicked off the scabbard, and it landed near the dead Native American woman. There would be hell to pay from the United Nations when they found out what happened to their skinwalker.

Sully rolled her shoulders and tried to get into her best fencing stance. It had been a long time since sword drills in the navy. The shape had resolved itself into a more or less humanoid form by now. In fact, if Sully didn't know better, she would have said it was a man floating across the bay toward her.

He looked human and wore several layers of thick, tattered clothing with little clusters of shimmering crystals growing on the seams. High boots, a long coat, scarves wrapped high around his face and what could only be described as a tricorn hat. The coat fluttered around him as the buffeting winds lifted him up. It was magic Sully had only ever seen used in demonstrations. Showy and wasteful with none of the stealth or efficiency of a simple traveling spell.

He landed on the pavement gracefully and, slightly muffled by the scarves, said, "You are the one they call Sullivan? You are the Irish witch?"

Sully kept her sword leveled. "What are you meant to be?"

He gave a stiff nod. "Forgive my manners, it has been a busy day. I am Magus Ogden, the last Mayor of Manhattan."

Sully pointed over his shoulder with her sword aimed at the thing in the middle of her bay. "That's Manhattan?"

He nodded slowly as though he were speaking to a child. "We are indebted to you, and you have our utmost apologies for the deceptions and the harm that we were forced to inflict upon your people. You must understand that we have been trapped in a very hostile place for a very long time. There were no means too debased to serve our ends."

Sully licked her lips—he certainly looked human. "All right Ogden, first off, lose the mask. Second, why don't you sound like a magus?"

He tugged down his scarves, and she saw immediately why he wore them. He had a thick black beard but it was run through with strips of scar tissue. His lips were jaggedly torn and badly healed, and his nose was missing a part of its tip.

He tried for a friendly smile but it looked more like a grimace so he abandoned it. "That was the first of the many trials that we faced.

When we found a way to reach out from the far realm, our magi believed that it would be a simple matter to have the seal upon our name broken. We needed only to present our problem to a magus on your side of the hells, and ask them to apply their intellect from the opposing perspective. Imagine our horror when we discovered what had been done to the magi in our absence. The drooling lobotomized wrecks have been coerced into burning away their reason with each simple spell that they cast.

"We had to throw ourselves upon fate's whim and hope that we would find a single lesser mind that could break the seal. Imagine our surprise to find you—a servant of the very Empire that had doomed us."

Sully grumbled at "lesser mind" but she lowered her sword. "All right, who the hell are you?"

APRIL 13, 1775

Ogden pulled his hat down low over his face as he strode through the gutters of New Amsterdam, past bawdy houses and soapbox preachers alike. In the taverns that he passed, there was a song being sung, and though he did not understand the Spanish words being bandied about, the rhythm of the drum made it painfully clear what the message was. The same message that rattled along the train lines across the colony. Revolution.

The massacre in the Boston Harbor had been too big for the Colonial forces to suppress. Four hundred men or more turned into fish and set loose in the ocean for protesting an unfair rate of tax. It called out for justice. Ogden was well attuned to the flows of magic—it permeated everything that lived—and he could hear the outrage pulsing in his own veins.

The Empire had banned all magic within the city limits, which was laughable. But then they had set a dome of magic over the city, so at least the seal against traveling spells could be enforced. A clear sign that the Empire was running scared of its own shadow.

Ogden ducked into an alleyway where two buildings leaned so far together that they touched in places at their higher stories. Plaster dust showered down on him as the people inside went about their rough business.

Manhattan was the richest island in the whole of the Colony, barring the governor's castle on Roanoke, and the people here felt the sting of the taxes levied against them less heavily than the starving commoners in their fields. There were no empty bellies here, no one was falling from horses or being mauled by the skinwalkers of the Indian nations who still ran around in the shape of mountain lions preying on those who settled out west.

This should have been the place where contentment with British rule ran the highest, yet here he was, on his way to a meeting in some counting house's basement, with a letter in his pocket from the desk of Magus Burr—a sorcerer who had played his cards so close to his chest that most would have sworn he held no position at all on the concept of self-governance.

The letter had been cleverly hidden inside a dove that kept battering itself off Ogden's windows for a fortnight before he finally had it shot down and brought in for study. The message was simple and clear: all magi unhappy under the yoke of the British should gather in Manhattan on this night to discuss what was to be done. There had been some rather cruel curses woven into the letter that would cut off his fingers or torn out his tongue if he had shared its contents.

Ogden knew that Burr was capable of even more creative curses than those, but the magus was a busy man right now, quietly planning a civil war that could send the whole of the Empire into a downward spiral back to another dark age, And that assumed that the bloody French didn't just swoop over the channel to the homeland and unleash their own version of hell the very moment the strategic minds of the Empire were turned elsewhere.

There was a brawl spilling out onto the street from the next barroom, and Ogden had to dither in the alleyway while the animals slugged it out. From the corner of his eye, he could see the redcoats doing the same. It made him wonder if there really was a web of detection set up over the city to stop all unlawful uses of magic, or if the Empire's pet spellhounds were just too lazy to intervene in a petty dispute like this. A gap opened up in the crowd and he slipped through unseen before he could find out one way or the other.

The counting house was not far ahead, a monstrosity of marble and flagrant opulence that amazingly hadn't already been chipped apart by revolutionary graffiti. Across the top of the lintel it read First Bank of America. Ogden shook his head at the thinly veiled jab at the Empire and then ducked inside through the layered illusion of a locked door. Inside, a trail of oil lamps on the floor led him to a rear room and then down to the dull glow and muttering voices in the vaults below.

Ogden did not recognize every magus in the basement. There were a great many of their caliber across the Empire and, with the potency of the natives' arcane defenses, many of them had been politely invited to the Americas until the situation was more settled. He counted at least two hundred magi and their assorted apprentices crammed into the cellar. There was only one chair in the whole place.

Near to the center of the room, and surrounded by a jostling circle of the most potent magicians on the planet, was the smug grimace of Magus Burr, looking like nothing so much as an overly content frog, stuffed to bursting with flies.

Ogden strode forward, and from a few of his fellows, he received brief clasps of the hands in welcome. There was a degree of deference there too—several of the younger magi, the ones who had been born here in the colonies, bowed their heads to him as if he were their school teacher. Peering at them in the dim light, he suspected that for several of them, he probably had been. That was good. Ogden's voice alone wasn't going to be enough to dissuade Burr and his cabal from their madness. The crowd shuffled back just enough for Odgen to be seen and Burr gave him a benevolent smile. "It is kind of you to join us. Even if the hour is late."

Ogden nodded curtly. "There was no possibility that I wouldn't wish to speak on this matter. Sir."

Burr chuckled. "You cut to the quick as always, sir. That was my intention all along. Civil discussion amongst peers is the only sensible way for us to decide things. The gentlemen in the city above us are free to argue in whatever manner behooves them, but I think that every-one here can at least agree that any decision reached by the popular opinion must be ratified by us for it to successfully proceed."

That was far too reasonable and clearly setting the bait for some later sophistry, but Ogden set his jaw and agreed amicably. As always, Burr sat smiling and nodding and saying not a thing. That had always been his way in every dealing Ogden had had with him. He set others into motion—planting the seeds of his ideas in them and then letting his marionettes dance to his tune when the time finally came to speak.

They'd had limited dealings through the years at the few conventions the Colleges held, and while Burr's intellect was impressive, his attitude was not suitable for scholarly pursuits. His puppets were flamboyant young magi, dressed up in bright colors that the redcoats could have spotted and remembered from a mile away. Among the British emigrants, there were many stoic supporters of His Majesty, King Henry, but their number dwindled the longer the debate went on and had withered in the face of the Empire's wild replies to calm complaints.

As a proportion of the population, the British were only barely a majority in the colonies at the best of times. With the Five Year War not long ground to a halt, there had been a flood of French refugees swelling the colony's population. The French loathed their new government with what was rapidly becoming a characteristic passion, and they spoke on the subject with great vigor in their prolific coffee houses. That concerned the overseers of the colony much more than the drunken antics of the Irish and the Spaniards. Raised voices and riotous arguments could be expected with liquor; when you heard them over coffee it was a sign of more serious troubles.

Magus Lafayette spoke for the French contingent and, whereas the other magi were on the subject of concessions that could be won by gentle resistance and writing letters, he had already moved on to discussing the ways that the colony could become a free republic with equal rights for all of its citizens. In contrast to Lafayette's flamboyance, Magus Madison spoke in soft tones that made the surrounding speakers lower their own voices and lean in closer to catch his words. He was a moderate and, like Ogden, he had been in the field and seen what full-scale magical warfare could do to a nation.

The young all cried out for war, and the old argued all sides of the issue relentlessly. The veterans of the Empire's earlier conquests—Ogden, Madison, Arnold and Charleston stood silently and let the roar build up around them. Their eyes met across the room as arms flapped around, and raised voices and emotions churned up the ambient magic in the room. There was sadness there; the veterans could feel the way the tide was turning and Ogden suspected that like him none of them wanted to cast death again.

Something was off with Magus Arnold. He seemed distracted—checking his pocket watch each time Ogden looked at him. He had it cupped casually in his palm as though it weren't an expensive extravagance. The basement had grown hot with so many bodies pressed in together. Ogden had shed his jacket and hat early on, tossing them into a corner on a heap of others. His waistcoats were now unbuttoned and his shirt was going the same way. There was sweat trickling down the faces in the crowd, but Arnold was still buttoned up as tightly as if he were meeting the Pope—even his gloves were still in place.

Ogden didn't say anything. He fell quiet as the arguments continued to rampage around him, and he started to slip through the room. He took the time to shake hands as he went, greeting the Scottish magi who had settled in the far northern reaches of the continent and the Roman ones who had made their homes in Virginia, until eventually he reached Arnold, the man whose adopted home city they were standing in right now. Ogden clapped him on the shoulder, making him startle and drop his watch, and before he had a moment to recover, Ogden grabbed his glove and tugged. The feeble illusion shattered. Arnold's fingerless stumps protruded from his shirt sleeves.

Although Ogden could swear he spoke softly, the whole room fell silent as he cried out, "Magus Arnold, what have you done?"

The Empire was on the lookout for anyone using magic without permission, so none of the hot-headed youngsters were given the opportunity to duel Arnold. It was probably for the best, even without fingers, Arnold was a veteran of the long and painful campaign against the Crow tribe and there was a fair chance he would have made mincemeat of those children.

The gathered magi fled up the stairs and out into the streets. Ogden joined the flight, but a glance back showed him that Arnold and Burr had not joined the fleeing mass, the two of them were still standing in the sweaty room—all hope of a resolution abandoned in the face of the impending danger.

Out on the street, people were screaming in a dozen different tongues. The French were claiming that the Royal Navy stationed in the harbor had opened fire on the city. The Irish were shrieking that the Indians were attacking. The Spaniards swore blind that it was the end times. And amongst them all ran drunken Englishmen, swayed to the opinion of whomever they were standing the closest to.

All that Ogden could be certain of was that there were no stars visible in the sky above; no clouds, nor any sign that the city was not completely enclosed in a pitch-black bell jar. Flows of magic coiled away from Ogden. Of the many reasons that magi usually kept far away from one another, magical interference was probably the least important, ranking far behind arrogance and the impossible truth that even a magus left alone in an empty room would somehow generate a bitter argument. But at the moment, it was exactly that interference that prohibited Ogden from interpreting the magic clearly.

Burr's secret convention was probably never going to have produced a consensus. The magi would have returned to their towers undecided on a course of action and waited for history to flow around them, as per usual. It took a catalyst like Arnold's betrayal to actually force a conflict.

Ogden was among the first to abandon any pretense that the magi had remained undetected. He cast his flying spell with consummate ease and drifted up above the crosshatch of streets and buildings to take in the entirety of what was happening. That was when the nearest redcoat shot him. The musket bullet caught him through the rear of his leg, ruining a perfectly good pair of boots and disrupting his concentration enough that he went tumbling back down to the street, only to be rescued at the last moment by a cushioning cloud thrown up by one of his peers.

Casting a healing spell on oneself was near impossible, and the other magi were rushing this way and that to escape the redcoats who were now on the offensive. The last thing Ogden remembered was the heat of blood flowing from the wound in his leg.

* * *

When Ogden woke from his brief bout of unconsciousness, he found himself propped up in the back of a hay cart a few streets over from where he had been injured, a small group of his fellow magi gathered around him. They updated him on the situation—there had been fighting in the streets between the redcoats and the magi. And after several hours, the magi had managed to annihilate most of the government stooges. Now the problem wasn't the redcoats—they had bigger things to worry about.

Ogden learned that the solid barrier spell that encircled the island of Manhattan had become porous, and several magi and civilians had volunteered to venture through the wall, investigate the situation, and report back. Once through the wall, they remained visible for a short time, encountering what appeared to be solid ground instead of the Hudson River, but observers reported that within minutes, they lost sight of the volunteers completely. None had returned.

Ogden was soon bellowing orders from the back of the haycart as though the command had been given to him. No one was to pass through the barrier until they could figure out what had happened; whether the island had been transported to some unknown location, and if so, where and why.

At some point, one of the young magi, a woman from Rome, came to perform a healing spell on Ogden's leg. With a hastily summoned walking stick in hand, Ogden and a few of the other magi made their way to the nearest edge of the island. Ogden could feel the magic thick in the air surrounding him—thicker even than when the Empire had placed the dome over the city.

It was at this magic barrier that enclosed the island that they encountered their first demon. It had a feline cast to its features, although it was entirely hairless, and in places it was covered in metallic thorns. It was also entirely wild with panic. The magi soon had it confined in a hastily drawn circle, and Ogden put it to question.

What they learned was worse than they could have imagined.

The demon's speech was slurred and it constantly shuffled around within the circle. Gradually its story became clear. It had been going about its demonic business within its own personal demesne on the hellish plane, when the island smashed through on its way to wherever this—its final destination—turned out to be. Ogden and the other Magi were astonished. Magic on this scale was almost always more simply performed with a wish—a deal with a demon, or a djinni from the Caliphate.

But the demon swore blind that its kind were not responsible, and it was well known that demons were entirely incapable of telling lies. Ogden also knew that the djinni generally emphasized the manipulation of probability, and he felt certain they lacked the raw potency required for something as substantial as the permanent transportation of an entire island to parts unknown.

Reports began to filter in from other places on the island: other demons that had been similarly dislodged and were now contained within circles of their own. The demon Ogden was interrogating kept digressing, trying to correct what it considered human misconceptions—such as the idea that demons were naturally destructive. It wanted to set the record straight. The behavior was chosen. The violence humans experienced at the hands of its kind was intended only to clear a foothold so that more demons could escape their own dimension—a valiant effort at colonization.

It was in the midst of this conversation that the bubble over the city melted away and the unfortunate residents of Manhattan first witnessed the blinding white expanse stretching out in every direction.

All hell broke loose. Civilians were going berserk, screaming and pan-
icking, many sprinting off into the desolation before they could be
restrained.

The demons were not much better: flinging themselves against
their containments and ranting about the things that even demons
fear. Nightmare creatures that snatched demons in their sleep. Abduc-
tions and experimentation by the creatures of the far realm. A realm
that was "CLOSER TO THE SOURCE" than their own demonic
plane, and further yet from humanity's reality. The demons believed
that Manhattan had been taken to this place.

Ogden had never heard of this far realm, but when he reached out
with all of his magical senses, he could not argue. There was a roaring
intensity where there should have only been ambient power.

* * *

It was on the second day of exile that the attacks began.

Civilians were going missing. At first, they attributed it to madness and fear, since the magi were unaffected. But at a hastily called
town meeting a month into their exile, it was no longer possible for
the magi to ignore the truth. People were not leaving Manhattan and
wandering off into the white expanse—they were being taken. When
Ogden listened to story after story told by the people of their lost
island, listened to the terror in their words, he recognized the pattern.
They raised walls. Conjured them from raw magic in a feat that would
have been near impossible on earth. But it was not enough.

When more went missing, the walls were raised higher. Guards
were put in place. Some went mad from staring out into the stark
abyss. Eventually, a permanent barrier was erected and it was then
that the creatures of the far realm became violent. The damage was
never witnessed as it occurred. Only on brief patrols outside the walls
were the strange markings, the strange growths and gouges, revealed.
By then, the demons roamed freely on the island as allies—there was
no advantage in violence, so they did not pursue it.

Sometimes, something made it over the wall, wreaking havoc until it found another victim to drag off into the desert beyond the barriers. Over time, living in terror became the norm. Marriages were conducted and children were born, each infused with so much magic that, within only a few years, they were the equal of any College-trained magus. There were few deaths, at least among the magi. The saturation of magic had rendered them more or less ageless and, with so much magic to call upon, sickness and want were things of the past. It could have been a utopia if the attacks would have just stopped.

Eventually the enemy was seen. Strange spindly pallid things with huge black eyes, bulbous heads, and few other features. They had a scent that reminded Ogden of nothing so much as a nest of rattlesnakes that he had once uncovered while divining for water. The creatures came in small numbers. Intent on abduction rather than warfare and so talented in magic and so steeped in the power of this place, that it was difficult to stop them.

But the magi were nothing if not resourceful. New strategies and spells were devised and every moment that was not spent in defense of the island and its people was spent plotting a way back home to safety. For two hundred and twenty years, every man, woman, and child strove for that goal and so went the siege of Manhattan until they saw the beacon.

There were few scouting trips made after the first century. The far plane was an empty desert in every direction as far as the eyes could see, and there were no resources to be harvested. If the enemy had a city, it was well hidden, and many suspected that the native's mastery of magic let them slip into pocket dimensions forged into whatever paradise they could imagine whenever they were not hunting humans or demons for whatever terrible purposes they pursued. Staring up into the endless white of the sky had driven many of the Magi to madness over the years but there were times when even Ogden's eyes were drawn up to that colorless expanse, seeking any hint of a star, any hint of a sky.

When sentry cries went up, it took him only a moment to follow after the magi flying up into the sky. The beacon that they rushed toward was little more than a black spot in the ceaseless white but that black spot gave him more hope than he had experienced in centuries. He flew to it, casting caution to the wind and closing the distance in an instant. It reeked of the hells, sulfurous and foul, but still he plunged into the cloud of blessed darkness with all his brothers in arms, even hearing the trills, shrieks and threats of the demons at its edges. He could feel home just beyond it, he could hear the siren call of earth in this tiny rift between worlds.

The way was blocked. A corpse had been stuffed into the crack, but beyond that lump of dead flesh Ogden could hear voices. Human voices. The magi joined their power and argued swiftly through the process of creating a spell. Then together, they cried out through the mouth of the corpse, saying the only thing they could unanimously agree on. "We are coming back."

The moment the words were out of the corpse's mouth, the rift began to collapse. Ogden and the others cast every spell that they knew to delay it, but whatever impossible power had punctured through the planes, it had only given them a moment. Ogden drew on the raw magic of the plane to which they had been exiled. He became a channel for it, pouring all that he could into the gap, but before their eyes, the aperture to earth snapped shut.

The black hole hung in the sky above Manhattan as a daily reminder of the opportunity that they had just lost, no bigger than a pinprick. The demons were delighted, at last they had a way to communicate with their home, some small connection to the planes above. The humans of Manhattan were less joyful but their resolve was hardened. It may have only been for a moment, but they had caught the scent of home and there was nothing that they would not do to get back to where they belonged.

AUGUST 1, 2015

Ogden spat out the highlights of his story with the bitterness of many recitations then returned to the beginning to fill in details. He did not describe how many times through the centuries they had fought, killed and died for their island but she could hear an all too familiar weight in his words. Sully stopped him when he was launching into the second century of condensed history. "Listen. This is fascinating stuff but you have murdered almost four hundred people."

He looked uncomfortable. "It saddens me that innocent people had to die. It was done to save a thousand souls condemned to the worst torments that you can imagine. They were the first casualties of the war that must be waged against the British if we are ever to be free."

Sully had sheathed her sword during the history lecture, but it was only now that she let her hands relax at her sides. "I know a lot of folk back home in Ireland who feel the same way as you, but you just made a dimensional breach the size of a small island. There's going to be a response to that."

Ogden squared his shoulders, and Sully felt the power rolling off of him in waves. "Let the British come. Our vengeance has been centuries in the making. Tell our story to the people. Tell them to rise up against their oppressors. There will be justice done this day."

Sully shook her head. "You aren't going to get the pride of the British Navy sweeping up the river. They're going to portal in swarms of vampires with the latest military gear, and they're going to chew you and your island people to pieces."

Ogden scoffed. "We have faced far worse than little dead men with guns. Every man, woman and child in my city is a veteran of the most brutal war humanity has ever suffered. Let them come. The only ones who would have the strength to best us are the magi, but it appears the current trend is for them to be lobotomized by those who were meant to exalt and guard them. Manhattan shall stand."

He held out bandage wrapped hand to Sully. "Will New Amsterdam stand with us?"

She had felt her heart thumping in her chest as Ogden told his story, but it was only now that she realized her hands were shaking, too, and it wasn't exhaustion or a concussion. It was rage—she was furious at what had happened to these people.

"That sort of decision is way above my pay grade. And you are under arrest. For murder, necromancy, conspiracy and whatever else the lawyers can make stick to you."

He scowled and power started to gather around him, but she held up a hand to silence him. "I'm happy for you to be under house arrest back on your island for now. The vamps are probably going to come execute you on the spot anyway, and that will save me finding a prison to hold you all in."

He was still frowning, but he answered cautiously, "Thank you?"

Sully shrugged. "Saves me some paperwork."

He squared his shoulders. "However, I cannot return to Manhattan until I have spread my word among your people. The world must know what the British did to us."

Sully shook her head. "No need. I've got you covered."

Newspapers were not unheard of when Manhattan had left the face of planet earth, although television had taken some explaining. Too much of what Ogden said was ringing true to Sully's own suspicions over the years, so she made a few calls.

The press descended on Ogden with the ferocity of a starving beast. It was just as well that they did, because if Sully's count was right then the entire fist of the British Empire was about to slam down on his little island within the hour.

Fortunately for Ogden, a dimensional breach the size of this one resulted in a delay in mobilization. They'd want to bring in every squad. In less than an hour, Odgen's story could be heard from every television and radio in the colony. Along with his sincere apologies to the families his necromancers had destroyed.

Sully wished he had left that last bit out as she hovered behind the cameras, fastidiously avoiding any attention, but he was intent on being completely honest from the outset. Between interviews, she snuck in the odd question of her own. "Bertie?"

He paused and then nodded. "The socialite? She expired of a drug overdose early this year. One of the young ones controlled her from then on. We needed to get the word Manhattan into your path somehow."

After another recitation she butted in. "And the one that Ceejay caught in Atlantic City?"

He smiled his crooked smile. "We could not complete the circle around the island without someone on the train bridge."

Sully wished the media circus was taking place over on the island instead of right here in front of her apartment building. But for all the panic the appearance of the island had caused, seeing the demons roaming its streets of the island might have driven the public into complete meltdown. Sully finally broke up the media frenzy with dire threats of violence and got another moment with Ogden. She nodded across the bay. "Get back to your island and shore up. I'm amazed that they haven't ported in to wipe you out yet."

He shook his head. "The spell that once prevented us from traveling beyond our island by arcane means has been cast over your city."

She opened and shut her mouth, eventually just shrugging. "Huh. That's handy."

The dreadnought came out of its portal in the open water off the coast of New Jersey moving at full steam toward the bay. Sully watched it coming up the river and didn't say a damned thing. Her cellphone was buzzing. She'd already missed a dozen calls from the Bureau, the governor, and numbers she didn't even recognize.

The ships launched their first barrage the moment they were in range. Huge meteors of lava launched toward the encrusted walls of Manhattan. They struck the island's invisible shields and deflected off. The first few ricochets landed in the water, forming new floating islands of pumice.

The next barrage hit a dockside warehouse that exploded into shrapnel. Sully's eyes widened, and she cursed under her breath. She dialed the governor's number. It was a testament to how badly things were going in the governor's office that not only did he answer the call himself, he did so on the very first ring. "Director Sullivan, I need your report immediately. Why has the media been involved? What in the nine hells do you think that you are doing out there, you stupid girl?"

Sully ignored him. "Call off the navy. Get on the phone or the radio or whatever you've got. Manhattan isn't hostile but it is protected. Bombardment is doing nothing to it, but it's destroying my city."

The line went quiet. A torrent of lightning arced from the port side of the dreadnought to bounce harmlessly off of Manhattan's defenses and incinerate a street in Brooklyn. Lord Price spoke far too calmly. "We cannot tolerate insurrection, Miss Sullivan. Not in any part of the Empire. Not in any measure. Not at any price. Kindly make your report."

Sully gritted her teeth. "I'll call you back with that report, sir. I've got a little problem to deal with here first."

She threw her phone into the bay and immediately regretted it. People were screaming past her now. Fleeing from the fires and explosions that were destroying New Amsterdam. One of them was wearing a uniform that Sully recognized, so she grabbed the poor man by an elbow and spun him to a halt. "Hey. Are the trains still running?"

He fumbled over his words. "Doesn't matter. It's happening everywhere in the city. Everything is burning. We've got to get out of here, lady."

She caught him by the sleeve as he tried to turn away again. "I don't care about that. Are the trains running?"

* * *

The lights and all of the electronics in her apartment had stopped working. A local transformer must have been hit in the bombardment. From the rate of fire that the dreadnought was turning out, it was hardly surprising. The whole city was going to be leveled at this rate. She grabbed her pens and her whiteboard and dragged them out into the early evening air. Smoke clogged the sky but it was still brighter than her apartment.

It had been a while since she had seen this done by her subway killer, but she still had the reverse-engineered calculations used to find him, so she dug into her pocket for her notebook and muttered some gentle charms to help it recover from the many times it had been doused in water over the last few days. She was miles away from where he'd drawn most of the circles used to create his thaumaturgical weapon of mass destruction, but she was betting that even in the damp tunnels, they'd still be there in some form. She worked frantically. The longer she took to do her math, the more likely it was that the trains would catch on to events on the surface and grind to a halt.

Using her sleeve, Sully wiped years of painstaking Dante calculations off her whiteboard, not without some regret. She needed room to work out the angles. Soon she was trying to make a sextant with her hands to judge the distance to the dreadnought—just like in the bad old days. By the end, she had shed her jacket and was sweating and scribbling her own circles on the much-tormented tarmac in front of her apartment, trying to forge connections where none had been before.

A cluster of shuddering red lights fired off from the ship, hitting a few streets over. Sully heard the desperate screaming, then a rumble and splash that she was sure was a portion of the block sliding into the water. She had been counting the casualties in her head without meaning to. She tried to shake it off. She needed to focus.

Running back into the apartment, she found the pocket watch the navy had given her when she was discharged and nearly dropped it in delight when she realized it was still ticking away.

Back outside, the streets were abandoned except for the omnipresent gulls that still circled, as if she were food. She started to cast, the basic parts of thaumaturgy were simple transfers of energy from one place to another; more complex ones changed the forms of the energy. This one was taking all of the kinetic force from four different places. Sully shuddered as she felt the circles linking up and wished she had the time to make something smarter than a direct channel with nothing but her magic to redirect it. She felt it in her gut when the circles connected, and when the trains passed over, it was like they were running right through her.

She shook as the momentum built up, gathered not just from that first moment the train hit the circle but from every moment it was rushing through. Sully channeled that rush of energy and hit the broadside of the dreadnought. The ship's shields shattered with a thunderclap and fragments flaked away into the sea. But the shields had still done their job, the impact was dissipated. That was why the boat only capsized instead of exploding into its component parts.

Sully couldn't help but cackle, even as she doubled over in pain. That had been worth it just to prove it could be done. The pride of the British Navy stayed afloat but the crew were too preoccupied with escaping to go on torching her city. Manhattan hadn't even raised a hand against the British, even though one of their pet demons could have resolved the whole situation readily.

The first people to come creeping back onto the streets by the bay were the locals, the ones too poor to live anywhere better. Immigrants, addicts and all the other losers of the British Empire. Her people. The reporters still lingering on the scene, looking for quotes were not her people. She faded into the background.

AUGUST 2, 2015

Sully was in her office at the IBI finishing her last tasks as Acting Deputy Director of the IBI. Safely tucked away in the deep leather chair, she signed off on her final reports and her letter of resignation. She folded the latter neatly, placed it into an envelope, and left it on top of the pile of closed files on the desk.

The case was closed. The Year of the Knife was over. Now she had to keep a promise to herself. Now she had to stop being what she had been all of these years and be someone else. Someone better.

On the plus side, her pension was going to be vastly improved, the acting director gig made sure of that. She had put everything into the reports. Everything that she had done, everything that she had allowed to happen, everything that she barely understood, and a full list of crimes carried out by people she was too conflicted to prosecute. Enough rope for the Governor and his lackeys to hang her with, if they were so inclined.

The island of Manhattan was safely nestled back in the Black Bay, its people and its demons were contained behind their own walls and barrier spells. It was practically a prison by itself, and Ogden and his people didn't seem inclined to stage a breakout any time soon. Sully shrugged to herself. It wasn't the job of the Director of the IBI to deal with something like this. The politicians would have to sort it out amongst themselves. She left it all on the desk for the next victim or volunteer. Then she took out a cigar and listened to the reports coming in.

There were protests going on all over the city and, while the red-coats were more than willing to attend every one, inciting riots by doing foolish things like opening fire on the crowd, the NAPD was begging the IBI for assistance in calming the crowds. Sully huffed out a cloud of smoke. Not her problem.

There were protesters outside the IBI building, too. Sully had coffee and tea sent out to them every few hours, and gradually, the story of what had really happened to the ship still bobbing upside down in the bay began to circulate among them. They drifted off to join other protests before long, and the stories kept on spreading. At least the newspapers were happy.

The telephone rang—the direct line from the governor's compound—and she seriously contemplated not answering it. She guessed someone had finally told on her. She forced a smile into her voice and answered. "Good evening, Lord Price."

There was a muffled sound on the far end of the line, possibly the phone changing hands, and then the dulcet tones of the governor's voice trickled down the connection. "I believe that we may have gotten off on the wrong foot, Director Sullivan. I do not honestly think that butting heads with one another is useful or that it benefits the people in our care. Don't you agree?"

He was showing more self-awareness than Sully could have expected. "Couldn't agree more."

He pressed on. "To that end, I wonder if I might borrow either yourself or some of your staff. Some of the citizens are becoming a little fractious on my lawn and, while it would be easier to bring in a show of force, I have heard that your department has been successfully diffusing these situations."

Sully covered the receiver, sighed heavily, and uncovered it again. "Of course. I'll be there as soon as I can."

He was smirking, she could tell. "Thank you kindly, Director. I am sure that this is the beginning of a far more profitable relationship for both of us. I look forward to seeing you."

Sully rang down for a car, skipping the pointless task of ringing around to see if there were any other agents still in the office. It was midnight and they would all be out celebrating the biggest case of the year being closed or, more likely, catching up on lost sleep. Sully had worked every one of them to their limits while she was Director. That was the problem with a coworker being promoted; they actually knew what you were capable of and expected nothing less. By morning, they would all be relieved that she was gone.

Her driver was an older agent, and they swapped some stories as they drove to the governor's compound, which was outside the city in an area of minor mansions and gated communities. The castle down in Roanoke was too isolated to be useful in the running of the Empire's interests, so it had been turned into a museum back in the seventies. The city's lights faded away until they turned off onto the governor's private road and had to stop.

The compound was set back from the road with a wall around it. The crowd of protesters that had gathered outside the wall was too thick for Sully's driver to get through, so she got out of the car and sent him home. She started elbowing her way through the mass of people. The crowd was angry. Sully felt it—like a dry electric heat in the air—exactly as Ogden had described it from that long ago meeting in the counting house.

It was easy to find the front of the crowd despite the dim light and the press of bodies around her, because that was where the yelling and jeering was the loudest. Sully could make out the words to bits and pieces of dozens of slogans she'd heard through the years. The crowd was chanting, "Set Manhattan free! Don't tread on me! Set Nova Europa free! Don't tread on me!"

There were redcoats lining the compound's walls. The governor must have recalled every one of them from their posts in the city and beyond. They had rifles and spells trained on the crowd.

Sully stepped up to the gates and tried to get somebody to look at her credentials. One of the redcoats—Sully recognized her as the gray-haired woman from Winchester Village—saw Sully and pointed her out to another redcoat with sergeant's stripes on his sleeve. There was a terse nod exchanged, and then Sully saw the woman adjusting her aim. The rifle was pointed right at Sully now. Words were being exchanged between redcoats along the line, too quiet for Sully to hear over the chanting, but she saw their shoulders tensing. She realized what was happening and threw up the biggest barrier that she could, but not before a volley of bullets tore through the crowd.

Only a few of the protesters had been killed but there were plenty of injuries and screaming; some people were scattering into the forest on either side of the road.

It was only when she felt something wet running down her shirt that Sully looked away from the barrier to herself. The bullet had gone through her chest, high up, beside the shoulder. She wasn't drowning in blood or dead so it must have missed everything vital, but she could still feel the black buzzing on the edges of her vision. She stumbled back a step and the barrier flickered.

Strong arms seized her shoulders from behind, and glancing up over her shoulder, Sully saw Ogden. Looking around, she saw others spread out through the crowd—men and women dressed in ruined clothes from another time, scarred and cold-eyed. They held up her barrier and cast other shields of their own to protect the protesters from the Gatling gun fire when it started. Ogden was saying something, but all Sully could hear was a high-pitched whine. Holding a hand over her wound, he looked at her with a question in his eyes and magic cracking between his fingers—that strange cool light she now associated with necromancy. Sully nodded for him to proceed and leaned into his chest as the pain came in waves.

It was easier than her first healing. Briefer and more skillful. Less like someone digging out a bullet with a rusty spoon and more like a surgeon making a delicate incision. It still hurt, but this time it felt like there was a reason for the pain. When she opened her eyes, she was surprised to find that it was still night-time and that she was still in the magus's arms.

He was holding her uncomfortably close and, judging by his ragged breathing and whatever was poking her in the kidney, he was enjoying it. Sully tugged his hands off and stumbled to her feet. The hole in her chest was gone, there wasn't even a scar. Sully scowled at that. "I didn't even have a bullet wound yet. You ruined my collection."

Ogden stared at her like she was a lunatic until she flashed him a smile, and he burst into laughter. The crowd was still milling around under the Manhattan magi's protection and now there was real fury in their cries. This wasn't an abstract event any more. Now the British had opened fire on a peacefully protesting crowd of their own citizens.

With her feet under her, Sully now found herself being patted on the back and pushed forward by every person she met. She almost missed having Ogden at her back for stability. Eventually she was facing the barrier. Behind her, the crowd was screaming. On the other side of the barriers the redcoats were lined up, ready to fire again the moment there was an opening. Above her, the crows were circling.

Sully squared her shoulders, cast her own defenses, and then let the barrier fall. It had been a long time since she'd fought with anyone on her side—she was used to taking care of everything herself. So, when the first flurry of spells came flying from the compound's wall, she was already readying counters when they were snuffed out in a flurry of dull flashes. The magi of Manhattan were there, protecting the people the way she was meant to, the way the soldiers on the wall were meant to. They would protect her flanks and let her do what she did best.

Sully stretched out her arms and unleashed hell.

A torrent of flames swept along the battlements and for every redcoat who managed to raise a protective shield, there were a dozen who fell, flesh charred, not even a scream escaping as the air in their lungs burnt away.

Sully was laughing and she couldn't stop until she cast a wild-eyed glance behind her and saw the fear on the protesters' faces. It stopped her in her tracks. She put her business face back in place and let her moment of doubt turn back into anger. She blew the gates off of the governor's mansion with a well-placed concussion spell and strode up the path without looking back. When the topiary started rustling to life, an entire menagerie of poplar tree animals reaching for her, she burnt them to their roots with a cascade of fire. From behind her, Sully heard the roar of spellfire and glanced back to see that the magi were making short work of the few redcoats at the gate who had survived Sully's initial assault.

Sully strolled right inside the marble atrium of the governor's lavish home. The two guards that had been held back in this position unleashed their evocations at such a pathetic rate that Sully didn't even bother to counter them. Ropes of bright flame coiled out from her hands, snatched their paltry spells from the air, and whipped them back across the room to where the redcoats hid behind pillars.

Sully didn't know exactly when she'd started thinking of them as the enemy. They were just people doing a job after all. It was probably when they shot her. She had always held a grudge about that sort of thing.

Sully could see a barrier hanging over a double doorway at the top of stairs. She couldn't rip it apart from this side—that would defy the point of the spell—but Sully wasn't just some Agent of the Crown, or a college-taught magician; she wasn't even just her mother's little witch. She was a soldier and she knew war like an old friend. In war, you learned to get around entrenched defenses or you learned how to breathe through a hole in your chest.

Sully took the stairs two at a time but at the top, she took a second to prepare before she blasted a hole through the wall beside the door, shredding the minor defensive enchantments that had been stitched into the stone and worn down with the passing of the years. The governor was behind his desk with his hands clapped over his ears. His haughtiness had fled, along with the contents of his bowels by the smell of the room.

To one side of him was a magus—one Sully had never seen before. He was an Indian boy who couldn't have been long out of his teens. He had gold jewelry through his nose, his eyebrow and his ears, and his head was shaved bald.

In the corner of the room, beside a hastily drawn circle, was a

greasy looking man who would have fit in on any Red Hook street corner. He had long hair, wore an orange leather jacket, and was trying to
summon a demon as quickly as he possibly could. The magus caught
her before she moved another step—a construct creature, whipped
together out of a grandfather clock and a pair of tall brass candle-
sticks, wrapped its makeshift arms around her before she could cast a
thing. Every time she squirmed the flames of its candles flared up and
burnt her.

The governor took his hands away from his ears and laughed
when he saw her caught. The burns were worthwhile just to see his
gloating face crumble a moment later when the construct fell apart
into its component pieces. Ogden peered through the hole in the wall.
He glanced from the destruction to Sully. "Your work?"

She shrugged. "Who else?"

The magus launched another attack: lightning in the shape of
kingfishers swept out from behind him in a starburst. If Ogden had
not hastily jerked bricks from the shattered wall to intercept the kingfishers, they would have dived straight into Sully's chest. She held up
her empty hands to the magus. "We aren't your enemy. We aren't the
ones keeping you in chains."

A flicker of doubt passed over the boy's face and that momentary
pause was all that Ogden needed to launch a whirlwind of needles
into his throat. The needles splintered into the Indian's fingers when
he grabbed at them in surprise, and when he spoke, the tiny needles
started to vibrate, flicking out more tiny shards that trailed sparks
between them. Fury set in his features; he tried to cast and the needles
responded violently, his throat exploded in a gory mess and Sully got
the unparalleled treat of watching his vocal chords twitching around
in the gap before he collapsed.

The greasy man had spent far too much time watching the action
when he should have been paying attention to what he was doing. He
had poured too much of his power into the circle, he emptied himself out completely and dropped cold and twitching to the floor as
the dimensional rift tore open. The demon that emerged looked like a

giant crow gone horribly wrong: black and oily with a jagged beak and six huge eyes shimmering with green light like a cat's at night.

Sully readied herself to drain the power from the circle but Ogden interrupted her. "No need. It is with us." He stepped forward and bowed to the demon. "Mol Kalath, blood of my blood. Your brood-mate holds our home in safety. Go south to the island of Manhattan, and you shall find it there."

The demon brushed over the hastily drawn circle smearing the chalk with its trailing wings. Then it returned the bow, in as much as a seven–foot-tall bird can bow. Its eyes flared when they passed over Sully and it said, "I HAVE LONGED TO MEET YOU IONA. SISTER FROM ANOTHER WORLD. SHADOW TWIN."

Sully backed away from it, shuddering, and held up her hands. "No thank you. Not today. I've got enough to deal with."

The demon clattered its beak open and shut as it laughed. "SOON, THEN. WHEN YOU ARE FINISHED AND THERE IS THE TIME. LET ME TEACH YOU WHAT WE ARE. WHAT YOU ARE. WHEN THE TIME COMES. I WILL BE WAITING FOR YOU."

Mol Kalath shuffled over to the bay windows behind the governor's desk and spread its wings. Lunging forward it burst through the glass windows, shattering them in its wake, and soared off into the night.

The governor was curled up on his knees, cowering behind his desk, when Sully turned back to him. His hands were clasped and he was shaking. "Please. I was just following orders. You have to understand. You served your country. You know that we must all follow orders."

Sully picked him up by the throat so that their eyes were level. "Your job was to take care of people. You failed. Now it's somebody else's turn."

She dropped him back into the puddle of his own filth on the thick plush rug and turned to Ogden. "Do you want to run a new country?"

He looked horrified. "I have had more responsibility in my lifetime than I could shoulder comfortably. I do not want to carry a whole nation's happiness on my back."

Sully shrugged. "We can hold elections once the fighting is done."

Ogden glanced at her with faint amusement. "Ah yes, so I would only have to command a divided nation, one that may not even carry out its threats of insurrection, through a war with the greatest of the imperial powers. Why would I turn down such an opportunity?"

The doors to the governor's office burst open, hitting the crawling governor in the face as he tried to escape. In strode Leonard Pratt, acting like he'd never abandoned Sully for even a moment. He glanced down at the sprawled governor and chuckled softly. "Sic semper tyrannis,"

He treated Sully and Ogden to a smile, as if he hadn't noticed that the room was covered in blood and half the walls were missing. "I hear that congratulations are in order, Miss Sullivan. You have solved your case and caught your killer. And this must be the gentleman himself." He turned to Ogden. "Congratulations to you too, Mr. Ogden, I understand that you have finally returned from your exile and are eager to resume your insurrection against the British. I am here to represent some interested parties who wish to expedite that process as much as possible and help the people of Nova Europa establish their sovereignty."

Sully groaned. "Of course you are."

Ogden glanced at Sully. "Who is this man?"

Sully fumbled for an introduction. "Sorry, this is Leonard Pratt. He runs with a lot of academics and political types that want us to be independent. And I've got a hunch it was his activities down in Louisiana years ago that accidentally punched a hole through to the far realm and showed you the way home."

The men looked at each other with intrigued expressions, and Sully snorted. Leonard took it in good humor and strolled around to sit behind the desk, ignoring the unpleasant smell. He took a sheath of papers out of his briefcase and organized them on the table into three piles.

He gestured to the tallest pile first. "This is a declaration of independence, a bill of rights, and the outline for a simple democratic process." He turned to the next pile. "These are offers of alliance to the free nation of Nova Europa from Ophir, Nippon, The United Nations of America and the Republic of South America. I expect more will follow once we have publicly declared."

He tapped the last pile. "These are pardons for all of your crimes against Nova European citizens and your written statement that you agree to my assuming the temporary role of Interim Prime Minister of Nova Europa until such time as it can secure independence. We will announce the first one publicly and hold the other until later, so that they appear a little bit less self-serving. And I'd like the two of you to immediately assume roles within my cabinet."

Ogden seemed to be weighing this all up before he nodded. "I would be glad to lend our strength to your cause, Mr. Pratt."

Sully said, "No. Nope. No way. I'm no politician."

Leonard held up his hands. "Of course, my dear. Your position would be General of the Nova European armed forces. The British will inevitably turn their violent attentions upon us in the near future, and it is my understanding that you would prefer to shield our citizens from the worst excesses of war."

Sully set her jaw and growled, "No thank you, Mr. Prime Minister."

He leaned forward on the table and sighed. "Minister Ogden, could you give us a moment."

Ogden smiled and dipped out of the room to talk to the gathering magi in the hall. Leonard tapped on the middle pile of papers again. "Miss Sullivan, there are certain political realities that you need to be aware of before making your decision."

Sully scowled. "I'm not going to be an officer, Leonard. I'm not going to send people off to die in your war."

He cocked his head. "The vampires will be leaving, Miss Sullivan. It is a contingency of our alliances with the United Nations and Ophir that all vampires are expelled from our borders. I have been granted a limited number of immunities to hand out among those undead who are too vital to the running of the country to be exiled."

Sully slammed her hands on the desk. "Don't threaten me you little cock-weasel. The first of your little toadies to show up at my door would go home as dust."

He raised an eyebrow. "So you would just murder innocent policemen? Over and over? I doubt it, Miss Sullivan. I doubt that the gentlemen from Manhattan would allow it either. Hard to believe that there are as many magi in the whole world as there are compressed into so small an acreage."

Sully leaned in close and hissed. "I hate you."

He laid a hand on his chest as though he were shocked. She grabbed him by the lapel and growled, "This isn't a joke. This isn't a game we're playing. From this day forward all of your bullshit about friendship is over. I hate you."

She snapped her forehead forward into his face and let go of his jacket. He rocked backward with the impact, flipping his chair over and landing on the rubble, piss and broken glass of his new office floor. By the time he was back on his feet with blood streaming out of his nose, Sully was scribbling her signature on the papers.

Ogden drifted back into the room and pretended not to see the state of the Prime Minister. He bent to work beside Sully, signing in his own elaborate handwriting as she finished. Sully recognized with a shudder it was the same script that was branded on poor Bertie Collinwood's dead hide. She glared again at Leonard and then dropped the pen on his desk with a clatter. "Congratulations, Leonard. You're the boss now. Don't screw it up."

She turned to Ogden. "Hey, are all demons on your side or just the relatives of your pet ones?"

Ogden raised an eyebrow. "I believe that our non-aggression pact extends to all members of their race."

Sully held up a hand to make him pause. "What I'm asking is, if we let a bunch of demons loose, will they attack who we want them to attack?"

Ogden tilted his head from side to side in consideration. "They are extremely trustworthy and we already have contacts with them across the planes. We could certainly talk to them about it. We share a common enemy, if nothing else."

Sully glanced at him. "Why do demons hate the British?"

Ogden almost smiled. "It is not the British but the allies they've called upon that troubles the demons. Our world is their life boat, their escape route from being so close to the creatures of the far realm. They do not want to see holes poked in that life boat. They do not want deals being made between the powers of our world and the far realm—"

Leonard interrupted. "Regardless of these wild accusations, you cannot mean to summon more demons into the world. Think of what happened to old Europe in the Great War. The land has been lost to all of humankind."

Sully turned back to Leonard with thinly concealed contempt. "We don't need to summon a thing. You actually just gave us the best answer to the problem. You're the best spell-breaker in the world, and we have a hundred magi sitting on their hands just waiting for the British to come. If it is going to be a war, let's take the first swing. Let's bring down the Veil of Tears."

SEPTEMBER 1, 2015

Sully had finally acquired a new apartment in one of the better parts of Brooklyn. The penthouse—all big windows and minimalist design—had been abandoned by a British loyalist who had fled for Britannia with his tail between his legs. While on one level, Sully loathed middle-class trappings—she'd always been the one in the basement apartment judging the one in the penthouse, not the other way around—even she had to admit that it gave her a good view of the city. Her city.

With Marie now a permanent house guest, Sully had paid a jaw-dropping amount from her new salary to get a special treatment put on the windows to keep out the ultraviolet radiation. Technically she supposed it was on the taxpayers' bill, but by this point, Sully was starting to think that maybe they owed her some hazard pay. With all of the other vampires exiled to whichever backwater Empire would take them, Marie had to keep a low profile. She bitched and moaned constantly about being held captive in the lap of luxury. There were places she wanted to go, things she wanted to do, but they were all in the public eye.

The theaters of New Amsterdam were overflowing with new plays about Manhattan, the Year of the Knife, the War of Independence. The cinemas would be right behind them—churning out propaganda about the birth of a new nation would keep them busy for years to come. Sully understood that the provisional government had even sold off the rights to her life story, provided they got to vet the film's contents first.

She smiled bitterly at that last part; Leonard had learned that from the Khanate—you can let anyone say and do whatever they like under your rule as long as the history books get your approval.

The first time Sully stopped Marie's complaining with a kiss, Marie had gone right back to it a moment later. By the fiftieth time, she'd just sighed and melted in Sully's arms. It turned into a game for them; every time Marie complained about anything at all Sully would give her an absent peck on the cheek.

They settled into their new life comfortably, falling back into patterns from the days before Marie had left—days that seemed like such a long time ago they weren't worth discussing. Songs from the old musicals that Marie loved so much filled the space, with Sully still singing to them off key in the shower.

Sully brought in a steady stream of adventurous takeaway meals from all over the city. She dreaded but ate them because it made Marie happy to experience the smells and to have the flavors described to her. At some point, Sully didn't notice exactly when, Marie started wearing a ring that she claimed she'd found among her old things. A ring that Sully recognized as the one she'd given Marie all those many years ago. They never spoke about it.

That night after sharing a bottle of wine, Marie drinking it vicariously through Sully's intoxicated blood, they fell into bed together a little earlier than usual. Before the clocks struck midnight, Sully found herself up again, cold and shivering after having her warmth sapped away by Marie's chill touch.

She picked up an abandoned Hawaiian shirt from the floor, wrapped it around herself for warmth, and walked out onto the balcony. She looked out over New Amsterdam, deafeningly loud and impossibly busy, even now, after all that had happened. It stretched off as far as the eye could see in every direction and, for tonight at least, it was safe.

ABOUT THE AUTHOR

G D Penman writes Speculative Fiction. He lives in Scotland with his partner and children, some of whom are human. He is a firm believer in the axiom that any story is made better by dragons. His beard has won an award. If you have ever read a story with Kaiju and queer people, it was probably one of his. In those few precious moments that he isn't parenting or writing, he likes to watch cartoons, play video and tabletop games, read more books than are entirely feasible and continue his quest to eat the flesh of every living species.